The Disciples
of Cthulhu II

Blasphemous Tales of the Followers

More Titles from Chaosium

Call of Cthulhu® Fiction

The Antarktos Cycle

The Book of Eibon

The Ithaqua Cycle

The Necronomicon (Revised Second Edition)

Singers of Strange Songs

Song of Cthulhu

Tales Out of Innsmouth

The Xothic Legend Cycle

R. W. Chambers' The Yellow Sign & Other Stories
(his complete weird fiction)

Robert E. Howard's Nameless Cults
(his Cthulhu Mythos fiction)

Arthur Machen's The Three Impostors & Other Stories

Arthur Machen's The White People & Other Tales
(forthcoming)

Joseph S. Pulver's Nightmare's Disciple
(original Mythos novel)

Miskatonic University® Archives

The Book of Dzyan

Call of Cthulhu® Fiction

The Disciples of Cthulhu II

Blasphemous Tales of the Followers

BENJAMIN ADAMS
SCOTT DAVID ANIOLOWSKI
A. A. ATTANASIO
DONALD R. BURLESON
WALTER C. DeBILL, JR.
HENRY LEE FORREST
C. J. HENDERSON
BRAD LINAWEAVER
GARY MYERS
WILL MURRAY
ROBERT M. PRICE
FRED OLEN RAY
BRAD STRICKLAND
ROBERT WEINBERG

EDITED AND INTRODUCED BY EDWARD P. BERGLUND

Cover Art by Harry Fassl

A Chaosium Book
2003

Cover art © 2003 by Harry Fassl. Cover layout by Charlie Krank. Interior layout and editorial by David Mitchell. Editor-in-chief Lynn Willis.

Our web site is updated monthly; see http://www.chaosium.com.

FIRST EDITION

10 9 8 7 6 5 4 3 2 1

Chaosium Publication 6033. Published in February 2003.

ISBN 1-56882-143-3

Printed in Canada.

Contents

Editor's Preface

In *The Disciples of Cthulhu* (DAW Books, 1976), I stated that there had been three generations of the disciples of Cthulhu. The first generation was, of course, begun by H. P. Lovecraft and the writers that were working at that time. The second generation began in the early sixties and lasted until around 1965. And the third generation began in 1969. Now this third generation continued until somewhere in the late seventies. And then Mythos writings went into a slump.

The distinctions of the succeeding generations is purely arbitrary at best. With the publication of the *Call of Cthulhu* roleplaying game by Chaosium Inc. in 1981, the stirrings of the fourth generation of disciples began, although not in a strictly prose sense. These stirrings were brought forth with the professional publication of scenarios based on the roleplaying game. After the publication of the first of the Robert M. Price anthologies, this group of writers began to move toward more formal prose presentations—actual stories of the Cthulhu Mythos, with a beginning, a middle, and an ending. This has continued, to include stories written around the *Delta Green* roleplaying sourcebook from Pagan Publishing, which is a cross between *Call of Cthulhu* and the television show *The X-Files*.

The beginnings of the fifth generation of disciples are not so easy to pin down, as they occurred entirely in an electronic medium—the Internet. Mythos writers would put their stories online on their individual website. The locations of some of these stories are still being discovered. However, the Cthulhu Mythos on the Internet began to be codified by means of websites devoted exclusively to the Mythos, taking the appearance of electronic magazines (ezines), although not necessarily dated and numbered like conventional print magazines. These ezines appeared in the mid- to late-90's and included Jim Hawley's *NetherReal,* Corey Whitworth's *All Things Dark and Dangerous,* Peter Worthy's *Mythos Online,* Ron Shiflet's *The Innsmouth Archive* (devoted primarily to Mythos poetry), and my own *Nightscapes.* All of these ezines are still online (although my *Nightscapes* is the only one to have been updated recently), although the Mythos material that has appeared in them has made the transition to the print media with small press magazines, such as Peter Worthy's *Al-Azif,* Ron Shiflet/R.S. Cartwright's *Dark Legacies,* and Tani Jantsang's *Cthulhu Cultus.*

I stated above that the dating of the beginnings of the fourth and fifth generations was purely arbitrary. As I stated in my "Editor's Preface" for the first anthology, "Whether or not there is a market for the Cthulhu Mythos stories, established and amateur writers will continue to write them for their

xiv   The Disciples of Cthulhu II

own and their friends' amusement and enjoyment. It is inevitable that one or more readers of this volume will be influenced into trying his hand at writing within the Cthulhu Mythos genre." Writers and potential writers have come under the influence of the work of H. P. Lovecraft in differing ways: 1) after reading Lovecraft; 2) after playing the roleplaying game and looking and finding Lovecraft; and 3) after reading Lovecraft and seeing what others were doing on the Internet. This has resulted in stories that are completely under the umbrella of this shared world of Lovecraft's Cthulhu Mythos and stories that only give reference to his creations as a way of showing that Lovecraft influenced them into becoming writers or better writers.

And herewith, in the present forum, we have representatives from the third and fourth generations of the disciples of Cthulhu. Walter C. DeBill, Jr. was represented in the first anthology in this series (the 1976 edition), as a member of the third generation, while Gary Myers's work appeared from Arkham House the year before, and Robert M. Price was represented in the second edition of the anthology (the 1996 edition). Also from this generation, although not professionally published in the mid- to late-70's, we have A. A. Attanasio, Donald R. Burleson, C. J. Henderson, Will Murray, and Robert Weinberg.

Our fourth generation writers are Benjamin Adams (who appeared in an early anthology from Chaosium) and Scott David Aniolowski (who was originally published with scenarios and then started editing his own anthologies). The stories by Henry Lee Forrest, Brad Linaweaver and Fred Olen Ray, and Brad Strickland are the first Mythos efforts of these writers.

We hope you enjoy reading these disciples' efforts as much as we did. And maybe one of our readers will find himself or herself represented in the next anthology.

Edward P. Berglund
Jacksonville, North Carolina
November 12, 2001

The Bookseller's Second Wife

by Walter C. DeBill, Jr.

"A MacLachlan & Co., Bookseller," said the gold letters on the big panes on either side of the door. The old book dealer was in an ancient brick building with a cement facade, just off the center of town in an area not slum, not prime territory to be propped up by subsidies. Not a place for an aggressive new business to get started; a place where the solid profit-makers of the past clung precariously to the present, each hoping to retire its band of proprietors and old hands gracefully before some random surge of economic change or new technological gadget made them obsolete. Nathan looked up and saw a dark figure move away from a dusty window on the fourth and top story; he thought he saw a rat jump back from a cornice.

A dreadful place to spend a youthful summer; his father's judgement upon him for graduating in art instead of engineering. His graduate fellowship did not begin until the fall three months away and the job market was just awful that summer. But he would have been content to live impecuniously at home and could have painted there, at least. There could be nothing but malice behind his father's insistence that he spend the summer assisting his great-uncle Alistair MacLachlan, a distant figure whom neither he nor his father knew well. The wages would consist of little above room, board and Greyhound fare.

Nathan set down his suitcases and knocked loudly on the door. The great glass panes, so vulnerable in this rough-looking neighborhood, were bleary with the grime of decades. He could see endless rows of tables piled high with disorderly stacks of books. Nothing stirred for a minute and he knocked again, rattling the long-paned door. He tried the doorlatch. It was unlocked. He maneuvered his bags through the doorway.

He was in a cavernous room with a ceiling almost twenty feet high. Most of the floor was occupied with books, with many of the stacks high enough to block his view. The walls were lined with bookshelves reaching almost to the ceiling, reached by tall ladders on rollers. Across the back of the room and half of the left-hand wall was a wide iron catwalk reached by a stair that appeared to be retractable like a fire escape.

Scurrying footsteps with a noticeable limp heralded a very short man with curly white hair and a seamed face with the startled eyes of the perpetual worrier. Instead of speaking to Nathan he turned and called, "It's him, Miz' MacLachlan, he's here!" and hared off like a bystander fleeing someone else's accident, leaving Nathan open-mouthed with a stillborn question.

Fiona MacLachlan appeared on the catwalk. He had seen her once years ago, at a big family funeral. She had been "one of the grownups" then, introduced and immediately forgotten, too old to be interesting. Now he guessed that she was in her thirties (a mature eye would have judged forty) and, in spite of this advanced age, strikingly attractive. She was tall and blonde and her green dress clung to curves that were full but not plump as she descended the stair. She did not yell at him across the room, but waited until they met at the foot of the stair.

"Welcome, Nathan," she said. "We are so glad that you could come." She had a trace of a foreign accent. "We are desperate for help, even though you have no business experience." The words stung him. His father was always taunting him with his economic uselessness.

"Well, I'll help you as well as I can. I guess even a painter can pack boxes and shuffle paperwork."

"Painter? Oh, yes—your father said something about that." Her eyes twinkled a bit; they were dark brown and appraising him as boldly as a coach eyeing a rookie. She made him quite uncomfortable.

"Let's go back to the downstairs office. We can have a drink while I tell you what's going on. You must be tired—surely you didn't carry those bags all the way from the bus station?"

He blushed slightly. "It's only eight blocks. I thought I'd save the cab fare." Actually, he was broke.

"Well, it's just as well you didn't call us. We don't have a car."

He left his bags at the foot of the stair and followed her through the maze of books to a large alcove at the rear. It was furnished with the dark heavy furniture of the nineteenth century, all recently dusted. There were a few small piles of the inevitable books but the place had obviously been tidied up. Fiona opened the rolltop desk against the back wall revealing several bottles of liquor.

"Do you like Irish whiskey? That's my favorite. And we also have Scotch."

"I'll try Irish," he said. He would have preferred a cold beer or a soft drink. He was thirsty after the stultifying bus ride and the long walk in the heat. The air in the alcove was fresh and moving, though it was quite warm. He guessed that they controlled the humidity for the sake of the books but not the temperature for the people. She mixed weak highballs from a pitcher of ice water and sat down at a big mahogany table with a cloth cover. He sat opposite her.

The little white haired man appeared abruptly. "Miz' MacLachlan, I can't find that 1892 *Golden State Encyclopedia,* it's not where you said and—"

"Don't worry, Pumphrey, we'll find it later. Nathan can help us look for it. Just go on to the next item on the list."

"Yes, Miz' MacLachlan," he said and vanished again into the maze.

"Pumphrey's the only help we've been able to keep for many years." She was eyeing him again, this time with an unreadable intentness. "We have to have somebody reasonably intelligent and also able to do a certain amount of physical work. Pumphrey's really good at handling the rare books that need special treatment but he's not so young any more. And now we have a huge order in, a big contract that we need desperately to get on our feet financially, and he and I just can't handle it by ourselves."

She was gazing out at the book-lined cavern now and there was a touch of weariness in her expression. She had strong clean features, he noticed, with none of the telltale flabbiness that so often marks the onset of middle age.

"Alistair doesn't do any physical work any more," she added. "Though he is completely alert mentally and handles all the special museum items personally except for the actual shipping. Actually that sort of business has really kept us going for a long time now. But we need this big book order to get in good shape financially. Alistair landed the contract through an old friend at the University of Montana. They're expanding their library system and we were lucky to get a piece of it."

"I don't understand," he said with a sinking feeling. "You mean you want me to stuff all this in boxes? Is that it?"

She smiled. "Not all of it. We need to start shipping the things we already have in stock right away and send out requests for the rest to the other dealers. That way they can start cataloguing right away. The only way they can get it all done in time for the fall semester is to get shipments from us regularly throughout the summer. Unfortunately, the first part is the hardest."

"You mean shipping the things you already have? How *do* you find them?"

"Unfortunately—sometimes we can't. It comes down to a lot of digging through stacks of old books."

"You mean you don't have records of the locations of all this stuff?" He looked out incredulously at the endless piles of books on the tables, on the floor in the aisles between the tables, on their sides on the lower shelves, in neater rows higher up, in piles again on top, nearly touching the ceiling. . . .

"You mean you just dumped them as they came in without making any records? Even an artist would know better than that!"

"Well, of course, we keep records!" she bristled. She took a pull on her drink. "Or at least we did. . . . Then Alistair became less active, Pumphrey got more and more scatterbrained, a lot would come in and something else would come up before we could log it properly. When an order had to be filled we were always in a desperate rush, we moved things around and didn't have time to put them back. And then some of the log books were destroyed in an accident. Our catalog got so out of date we haven't mailed it in years. Our best stock isn't in it, half of what *is* in it is gone and we can barely locate the rest." The sharp tone had trailed off into despair.

"So," he said, and savored a sip of his whiskey, "you hired me to spend the summer scampering up and down the ladders like a squirrel and packing boxes."

She smiled and cocked her head. "That's about it. Not what you would call an artistic job. But you look able enough, even if you don't know a thing about the business. We can't pay you much, but with room and meals furnished you can save most of it."

He stared gloomily out at the appalling chaos throughout the room and felt the whiskey spread through his veins. He wanted to be somewhere else, anywhere. He wanted to reject his father and his father's judgement on him. He could drag out the summer, playing the idiot she thought him, surviving somehow to flee back to the world of art and intellect that had beckoned to him. But—

He also wanted to show this woman, so irritating yet so appealing, that he was not a nincompoop at all.

Fight or flight—

He chose to fight. "Why don't you put it all on a computer? It's not that hard, you know."

"A computer?" Her eyebrows went up in surprise. "But they cost thousands of dollars. And I don't know anything about them and neither does Pumphrey. Or Alistair. We can hardly afford ledgers."

"You could get one for about five hundred that would handle this mess for you. I could show you how to get started. My roommate had one and I learned a bit. By the time we get on top of this order we'll have looked in just about every nook and cranny of the place. If we start making notes and buy a machine as soon as the University makes a payment—they *are* paying something before fall, aren't they?"

"Yes, of course. But are you certain—?"

"Well, we've got plenty of time to talk about it," he said, enjoying a secret glee. "It won't hurt to start making notes on where things are located, will it? Whether they wind up on a computer or not. Well, when do I start?"

"I'll show you your room upstairs. Then if you're ready we've got plenty of lists. . . ."

An hour later Nathan sat perched atop one of the high ladders where he had climbed in pursuit of a seventeenth century grimoire looking out giddily over the vast room. The gilt-lettered panes that had seemed so tall from the street were below him now, myriad runnels streaking their length from the evening thundershower outside. The air had gotten gradually cooler. He felt Alistair's presence behind him as a sudden chill, almost an electric tingle on his skin, even before he heard the dry cough. When he turned his uncle was on the catwalk, behind and a little below him.

He stood motionless, peering intently at Nathan and, after the little cough, made no sound. He wore a black suit of old-fashioned cut and leaned on a stick whose golden head was cast in the shape of a gargoyle. His wispy white hair bushed out as though electrified and his intense expression might have been a smile.

Although he was no more than twenty-five feet from Nathan and the silence was marred only by the patter of rain, he felt it would be somehow inappropriate to hail the old man across the room. He made his way gingerly down the ladder, threaded the piles of books and climbed the iron stair to meet his silent host and patron. When he finally faced him he found himself tongue-tied.

"Hello, Nathan," came the voice at last, exceedingly thin and dry yet resonant, like the whisper of an operatic baritone. "I have needed you for a long time." The mouth was small and pursed, the teeth tiny and sharp. "Your youth will be of great benefit to us here. Your strength, your intelligence . . . this place has seen no youth for much too long."

Still Nathan's tongue was dry and still. Alistair was definitely smiling, not so much in the mouth as in the eyes, which were of a feline yellow. Of every feature of the ancient's appearance, only the eyes did not tell of age; they were timeless.

"We will make good use of your youthful vigor here, nephew," he said, and then he turned and moved slowly and deliberately back into the hall that led off from the catwalk into the warren of old rooms and corridors, apparently unconcerned that Nathan had never spoken. And ever after Nathan felt his presence there, permeating every stone of that place.

Later, when Nathan fell asleep in his tiny second floor room to the distant roll of thunder and the spatter of rain in the alley outside his window, he dreamed of great yellow eyes, and falling, and of a strange sickness that made him feel weak and old.

For the next two weeks Nathan swam in a sea of first editions and "half morocco binding" and "slightly foxed pages." The faint dusty smell of the books, mild and not unpleasant, was always with him day and night. In a surprisingly short time he began to find his way through the endless stacks confidently, acquiring a vast amorphous knowledge of the untidy book-trove. Alistair he rarely saw; he took his meals in his room and only rarely appeared on the catwalk to look out over the work, a presence more felt than seen. Pumphrey was always quietly scurrying among the piles of books, almost never speaking more than a few words at a time and all of them to Fiona.

Nathan genuinely enjoyed the quiet and the solitude of the work, but after a stretch of an hour or two he would find himself looking for an excuse to talk to Fiona.

She seemed to welcome his conversation, like someone rediscovering the joy of companionship after a long enforced loneliness. She soon found that Nathan was a real asset in filling the big university order and treated him with a new respect. Like Nathan, she spent long days hunting books, even climbing the great ladders (Pumphrey was afraid of heights), typing lists, packing boxes. She wore jeans which looked fine on her firm ripe figure; it became apparent that she had dressed up especially for his arrival that day. Pumphrey lived near the shop but off the premises so the two of them ate together and talked about the order and the computer project, which Alistair had half assented to, and of Nathan's youthful enthusiasms which seemed to stir her oddly. At his suggestion they ate out twice, at nearby restaurants. They left almost furtively, after Alistair had been served in his room (Fiona slept in her own room) and she seemed delighted with this simple pleasure. There was no television set in the place and Nathan finally enticed her out to a movie where she seemed to rediscover the basic experience of laughter.

It was the night after the first big shipment had gone out that she came to his room. The excitement of meeting the goal and proving his worth had vanished like a bubble, the vision of the long stifling summer lay upon him like a shroud. He had showered off the dust of the books and lay on his narrow bed, listening to the first drops of rain.

She did not knock. She opened the door silently and held a finger to her lips, cutting short the blurted greeting on his startled tongue. She closed the door soundlessly behind her and came to him. She wore a diaphanous peignoir; she untied the sash and let it fall open. Firm breasts, flat stomach, a profusion of blonde body hair; no words, no proposals, no assent, their bodies entwined and explored with rapt abandon. Soft eyelashes, mobile lips, hard nipples, hips both muscular and downy-soft, all as new and amazing as if he had never touched or imagined a woman before in any dream or incarnation. The college girls he had known, with their coquetry and self-conscious sophistication seemed like spoiled children playing "doctor." For an awful moment his own self-consciousness surged up and he wondered in panic if he would be able to respond to this fierce, knowing, *total* woman, but when she mounted him on that narrow little bed and took him deep and hot he found that his own body knew precisely what to do and when and it mattered not what he thought or felt. He willed nothing and all was perfect. When she left him the rain had stopped and there was dawn-glow in the sky.

For Nathan the weeks of that endless summer crept on in dream-like slow motion. On the one hand the work in the labyrinth of books became less oppressive and more interesting as the old bookseller's store became the one place in space and time where he wished to be; on the other, time hung in the air about him like stagnant smoke as he waited for the next time of passion in his little room. Only then, in embrace with her flesh and hair and musk and whispered voice, did time swirl and rush with abandon.

Fortunately the peculiar arrangements of the old bookseller's household made it possible for her to come to him more nights than not. Although Alistair did not seem at all feeble and obviously dominated Fiona and Pumphrey completely, he lived the life of a recluse, appearing rarely and speaking little, taking all of his meals alone in his room. Fiona slept in an adjacent bedroom on the fourth story so that, even though her husband's room had been lined with cork in the distant past and was largely soundproof, it was out of the question for Nathan to go there. But it was safe enough for her to tiptoe down to him after the shop had been locked for the night. Pumphrey lived off the premises nearby and was gone by seven each evening. Once the work was done for the day and Pumphrey let out like a pet cat, the doors would be locked and, unless Nathan was going out for the evening, the stair to the catwalk pulled up. The city had more than its share of violent crime and this unusual security precaution didn't surprise Nathan as much as the survival of the great glass panes of the window on the street. Thus their trysts were almost nightly.

Those delicious summer nights were long and sultry and in their murmured conversations he learned as much about his exotic lover as she was willing to tell him. She had been married before and had come to Alistair as a mature and forceful personality, attracted to him by his knowledge and power in the eldritch lore of subterranean

magic. Fiona had been steeped in such things herself before she met
him, as had his first wife, Cordelia. In reply to his timid hinted questions, she discussed the physical passions of the first years of their
marriage frankly, mischievously amused at Nathan's embarrassment.
Yes, Alistair had been an attractive lover in those days. Though no
longer young he was physically vigorous and his powerful personality had been fascinating to her. Their lovemaking had been enhanced
by the atmosphere of ritual magic and the use of esoteric drugs. But
for many years now, Alistair, though still physically strong in most
ways, had shown no interest in her as a woman. He remained strong,
she said, but not youthful. Now she feared him but feared more to
leave. His first wife had disappeared under mysterious circumstances.
Alistair had given out that she had first gone on a long trip, then
decided not to come back. The fear in Fiona's voice and expression
when she whispered of this convinced Nathan that she knew (or suspected) more than she would tell him.

At first Nathan was too infatuated and fulfilled and flattered to
question their relationship; like a naughty child he felt exhilarated to
be breaking all the rules and the rewards were too overwhelming
even to consider turning down. But as the summer went on he began
to chafe at the deception of the old man. It was his pride more than
his morality that prickled; he began to feel sneaky and cheap. He felt
trapped as she did, oppressed by his surroundings but having no
money and no job prospects elsewhere. He assumed her trap was the
same as his; her references to the black arts and her subtle signs of
physical fear puzzled him briefly and passed from his mind. And so
Fiona began in her own oblique way to educate Nathan in the realities of their enclosed world.

Fiona made out the lists of books for him and Pumphrey to
retrieve, as well as for herself. At first he thought she was just giving
him the most strenuous assignments, most of the ladder work and
the dustier corners of the room. But soon he noticed a pattern to the
spaces he was sent to comb and a distinct trend to the titles he
sought. On the tables in one of the less accessible corners and in the
lower glassed-in cases was an enormous cache of modern authorities
on mythology, folklore, witchcraft, ritual magic and kindred subjects
in frayed dust jackets and sturdy uninspired cloth edition bindings.
Margaret Murray's *The God of the Witches* was there in multiple copies,

as were her *Witch-Cult in Western Europe,* Montague Summers' *History of Witchcraft and Demonology,* and many others. The complete works of the bizarre magician Aleister Crowley had pride of place there.

The first cases high enough to need a ladder contained 18th and 19th century treatises and translations of older sources, many privately printed, with leather corners and gilt-lettered spines and yellow-spotted pages: *Malleus Maleficarum,* the Ashwin translation of Remigius' *Demonolatria* and the rare *A Warning to Those Who Delve* of the mysterious Squire Phillip Howard . . . and works of similar vintage were stocked in depth. Another category here that puzzled Nathan was a profusion of titles concerning Indian religion and yogic practices.

But when he mounted the rickety ladder to the topmost cases and the dusty individual boxes on top of them, he began to realize the full extent of the old wizard's store of infamous lore. Indeed, this had been the object of Fiona's lesson, for she often directed him in furtive tones to "inventory" just these regions, when nothing had been ordered from them. There, as he perched on the flimsy ladder glancing frequently at the door where Alistair might appear, he found nothing newer than von Könnenberg's *Uralte Schrecken* with its plain black leather binding and silver lock; Dr. Dee in a great Elizabethan folio with the royal imprint and a Latin title in gold on the front edge; Ludvig Prinn in brooding black-letter; the much debated Count Cagliostro in a magnificent private edition full of engraved diagrams, decorated in gold filigree, echoed on the edges; a manuscript in Hebrew on parchment enclosed in heavy wooden boards covered with plain leather, with an inscription in French on the front endpaper containing the words "Abra-Melin" and "originale" . . . every dark soul who had dared the forbidden arts for centuries was there, in the original or in translation. And the old man's trove did not stop there. The boxes on the top contained manuscripts and incised clay tablets at which Nathan could only shudder. Fiona referred to these as Alistair's trading stock; in his unseen chambers he had copies of everything here that he considered of value and more that he would never sell to any public institution.

As the outlines of the bookseller's monstrous collection became clear to him, Nathan was shocked; yet he could only see it in terms of hysterical gullibility, the common delusion of a group of frail old men. He was amazed to see that Fiona did not react in the same way as himself; she was always tense and deadly serious when she spoke or hinted at Alistair's strange predilections. She in turn seemed puzzled at his casual attitude. Her hints and subtle pointers began to direct him toward the side of Alistair's business which they referred to euphemistically as "special museum items."

He was aware that these objects were an important part of the business and had often seen Fiona and Pumphrey carrying packages out to the parcel service truck in the alley behind the business. Now Fiona began to leave the special account books for these items under Nathan's nose when he visited her alcove office. The titles and descriptions told him little; "fragment of a statue," "probably South Pacific origin," dimensions. What struck him immediately was that the prices were always quoted ridiculously high and that the finished deals almost always showed the prices reduced drastically because of items taken in trade. Too, the items almost never went to museums; the buyers and traders were individuals, often residing in foreign countries. The prices asked and sometimes paid were enough to convince him that Alistair and his kindred spirits were morbidly serious about their eccentric pursuits.

He suspected that she would soon show him more and sure enough, one day she asked him to ship a museum item. The invoice said "dagger" with the usual uninformative description. She led him quietly through the books to an alcove in a side wall. There were many of these alcoves, all populated with books, and all of them contained at least one locked door. He had assumed these led only to closets but that day Fiona produced a key of antique design and opened a heavy door to reveal a rickety wooden stair leading down. An old ceramic switch clicked and an unshaded bulb glared at the bottom of the stair.

She descended slowly, her head cocked slightly as though listening for some faint sound. Nathan followed gingerly, wincing at each tiny creak of the stair. At the bottom she turned to him with a finger to her lips. Her eyes were wide and dark and once she licked her lips nervously as she looked left and right down long hallways and peered ahead into the gloom of a third. She led him off to the right in a direction he knew must lead under the neighboring building. Later she would tell him that Alistair owned most of the buildings on the street and that there were many ramifications to the bookselling establishment, more than she cared to explore. The neighbors were afraid of Alistair and usually only too glad to sell out and move on; they knew they would be lucky to get anything for a property in this area and it was rumored that those who fell foul of the old bookseller encountered bad luck and ill health.

The door she chose was on the left, so far down the gloomy passageway that Nathan wished they had brought a flashlight. There was a second key for this room and another of the old-style switches and she took the odd precaution of closing the door behind them. The walls were lined with rough wooden shelves, all loaded with wooden boxes of various sizes and shapes. There was a deal table in the center of the floor. With silent gestures she showed him the catalog number on the invoice and a matching number pencilled on the outside of one of the boxes.

He brought it to the table. The top had been unfastened, opened, and inspected on arrival and never resealed. Inside was an object of a powerful, morbid beauty. It was a dagger fifteen inches long. The blade, of tempered steel, was only slightly marred with pinpoints of corrosion. For a few inches near the point it was discolored with a faint bronze cast that was iridescent in the light. The haft was decorated with bloodstone, the ebony handle intricately carved with a filigreed inscription. From his recent browsing Nathan recognized it as the Enochian script used in the rituals of witchcraft.

Before carrying the box upstairs, they silently viewed the contents of a dozen or so of the boxes on the shelves. Brass censers, pottery vessels of primordial design, a polished ceremonial bowl crusted with an unknown material, all in perfect condition, effigies of demons and maleficent gods—the worst of these was a figure in malachite, a thing with wings and claws and tentacles for a face. Here for the first time Nathan's body, if not his conscious mind, realized that there was something to fear in this place.

The brooding tension was broken by a scampering rustle somewhere outside the room. Nathan jumped, then almost laughed until he saw that Fiona was standing rigid with her mouth open and her eyes wide with terror. He placed a warm hand on her shoulder in a gesture of comfort and to his surprise she turned and clasped him in a desperate, passionate embrace and kissed him long and hard.

When she relaxed, he asked, "What . . . ?" in the lowest of whispers.

"Rats," she murmured, "just . . . rats. Let's get out of here." And they did, taking the dagger in its box and locking the doors behind them. But Nathan found it hard to believe that this woman, so strong and intelligent, could be terrified by mere rats.

She gave him no more assignments handling the "museum items." Apparently that would not please Alistair, and Pumphrey, who was curious and resentful of Nathan, was likely to tattle. She did tell him that there were many rooms full of such objects in the closets and cellars and that the most important ones were on the fourth floor with Alistair's rooms.

It was after the incident of the rats that she began to direct him to certain passages in the more arcane books in Alistair's collection. She would send him to get something in an obscure alcove and there next to it or underneath it would lie a book he recognized as especially rare, something that certainly did not belong on a table in a humble alcove, something she must have fetched surreptitiously from a high shelf or a locked room. In it would be some innocuous scrap of paper unobtrusively directing him to a particular passage. An hour after he had read it the book would be gone from the alcove.

The first dozen or so were in books on Indian mysticism, originals or reprints from the early days of British imperial control of India. They told of a secret teaching of southern Indian origin which combined certain forbidden yogic practices with ritual magic. Orthodox religionists had despised and condemned it because of its aggressive nature and because its primary goal was prolongation of one's own life by preying on others, all in total opposition to both Hinduism and Buddhism.

Like Buddhism, the teaching had travelled north to Tibet and China where it had both influenced and been influenced by Taoism, with its ancient herbal lore and obsession with immortality. A darker strain of neolithic shamanism from northern Asia also made its mark, and the cult was linked with the dimly menacing names of Yidhra and 'Ymnar. Nathan had seen those names, in crumbling leather-bound manuscripts on the highest shelves and inscribed on objects of doubtful purpose in the locked room below. As he read on in the works of fabled nineteenth century scholars of the occult, he found that the cult had indeed invaded European culture and spread worldwide in an underground network of wizardry. He began to sense a direction in Fiona's clues.

Von Könnenberg's 1854 *Uralte Schrecken* (in Crowley's London translation) was the most modern source to shed new light on the cult. In his time, its practitioners were known as the "masters of the life force" and were profoundly feared by the occultists who knew of them. Although having little power in the areas outside their special interest, they were known as deadly vampire-like beings who destroyed others in order to live to abnormal ages, although even von Könnenberg with all of his erudition did not know precisely how they harmed their victims. Their control of the life force was so great that they could actually bring about physical transformations in all orders of life forms, which may account for the recurrent stories of keeping demons or familiars on their premises. The mad lama of Prithom-Yang may have hinted at this when he wrote of a mysterious ascetic who kept about him ". . . that which walks but cannot speak, and that which speaks but cannot walk."

The implications of a group of fanatics, intelligent, amoral, obsessed with prolonging their own lives at any cost, believing every word of these ancient horrors and prepared to act on them . . . Nathan began to feel menace in the air, to become watchful and wary, to listen for faint sounds. Pumphrey's rabbit-like nervousness was no longer ludicrous and Fiona's quiet fear no longer seemed meaningless.

Yet their apparent entrapment, both his and Fiona's, still seemed unreal, and their deception wrong. She sensed this, in the sultry closeness of their evening trysts, and continued to try to convey the depth of her fear and the gravity of their jeopardy.

His attention was directed to a particular item in an account book he had not seen before, one normally kept out of sight of any casual visitor to the shop. A big folio-sized leather-bound tome of a design he was sure had not been seen since the turn of the century, it contained accounts going back to 1864, only a few items per year, usually quoted at fabulous sums. The descriptions of the items were innocuous and uninformative, those taken in trade for them equally so. The item she evidently wished him to see was the latest entry, first listed in March of that same year. It was styled, "Elizabethan diary.

Folio. 99 pp 1 blank leaf. Contemporary undecorated pigskin over wooden boards, some wormholes, two clasps. London, 1580," with some vague comments suggesting a dreary picture of country life recorded in a largely illegible nonprofessional hand, and there was no record of its acquisition. Nathan could hardly imagine a less intriguing description. It was listed for a quarter of a million dollars and there was a list of six sets of initials of individuals to whom it had been offered. Beside four of them were small marks which he took to mean they had rejected the item. There was a set of coded entries that seemed to indicate that the other two had made offers considerably below Alistair's asking price. These entries had covered the period of Nathan's presence in the shop and entries continued to be added as offer and counteroffer were made. Then one day Fiona, taking care that Pumphrey was not within earshot, showed him a new entry. The "diary" had been exchanged for $10,000 and a "chest, carved and inlaid, medieval, prob. Flemish origin," which item, presumably, was worth approximately $240,000 to Alistair.

As usual Fiona refused to discuss the matter openly, but she did tell him, in careful murmurs, that the initials "K. v. S." stood for Klaus von Schleiwitz, that he was the most feared man in Vienna, and that under no circumstances would the diary be shipped until the chest arrived.

During the two weeks it took to arrive, she gave him no more clues or readings, leaving him to build his curiosity with speculation and ponder his depressing situation, his seeming helplessness in the face of a frustrating trap. He was not the only one affected; there was a tension in the air and Fiona and Pumphrey were both even more taciturn than usual. When the United Freight truck pulled up in the alley and a voice announced a package from Vienna it was as though an electric charge had galvanized every molecule in the building.

Nathan wheeled a heavy dolly out behind the truck. The rough wooden crate, fully six feet long and one and a half wide and deep, sat alone in the center of the truck. It was a bit lighter than it looked and no help was asked or offered in loading it onto the dolly. Seconds after Fiona scribbled a signature on the driver's clipboard the truck roared off down the alley leaving Nathan and Fiona alone with Alistair's sinister prize.

Pumphrey disappeared completely and it was Nathan's back at risk when Fiona directed that the thing be taken downstairs. She had to move books here and there to clear a path for it as she led him back to the alcove that led to the basement storerooms. The rickety stairs groaned ominously under the weight. Nathan glanced back once and saw Pumphrey's frightened face peering around the door frame and again to see Alistair looking down with shining yellow eyes and a leer of triumph. Fiona directed him to a room to the left, where another dingy bulb illuminated a litter of empty shipping crates and excelsior and styrofoam packing. Then, with his curiosity at a fever pitch, she thanked him, picked up a pry bar and sent him to cool his heels upstairs. He passed Alistair on his way to the stairs; Nathan might have been invisible for all the notice the old man paid him. He heard the screech of nails pried out of dried wood before he reached the top of the stairs. Furious, he stamped out the front door and walked energetically and aimlessly for two hours.

When he returned Fiona was working as usual in her alcove office. She was tense but not too taut to be sympathetically amused at his frustration. She quickly shushed his questions and asked him to help ship the "diary." It was in another room below, this time to the right of the stairs. He noticed that the air of listening was back, though he could hear no rustlings or scurryings in the labyrinthine undercellars.

He saw immediately that he was not really needed; she had brought him for his own education. The small crate sat in the middle of a work table along one wall. It had been carefully prepared for the long trip to Vienna and nothing remained to do but nail it shut. She motioned to him and he carefully lifted the wooden lid, then the lid of the stout cardboard carton inside.

It was huge; wide, long, thick, between heavy boards clad in black calfskin. The heavy leather covers were cracked and rubbed and there was no title on the outside—a plain book for its time. Inside the text was easily legible, in a graceful Roman typeface, though the Elizabethan English was difficult for Nathan to follow. It was not a diary at all but a printed book, attributed to Dr. John Dee and purporting to be an English translation of a medieval Arab work entitled *Al Azif,* which Dr. Dee translated as "Ye horrors cried by ye insects in ye night." The colophon at the back was in French;

it contained no names and indicated that a mere 169 copies had been printed, a puzzling number.

Hesitantly Nathan turned the pages and saw again and again the most dreaded names of his earlier readings, the most appalling horrors of the earth's immemorial past and precarious present and unknown future faintly echoed in the tones of human speech and the runes of human writing, names like Nyarlathotep and 'Ymnar, Yog-Sothoth and Ngyr-Khorath, Mlandoth and Azathoth. There were awesome assertions about the course of history on this planet as the primordial life-force created in the chaos of the universal beginning unfolded, often in the most hideous forms, and chilling speculations on man's ephemeral role in the awful pageant.

Nathan paled and closed the book of his own volition. They carefully sealed the crate and together carried it by taxi to the shipping office, a most unusual measure in the frugal MacLachlan household.

That night when it was time for Fiona to come pull up the stair, Nathan heard two sets of footsteps pass his door. The sound of the stair rolling up on its runners didn't come. He turned off the lamp and waited silently in the dark. He silently went to the door and opened the latch, holding the knob but not opening the door. The soft shuffling footsteps that crept past him would have been inaudible from the bed. He eased the door in enough to open a hairline crack.

Fiona and Alistair, silhouetted by the light from the stairwell at the end of the hall, were carrying a short stretcher. Fiona, at the front of the stretcher, was walking backwards but did not see Nathan's door move. Alistair's back was no more than four feet from the door.

The object on the stretcher was over five feet long and covered with a blanket. It was lumpy, its shape indeterminate. A fold of the blanket had fallen away to reveal a rigid clawlike mummified human hand.

For the next few weeks Alistair was abnormally active. He was queerly energized, appearing at unpredictable times on the catwalk to summon Fiona for some special task or just to look around aimlessly and pace mechanically as though in a frenzy of wordless mental activity. He often sent Fiona up the ladders to the highest treasures and there gave her gestured directions, always unspoken. When he did speak above a whisper it was often to tease poor Pumphrey, who was

palpably afraid of him, with cryptic references to "finding new uses"
for him. Nathan often heard noises from the floor above his bedroom
and higher late into the night. It was after one of these marathon fits
of activity when the old man was sleeping exhausted well after noon
that Fiona took Nathan up to the fourth floor to see the erstwhile contents of the "chest, carved and inlaid."

In mid-morning she gave him whispered instructions to slip up
to his room. After five minutes of suspense came the soft footsteps
down the hall and a barely audible pat on the door. When he opened
it she signalled for silence. She led the way to the stairway at the end
of the hall and set the style for their slow catlike ascent. They crept
past the featureless third floor hall and on to the top of the stair.

Here the silence was thick and turgid, the two lovers could hear
every breath. There were no footfalls as they crept through the old
wizard's lair, only the faint creakings of the floorboards. It was a very
long hall, extending across the width of the book room below with
many doors on each side, lit only by a small bulb in a sconce halfway
down. There was a mangy carpet runner on the floor, a few decora-
tions on the walls, prints of Aubrey Beardsley, a copy of a Goya. As
they moved past the lamp he could tell from her manner that it
marked the door to the old man's cork-lined room.

At the second door from the end on the left she stopped and produced a key from her jeans. The well-oiled hinges made no telltale
sound. It was a long room with three windows overlooking the alley
below. The heavy curtains were tightly drawn except for a narrow
strip in the middle window which gave the room its only light. Fiona
turned on a small table lamp. The room was a study furnished in the
dark heavy style of the 1890s. There was a faint smell of incense and
the paraphernalia of ritual magic and witchcraft lay about as though
casually discarded in the middle of a game—censers, herbs, vials of
curiously colored infusions, cabalistic diagrams on parchment. On a
long table near the windows lay the blanket-covered object he had
seen in the hall.

She waited for him to come stand at the head of the thing before
she touched the blanket. She pulled it back delicately, disturbing
nothing. The mummy was a foul gray-black color where the skin
remained. In many places it did not. Someone had cut an oval hole
in the skull, a long time ago by the look of it. Yellow-gray bone,

cable-like tendon, hard blackened muscle were all visible on the man from the chest, "medieval, prob. Flemish origin." The blackened lips remained drawn back from carnosaurian teeth and the great black hollows where the eyes had been stared up with hypnotic power. It took an effort to break eye contact with those sinister hollows.

The mummy was shrouded in the tatters of a garment with many gathers like a judge's robes. He had obviously been explored thoroughly since exhumation, as though he had taken some object of great value or power to the grave with him, though the neat incisions and minimal disturbance of the shroud did not show the random vandalism of the typical graverobber. Alistair had done some work here; some of the cut edges were too crisp to be very old.

When she finally replaced the blanket she made sure it held no new fold that might alert the necromancer. She gestured Nathan to another table that held two open books and an amulet made of polished bloodstone. The amulet was intricately inlaid with a design in gold; through the ornate whorls and filigree Nathan recognized the sign of 'Ymnar. One book was a battered but complete copy of von Könnenberg's *Uralte Schrecken* in the original German edition. Nathan could not read German but the name "Nicholas van den Poel" occurred repeatedly in the text. The other book he recognized immediately as another copy of the dreaded volume that had been exchanged for the ancient sorcerer's remains.

They disturbed nothing as they left and locked the door as silently as they had entered. To Nathan's surprise she led him to the left, to the last room on the end. It was unlocked. Again a small lamp lit up an old-fashioned sitting room, this smaller and lined with glassed-in bookcases. But on close inspection he saw that they contained row upon row of little doll's heads. A museum-type plac-ard, looking almost silly in a private home, labelled them "SOUTH AMERICAN CURIOS." Looking more closely he saw that they were shrunken human heads, with the lips and eyesockets sewn shut in the Jivaro manner. All of them had long white or gray-white hair and, in spite of the distortion caused by shrinkage of the skin after the skull was removed, he could see that all belonged to very aged individuals, with Caucasoid features. She led him back out as soon as he had seen this.

Their cautious retreat downstairs was maddeningly slow. She was even more tense as they passed Alistair's room. She seemed to be listening intently for the faintest sound from within.

When they reached Nathan's room she led them both inside and went almost limp with relief. At her urging they took the unusual risk of making love in the daytime, with Pumphrey on the premises and Alistair likely to stir at any time. He had noticed the aphrodisiac effect of fear on her before and this time it was overwhelming. Afterwards she began, in haunted whispers, to complete his education.

"He is a kind of vampire, you know. A vampire and a necromancer and many other horrible things. Legend has only the palest names for the hideous things an evil man can conjure up. He sucks the life force like a vampire drinks blood, leaving his victims drained in body and spirit. If the transfer does not kill them he murders them himself to keep them from talking. You have seen his trophies. Only rarely does he leave them alive. Pumphrey is thirty-one years old.

"But now he is desperate. He has done it too many times. The methods he knows no longer work for him, and he is aging. There are more powerful methods. But the masters of the life force are selfish, evil creatures. They share nothing willingly, give nothing for no return. He has driven a hard bargain to get the unholy relic of Nicholas van den Poel, but the reward will be centuries more of Alistair's evil life."

"But how?" he gasped. "The amulet? Was it in the chest? Any grave robber would have taken it."

She gave him a peculiar smile. "I don't think any ordinary grave robber could molest the remains of the likes of van den Poel and live to tell about it. The amulet was hidden within the corpse. I don't know how it got there, any more than I know how or why he died in spite of his power, but I know that the remains of the great sorcerers are prized by those who still live. Religionists speak of a soul, mystics of Akashic records, scientists of memory molecules—I don't know how it can happen but I have seen it happen—soon Alistair will succeed and raise the dead shade of Nicholas van den Poel and torment it until it teaches him new ways to prey on others to keep his evil self alive for many, many centuries.

"And when he learns this, Nathan, you and I will be very close at hand. We will be tempting and convenient."

That evening Nathan was encouraged to go out to a movie alone and after his return the faint sounds from the fourth floor continued almost until dawn. He never saw Pumphrey again; Pumphrey had evidently been even more convenient than Nathan or Fiona. The change in Alistair was immediately apparent. He came downstairs more often during the day, there was a new spring to his step, he actually showed an interest in the day to day workings of "A. MacLachlan & Co., Bookseller." Coupled with the abrupt disappearance of Pumphrey, who was said to have resigned quite suddenly, the effect was terrifying. And yet it took two more incidents to convince Nathan that he and Fiona must strike for freedom.

The first was the cancellation of Nathan's fellowship. The college was on the brink of bankruptcy and had cancelled their graduate program altogether. Nathan had been lucky to find financial support even from a small college on its last legs. He would be lucky to get another chance, even in a year. He had no illusions about the value of his bachelor of fine arts degree in the job market. Suddenly the gray moment of the present was no longer finite; unless he did something he hadn't thought of yet he would not be leaving at the end of the summer. The thought of Pumphrey scurrying among the books year after year made his stomach feel like cold lead.

The second was the occasion of Fiona's punishment for falling behind on the library order in the unnerving days following the arrival of the chest. It was a sultry evening, a week or so after the departure of Pumphrey. The stifling days of early August were upon them. An afternoon shower had turned the city into a steam bath without lowering the temperature at all. He showered for the second time that day and lay on the bed in his shorts waiting for his lover to feed the old man and steal down for the tryst they had both hungered for all day. As the late summer light waned with eery slowness, he smoked cigarettes (a new habit) and tried to interest himself in a novel he had started a month earlier. When her usual time to appear came and went he thought nothing of it; knowing how she shared his anticipation the wait would only make the consummation more delicious. Could something have gone wrong? Could the old sorcerer have claimed his long-neglected conjugal rights? Nathan's hearing, grown morbidly keen in that quiet place, heard faint muffled sounds from within Alistair's soundproofed lair;

he was sure he heard Fiona's voice raised in what might have been an argument. He gave up on the novel, did pushups, sponged himself with a cool damp cloth, smoked more cigarettes, fiddled with the electric fan to clear the air. . . .

When she finally came he was lying on the bed again. She wore the peignoir and slipped in without knocking as on their first night together. When he jumped up she motioned him back with an outstretched hand. Her eyes were red and puffy. She moved stiffly over to the window and stood looking out at the alley, body taut and erect. Nathan stood still behind her, not sure what to do. Once she threw back her head slightly and her body shuddered from head to toe.

Without turning she unfastened the peignoir and let it drop to the floor. A row of fiery red welts ran from her neck all the way to her knees. The stripes had been fiercely, methodically laid on; they were almost perfectly parallel and evenly spaced except for her bottom, which had been crisscrossed at least three times. Alistair had been very thorough.

Nathan was paralyzed; he felt horror, he felt shame, he felt anger in a bewildering vortex of emotion. She turned and spoke.

"It is time now," she said. "We must kill him, before he destroys us."

And after they had exhausted each other with consoling passion she explained what they must do.

They waited a week. During the punishment Alistair had taunted her with her interest in "the boy" and Alistair had hidden ways of finding things out; it seemed wise to stay completely away from each other for a while to lull his suspicions. Too, they were both shaken, as much by their own decision as by the brutalization of Fiona, and needed time to steel their nerves for the deed. So for a week they hardly spoke to each other and did not meet at night. Nathan tried to look bored and sullen, an easy task as Fiona and Alistair gave him more and more work to do. Fiona looked cowed and listless as she pressed Nathan to meet Alistair's demands, but after three days the stiffness had gone out of her movements and Nathan could see, when Alistair was out of sight, a panther-like energy growing in her.

On the appointed day he did not speak to Fiona at all. He went out alone for an early supper. When he returned in the twilight and let himself in he heard the chink of a dish in the downstairs kitchen.

He made his way through the books and into the narrow hallway that led to it. Their eyes met; the spark that passed between them would have been obvious to any observer. Alistair's dinner, which was to be his last, was on a lacquered tray, ready to be placed in the dumbwaiter. A breaded cutlet, peas, corn . . . and a cup of hot chocolate, sweet enough to mask the taste of the powder which would tranquilize him into a drowsy, vulnerable torpor.

"I'm back," Nathan said, and went up to his room.

Minutes later he heard the clang and whirr of the stair being pulled up on its rollers. Fiona padded by his door, moving quickly. She slowed on the stairs, peering carefully down the unlit third floor hallway, mounting the last flight of stairs a step at a time, listening, looking. The shadows held more terrors for her than for her young lover; to him she had only hinted at the powers at Alistair's disposal, at the weapon he could command, at the unnatural means of acquiring information, at the allies he might summon . . . like those below in the cellars. She had to force herself to move at her normal pace down the corridor toward the lamp ensconced between the dumbwaiter and Alistair's door, all the while listening, imagining shadows where there were none, so totally conscious of her own sound and movement that she could hardly walk. She slid up the door of the dumbwaiter and began pulling on the rope. As Alistair's final meal floated up out of the darkness she quailed for a moment, wondering if she could go through with it, thinking of the consequences of failure, at the hands of Alistair or the law. She could say she forgot the chocolate and go on as before. But she was too stiff with fear to change her plan now. As she lifted the tray and faced the door the strength was running out of her legs and she wished she had gone to the bathroom. She held the tray with one hand and opened the door with the other. She realized that her cotton-dry mouth was open and her eyes bulging and fought for control of her face while she fumbled through the doorway and closed the door behind her.

The only light was from the little opaque-shaded table lamp next to his armchair across the room. He sat there looking very small, shrouded in a voluminous robe with a hood. He did not speak or move. She stood for a moment screwing herself up to approach him. Something warm and furry embraced her ankle and nuzzled her with sharp little teeth. She made a hoarse gasping sound and dropped the tray.

Nathan heard nothing after the rattle of the dumbwaiter. Even the usual distant traffic sounds of the city seemed hushed on that sultry August evening. He stayed up on the bed fully dressed and tried to distract his mind from the anticipation that tried to overwhelm it. It was impossible, of course, not to think about the coming crisis but at least he could stifle the compulsion to go over and over every detail in his mind's eye. Alistair had unknown ways of learning others' thoughts, true, but some thoughts were more dangerous than others. Imagining one's own movements was the worst; that was why the sullen-looking little automatic lay on the bedside table. His entire nervous system itched to pick it up and fondle it and uncock and unload it, load and cock it again. Guns were strange to him, he could not be sure of the processes so new to him. Ease off the safety, point the barrel, squeeze the trigger—that was all that mattered now, he told himself. When the old sorcerer's heart and brain stopped, all the evil conjured by his will would surely cease.

When the time came he stood up and felt his heart race. He took the gun off safety and managed the door with only the subtlest of sounds. Unlike Fiona, he moved silently and his fear, more physical and less uncanny, made him want to rush to be done with it. Movement was a release that calmed him and cleared his mind; he remembered which steps creaked. Faltering or failure never crossed his mind.

On the fourth floor the lamp by Alistair's door was on as usual. The shadows did not stir; the way was clear. As he approached the door with exquisite stealth he felt a first shock of surprise—the sliding door to the dumbwaiter shaft was still open. She must have forgotten it in her excitement. He stood squarely before the door and took deep quiet breaths. Alistair would be sitting in an armchair directly in front of him, about twenty-five feet away. He felt his gun hand trembling as he reached across with his left to grasp the knob.

He flung the door aside and rushed across the threshold, bringing his left hand up to the gun pointing at the shadowed blur in the chair. The first roar and flash were stunning, the second more so. The blurred thing jerked twice like a straw man. The third roar toppled

it with half the face in the lamplight; half the eternal grimace of
Nicholas van den Poel.

Nathan's knees turned to water as his comprehension reeled. In
the chair the folds of the rotted shroud were moving. The thing that
rose out of its folds resembled a hooded cobra, yet it had a face, a tiny,
evil face with piercing ruby eyes and a piglike nose and a mouthful
of needle-like fangs and it laughed a high-pitched sneering laugh.

Run. His body made the instant decision, impulses rushed to
every muscle—then he heard a muffled squawk and lurched. There
was an alcove to his left and in the dim light he saw Fiona's face, eyes
enormous with terror. She had been gagged, stripped and her hands
tied to some fixture depending from the ceiling. She was stamping
her feet in a parody of sprinting. A small agile thing was clinging to
her leg, easily riding her wild gyrations. Alistair had thoughtfully
placed cushions under her feet to spare Nathan the sound of her
stamping during his long wait.

He ran to her and jerked the thing off her and flung it across the
room. It clung tenaciously, like a tick. Fiona shrieked when it came
free and blood ran down her leg from the point where its mouth had
been. The rope was knotted to an open hook. He heaved and raised
her enough to clear the point. He pulled her into the room, toward
the door. She had been thrashed again, this time haphazardly, desul-
torily; Alistair, too, had passed a long hour waiting. And there were
smears of blood where his monstrous pets had nibbled at her.

The creature was staying a couple of paces in front of them, scut-
tling back and forth sideways as though at bay and tittering. Two
more swarmed out from under the chair and scrambled toward them.
They were furry with short tails, about the size of weasels and equally
vicious. They ran low on all fours but stopped to dance in front of the
terrified pair on hind legs with arms out like wrestlers. The faces were
short and much too human, except for the long pointed teeth that
grinned in deadly mirth. There was a musky smell like a tomcat, but
worse. More emerged from the shadows around the room. More of
the serpent things were appearing too.

One made a dash at Nathan and retreated at a reflexive swipe
of his foot. Another darted at Fiona, who moaned and ducked
behind him. He pointed the gun at it and closed his eyes as it roared.
Its head was a red pulpy bulb, but still it groped for him, pressing

the bloody remains of its head against his leg, then cavorting off aimlessly like a waltzing mouse. Nathan shuddered and moaned, too. He panicked and fired at the row of grinning teeth until the slide of the automatic stayed back and the trigger didn't click when his finger jerked on it.

Then the tittering and the sneering laughter ceased and they heard a dry cough. The foul menagerie fidgeted and looked from their quarry to their master and back again.

Alistair stood in the archway at the back of the room and leaned on his cane. He looked more alive than Nathan had ever seen him, an evil Einstein with the glowing eyes of a tiger. He was certainly smiling now, mostly in the eyes.

"Well, well," he said, in that dry hollow voice of his. "It seems that your plan has failed. And mine has succeeded.

"Did you think me too feeble to observe your fatuous passion? Or too stupid? I have watched you at your work many more times than you have seen me. And my little friends have been very busy indeed, watching and tattling. Did you know they could speak, Fiona? I commanded them all to hold their vile little tongues in your presence, of course. I have never been foolish enough to trust you, my dear. But their brains, though small, are more human than otherwise.

"You, Nathan, are more forgivable in your foolishness. You could not know how a powerful will can command the eternal life force, how the life force can transform matter. If your lover told you you could never accept it. Yet it is the plain truth, as you see.

"You see here the dregs of the biosphere salvaged and combined into the most enchanting companions and helpmates." The weasel things were starting to titter again, softly.

"Stray cats and dogs, ferrets, rats, human derelicts and criminals—I wasted nothing, you see. The human specimens are quite lucky to be alive in any form. I had drained them. Like Pumphrey.

"Did she tell you about that? About what you faced when your plan failed?"

Fiona whispered and Nathan's fear took on a new dimension.

"I used to drain them, like a glass of sherry. The method was simple, I won't bore you with details. I would become strong, vital. They would wither. I could see it first in their faces, their carriage. After a week or two the physical signs became unmistakable—the hair white at the roots, the sagging flesh, the doddering walk. I could have taken it all, all their life force, and left them dead. Yet I did not. I combined the remains of their human psyche with the vitality of wild and feral beasts, leaving them enough brain to be useful to me. And the results you see before you, hungering for your flesh. But have no fear; they are completely under my control, and I hunger for something less tangible."

The hollow timbre of the ancient's insidious voice held Nathan in trancelike fascination.

"The methods I used to drain these souls will no longer work for me, you see. That is why it was necessary for me to . . . consult a colleague. About more sophisticated methods."

At that obscure witticism the necromancer burst into cackling laughter, ending only when he had to catch his breath.

"And old Nicholas, you see, had no desire to help me. None at all. And no gratitude for letting his shade come into the world of the living, if only for a brief hour or so. But I was persuasive. Yes, very persuasive. I can be very persuasive, can't I, my dear Fiona?"

Nathan felt her shudder behind him.

"At last I was able to make him reasonable, and tell me, in Latin, that which he had known centuries before my birth. And now I have the means to continue my most agreeable life for quite a long time. Even longer than poor Nicholas, who died untimely of his own errors. I do not make errors. And that is how I came by my new toy. It is beautiful, is it not?"

With that he held out his cane, pointing it at Nathan, and for the first time Nathan saw that it was not his usual gold-headed cane but a darkly beautiful rod of murky crystal, inlaid with a filigreed inscription entwined around the sign of 'Ymnar. He felt Fiona let go of him and retreat from Alistair's thrust and instinctively did the same. Alistair moved slowly forward behind the enigmatic staff, savoring the moment.

"Not a mere walking stick you see, but a funnel. For the life force. From you to me."

And he advanced hurriedly toward the hapless pair, the grinning beasts scattering to make his passage, the rod thrust out like a rapier. Nathan felt Fiona shivering behind him; he was beyond rational thought, seeing only the rod and the image of Pumphrey, hopeless

Pumphrey with his grizzled hair and his seamed face and his limp. There was no decision made, no conscious thought before he hurled the empty gun at Alistair and it was only luck that jabbed the pointed corner of the slide squarely into his left eye.

He dropped the rod and clutched his face, reeling backward and roaring with pain. The beasts all stared at him stupefied. Nathan was out the door in an instant, pulling Fiona by the wrist and slamming the door after them. It took but a moment to free her hands from the rope. They started toward the stair, then stopped when they saw the shadows move there. The horde of snake-things that came crawling up into the hall looked dazed and clumsy but they still glared balefully at the fugitives.

"The fangs," cried Fiona in a quavering voice, "venom. . . ." She clutched him and trembled again.

The dumbwaiter next to them was still open.

"Quick! In here!" he blurted and grasped the pulley rope. "Let yourself down. It's the only way past them!"

She needed no urging. Alistair's groans were fainter and more intermittent through the cork-lined door. She swung her legs over the sill, sat on the platform, and took the rope. Nathan closed the sliding door leaving her in total darkness.

He looked at the squirming mass creeping toward him. Behind the door the muffled groaning stopped. He took a deep breath and ran for the stairs. Beady eyes and needle-fangs caught the lamplight as he ran and his first great leap carried him twelve feet over a hissing chorus. He landed on something that squashed and cursed him in a squeaky parody of a human voice before it died. The second leap took him to the top of the stairs where he stumbled and rolled down over a dozen wriggling bodies. The hissing and squeaking behind him were furious.

He landed with his eyes a foot from a tiny face that reared back to strike. He scrambled back and felt fangs graze his hand; he felt two thumps against his pants leg before he got to his feet and went pounding down the stairs clear of the serpents. His hand and two spots on his left leg were needle points of pain, spreading like slow fire. He was limping by the time he reached the second floor and heard Fiona screaming in the dumbwaiter shaft.

When Nathan closed the door on her the darkness was total. She sat huddled on the little platform, bowed in the center with her weight, and let the rope up hand over hand while the platform jerked and slid a few inches at a time down the seemingly endless shaft. Her mind was frozen in wordless fear, the inky blackness a threatening ocean around her, the distant vibrations of Nathan's progress a cryptic rumor of disaster. She had no sense of how far she had descended when suddenly the blackness was not total. She puzzled for an instant, then looked up at the bright trapezoid of the fourth floor far above. A small shape clambered over the sill, then another. The rope quivered in her hand. She let go and plunged three feet before grasping it again, searing her palms. She screamed hoarsely, methodically, rhythmically, her entire organism enthralled by the primordial function of the trapped animal, flight gone, fight gone, waiting to be devoured.

When Nathan opened the second floor door she was a foot below him. He dragged her out limp and screaming with four of the horrors gnawing at her like leeches. He himself was badly bitten pulling them off and throwing them down the shaft. He had to drag her to her feet and pull her down the hall.

He had never lowered the stair before and the mechanism baffled him. He shouted for her to help, but she stood at the rail staring openmouthed at the darkness below. He looked down and saw movement. Something, no, many things, were jumping up and down as though eager to get at the pair on the catwalk. The largest of the lot was as large as a Doberman; their shapes reminded him of rats. They began to chatter like monkeys.

"He let them out! He sent one of them to let them out!" she gasped.

Then with a scurrying rush the catwalk was full of squeaking and hissing forms pouring out of the hallway onto the catwalk and he and Fiona were climbing up on the rail. Nathan leaped for a ladder eight feet away, barely saving himself from a long fall; he had forgotten the pain of the serpent bites but now his left leg and arm were numb and hard to control. Fiona lost her footing and fell with her hands gripping the rail and flailing her legs wildly as the great rat-thing leaped at her and the others crept within a foot of her face.

And then the squeaking and gibbering and thumping died away to a low rustle and the things on the catwalk drew back as their master appeared.

He held his left hand over his left eye and in his right he held the rod inlaid with the sign of 'Ymnar. The urbanity, the cat and mouse teasing were gone; he glowered at her with his good eye, hatred undisguised and uncontrolled. His voice was a foul hissing shriek.

"Whore! You FILTH! You PIG! You came crawling to me begging for life and youth, begging to learn how to suck the life from others to prolong your filthy existence, you ignorant slimy pathetic little WITCH! And after fifteen years of youth that I gave you, not yourself, not your own power, but mine, you betray me with this CHILD and then try to destroy ME! Did you think me blind and deaf, did you think me an imbecile?

"Very well—life you shall have. Life, like Cordelia before you. You shall join her! But—not too much life. I shall have the best of you."

He advanced holding the rod before him, aimed at her heart.

"You shall nourish me, and then you shall join her and her friends and you shall help them guard my treasures at night. I shall leave you enough of the life force to live for many years and to remember who you are and what you once were. But very little of your body—you shall have plenty of vigorous new bodily material, most of it rodent. I find that very fitting. But for now I want Cordelia and her companions to have most of your flesh." His voice rose to a bellow. "Do you hear me, Cordelia?" And the great rat-thing began again to leap up to snap at Fiona's heels.

Hypnotized by the scene before him, Nathan was unaware that his left leg and arm were completely numb or that he was drooling from the slack left side of his mouth. When the rod of 'Ymnar pressed against Fiona's chest there was a sensation like a subsonic hum and a crimson glow that enveloped the wizard and the rod and its victim. She gaped at the necromancer, wide-eyed and open-mouthed, her thrashing legs slowing, her horrified face growing seamed and withered, her hands weakening. There was no strength left for a final scream as her hands began to slip, and when Nathan finally lost his balance, there was no response to his reflexes and they both plunged to the floor below.

When Nathan finally came to full consciousness he knew that he had been out for a very long time, that he had been drugged, that he had dreamed long, that there had been much pain but that it had acquiesced to a dull ache that pervaded his whole body. The face before him was one that he had seen before in dream, a beautiful heart-shaped face framed in raven hair over emerald green eyes, beautiful but cruel, passionate but cold.

"Who . . . ?" he stammered. "Who . . . ?"

"I am Firenza," she said.

She added, "I am the bookseller's third wife."

There is a permanent economic recession in that city and now and then a young man desperate for employment answers the uninspired ad deep in the classifieds and reads the gold lettering on the big panes on either side of the front door. He may be repelled by the gloomy aspect of the place and leave immediately, or he may knock. The creature that confronts him through the glass, the seamed face beneath grizzled hair, the limping gait, the frightened visage curiously scarred about the neck and face, may drive him away forthwith.

Or . . . he may enter. ✳

Eldritch

by Brad Linaweaver and Fred Olen Ray

When he was seven, she [his mother] confiscated a copy of H.G. Wells's novel *The Island of Dr. Moreau* lest its gruesomeness harm his delicate nerves.

—L. Sprague de Camp, *Lovecraft: A Biography*

THE NARRATIVE OF JOHN REYNOLDS

All that could be said in favor of the long voyage from Africa was that I finally got my sea legs. The accommodations in the old tramp steamer were ragtag. Normally I never would have entertained the idea of traveling under these conditions, but business in London could not wait any further delays. As it stood, the voyage would take up the better part of six weeks.

The cabin was small and musty with an overpowering stench of tar and pitch. In the middle of June, it felt like a foretaste of hell. God, it was hot!

In truth, I doubted that I would make it back to Soho by August. I spent considerable time trying to convince myself that the old tub was seaworthy enough to make the trip around the Cape of Good Hope. The *Marie D'Artain* was a piece of nautical rubbish. The sides of the ship were weathered, the paint long since cracked and peeling. Even the metal fittings that held the vessel together were rusty with age.

Under the circumstances, it was astonishing to discover that the crew was in a more dilapidated state than the ship. Some of them were such perfect caricatures of ragged seafarers that they looked as if they'd just stepped out of the wild and delirious tales told in gentlemen's clubs in London. These were men who had lost fingers, eyes, and even limbs in pursuit of objectives I little doubted were questionable. I didn't want to test my mettle against any of them in a brawl if I could possibly help it. Nor did I like the idea of my back turned to them.

At least the captain was a man of strength and seriousness—a Lucifer to this crew of lesser demons. Like them, he was aged and weather-beaten by a life as unrelenting as the tides of the sea. Unlike them, he had a focused mind. If not for his presence, I would never have signed on as the only passenger; and even a capable captain seemed inadequate insurance for such a voyage.

I counted myself fortunate that after using the last of my gold to pay for passage, I still had resources—two hundred pounds of raw ivory, a shipment sufficient to keep Brighton street jewelers scrambling for six months. There might even be a promotion in it for me. This was easily the largest and finest shipment of White Treasure to come out of the delta in three years.

As I sat in the reeking cabin, feeling the gentle rocking of the ship, I allowed myself to finally ask a question I had put out of mind until now: Did I deal fairly with the natives? Even though the tusks were of little worth in their eyes, I couldn't help but feel that I stole from them. Naturally they fancied the oddest and most useless goods I'd been able to acquire to barter with them. One chieftain actually pined after a cricket bat, which I was happy enough to let him have—although I'm sure he saw it as a war club (but then, his perception may not have been so far off the mark).

At least the black faces that floated through my uneasy dreams were to be preferred over the unshaven white masks of the surly crew. One crude specimen in particular, the cook's assistant, always leered at me with the most malignant expression. There was something almost animalistic about the man that made me feel a loathing that I never had with any of the tribesmen. His face put me in mind of certain stories I'd heard from this part of the world.

In short order I stopped worrying about unwholesome impressions because I had far more material concerns: storm warnings! One did not have to be a sailor to understand the portent of creaking timbers and clanging chains. The wind was picking up, but so far there was no rain. Only once did I become seasick from the rocking of the old tub. I considered it a great victory that I made it to the railing. The lodgings were noxious enough without my adding to the reek of the atmosphere, but I gladly sacrificed my best shirt to the sea. It would never be my best shirt again and I was grateful to be rid of it.

I'm certain that I would have faced the storm with equanimity if not for the suffocating confines of the tar-scented cabin! My small port window remained sealed tight, adding immeasurably to the staleness of the air.

When my stomach finally settled down, I started wearing my jacket, despite the stifling heat of my quarters. The leather, fleece-lined short jacket was the best buy I had made in Nairobi. It became a point of honor with me to walk the boards and acquit myself as well as any of the bestial crew.

In any event, I didn't stay very long in the cold night air, because I was drawn to the light shining in Captain Marsh's pilot house. A quick climb up the short ladders showed me he was at the wheel. As usual he was receptive to company. Perhaps he found me pleasant to look upon simply because all my digits and ears were still intact.

I knew a little about his background already. An American hailing from Innsmouth, Massachusetts, he had received some education. He did a lot of East Indies trading and claimed to own several other ships. He also had good taste in tobacco for such a rough seaman, if I could judge from the rich aroma filling the pilot house from his briar wood pipe.

"Good evening, Captain," I said, pushing wide the door as I entered.

"Can't sleep?" he asked, biting down hard on the stem of his pipe as I nodded. "It's these waters," he went on. "Does it to everyone."

"How's that?" I asked, taking note of his smile. No doubt I was just what he wanted at that moment: a receptive audience.

"There's things about this stretch of ocean that don't sit well with me." I sensed a sailor's tall tale coming on with plenty of salt and brine. An excellent way to pass a spell of insomnia; or just to get the hell out of my cabin. I urged him on and he was only too willing to comply.

"You can't see 'em at night," he continued, face partly obscured by a wreath of pipe smoke, "but there's a string of islands to the west of us, in the blackness. No one stops there. Never been there myself and I don't want to. Lots of stories circulate 'bout them islands. And one in particular. Can't say as I believe 'em, but if you got no business there why take chances?

"Well, once there was a storm through here and we was caught in the squall. Nothing we could do made any headway, so we just battled on, trying to move up the coast. When the wind and rain finally let up I discovered we'd gone nowhere. We're still right here and we got damage to take care of below deck before we dare go on. Rufe and some of the boys was down in the hold doing a quick patch job on some weakened timbers . . ."

Here I interrupted his narrative to inquire as to whether or not this "patch job" was in fact the makeshift metal sheeting I'd seen nailed to the inner hull as I passed out of my cabin. "Yes," he replied. "But don't you worry about it. That job's held for the last few years and it'll hang on a few more. It wasn't the damage that bothered me that day, but the wreckage floating about the ship. That wreckage gave every man aboard a case of the shivers."

"Wreckage?" I asked. "You mean from another ship?"

"No other ship was anywhere to be seen. Near as I could figure the stuff had washed a'sea from islands to the west. Besides, it was nothing like ship scuttle, but tables and crates of instruments—wooden cages—you name it! Everything but Davy Jones' locker. All of it drifting with no one but us to salvage it."

"Did you collect the materials?" I asked.

"One of the boys . . . Curtis, I believe . . . fished something out of the debris, but it wasn't no manmade object. He pulled the thing out of the drink with the long gaff. At first he thought it might be a lady's fur coat . . . but then we figured it had to be a drowned animal of some sort." Marsh's eyes grew wide as if seeing the long-ago sights once again, and he took a deep drag of smoke.

"So what was it?" I asked impatiently.

The older man looked long and hard at me before answering: "A monster, Mr. Reynolds. It was a beast spawned in hell."

By this point the captain had hooked my interest as certainly as he might reel in a fish big enough to satisfy any sailor's fantasies. "Can you describe it to me?" I urged.

"I might," said the weathered seaman, reaching beneath the steering cabinet to retrieve a half-emptied bottle of whiskey. Uncorking the sour mash, he turned the bottom up for a long draw. The label showed it to be a product of the Tennessee state of America. I reckoned the bottle had traveled far to be here tonight, but, despite his hospitality of offering me a portion, I declined. I wanted nothing to weaken or distract my attention as I again prodded him for a description of the monster.

"For starters," he resumed, "it was good and dead. But it was hard to believe that anything like that could have ever been alive. Why, it looked a bit like one of those dried up freak show mermaids you see in the dime museums. You know, the kind of critter where some taxidermist has taken two kinds of animal and sewed 'em together into one sorry looking monkey-fish!"

Although I had never been even remotely anxious to view such a carnival monstrosity, I found his recounting to exert a strange and morbid appeal. "You'll understand what I mean when I tell you this thing was a crazy-quilt type of monster—like several different animals all fused together. There were arms or legs, maybe six of them, sprouting out of the body like dead tree limbs with claws like a lion. Half its face was short-snouted like a hyena, but it had the eyes and ears of a great cat! The body was leathery and near hairless with the toughness of rhino hide, but there was no tail."

The captain caught his breath and stared out through the window. I didn't doubt that he was remembering the thing so vividly that it was the same as if it was with us in the cabin. Then he surprised me again: "I haven't told you the oddest thing, Mr. Reynolds. There were knife wounds all over the carcass. The monster had been butchered before the storm washed it out to sea. And the nature of the wounds makes me think it was killed in some kind of ritual. I'm afraid I know what kind!"

He paused. I could tell that he wanted to say more, but it was as if an invisible barrier had been thrown up between us.

"What kind of ritual?" I dared ask.

He answered my question with a question. "Mr. Reynolds, have you ever heard of Shub-Niggurath, the Goat with a Thousand Young?"

"I can't say that I have, Captain."

For a long time, he puffed on his pipe. "Pray, sir, that you never meet any of her children."

By this point I was beginning to think I'd been too hasty in turning down the drink. "What became of the thing?" I asked.

The captain seemed relieved to return to the subject of one palpable horror. "Curtis wanted to save the monster. Put it in salt and sell it to the circus when we got to England. Trouble was that half the crew was spooked by the thing and I wasn't happy about having it on board myself. More drowned monsters were floating by on that cursed day. I ordered it tossed back in the sea to join its companions. And since that day I've always charted my course past that string of islands on the darkest night of the month. I know you can't see 'em; but they're out there."

On that note Captain Marsh finished his bogey tale and stared through the dingy glass window into the blackness. After a moment he relit his pipe, which had gone dead. He just stared out into the night, his desire to talk also as dead as ashes.

So I left him to his thoughts, stepped out onto the lightless deck of the heaving ship. I was determined to hug the rail for a few moments and strain my eyes westward, in search of the islands Marsh swore were out there. I've always been fascinated by the juxtaposition of the beautiful and the ugly. Maybe it goes back to when I used to frequent carnivals in my youth. Whatever the reason, I couldn't shake the idea that there might be an island with creatures on it worth more than all the ivory in the world.

Curiosity may have saved my life. Leaning over the rail put me in position where I heard an ominous sound. A low, rumbling sound coming towards me with due speed. Out of the gloom I saw a handful of sailors approaching. They were the sorriest specimens of humanity I'd seen . . . up to that point. And they were coming right at me with blunt objects in their hands and scowls on their anthropoid faces.

Two of them pounced, pinning my arms to my sides and before I could even utter a cry of surprise, a third dirty bastard clubbed me over the head with something that looked like a rapidly moving straight iron. I was sure I was a goner, but I only blacked out for a moment before being brought to by a blast of water.

The scoundrels had thrown me overboard!

At first I could not let myself fully believe how dire were my circumstances. I even called for help. But then I heard a gunshot and to my horror saw the body of Captain Marsh plunge into the sea near me. The mutineers were not about to throw me a raft. I counted myself lucky if they thought I had already drowned.

Years ago I had learned the advantages of floating on one's back when in the ocean so as to conserve strength. I let myself drift and tried to be silent as death.

Lifting my head, I saw the black bulk of the ship receding sluggishly towards the horizon. It would probably be the last I ever saw of the steamer and my white cargo; and perhaps the last thing I saw in this life if all luck had deserted me.

Although not a particularly religious man, I found myself praying that Captain Marsh's dreaded islands actually did exist. Whatever dangers might await me there seemed a small matter when the alternative was drowning in the open sea.

When the ship was finally out of sight, I turned over and gave a few gentle kicks, heading in the most hopeful direction—I remembered the last sighting of the steamer's lights. I swam for what seemed an hour, drifting as much as I could without losing my bearings.

My head ached horribly, but I suppose I was fortunate to be so close to the ship's rail at the time of the attack or it might not be aching at all. The water was temperate, which made survival easier, but I couldn't stop thinking about the possibilities of sharks. I floated and swam and prayed. When I began to feel that all was lost, I heard the sound of waves rolling harshly against a rocky shore somewhere in the blackness ahead.

In between mouthfuls of sea water, I amused myself with a vision of wringing the life out of my employer. It's a pity that very few precious stones abound in England. Much like spices, one has to travel abroad to gather them . . . to India, China, and even America. My position required that I visit every rotten hell hole this earth had to offer in search of rarities. And now *this!* I couldn't imagine anything worse, which speaks volumes for my lack of imagination.

Homicidal thoughts for my employer were an inspiration. They kept me going past the point of exhaustion when it seemed that I could not swim another stroke. I imagined him drowning; then I imagined him being devoured by a shark. Then I decided, that given my situation, I should not dwell too long on such grisly details at the moment.

I had been so caught up in my fantasies of revenge, and my heartbeat had been so loud in my ears, that I had not realized there were sounds of crashing waves growing nearer with each stroke. Suddenly I realized I might actually survive this ordeal.

With great joy I made my way to the rocky shore of Marsh's devil island. But actually emerging from the water onto that jagged coast would be a miracle of perseverance. The tow of the waves picked me up a good fifty yards out and swept me towards the sharp stones forming a wicked-looking shoreline.

In an instant I realized that all my efforts to reach the island alive might well have been wasted. The waves that rushed me on towards my only hope for salvation could very easily kill me. The knifelike surface of the rocks reared up menacingly against the sky like the mouth of some huge serpent that threatened to swallow me.

As the waves rushed towards the jagged outcropping I tried to relax, despite the body's natural inclination to tense up. I barely remember it now. One moment I was fifteen feet away from the nearest boulder and then I was tasting my own blood as I was smashed against the rocky surface. If I had not had the foresight to wrap my arms about my head, I might have suffered a concussion.

The second time the wave brought me back to the boulder, I struggled to find a hold on the craggy surface. There were only a few seconds of calm before the next wave would crash on me from behind. My fingers dug into a crevice just as the second wave struck with less force than the first. I did not waste the opportunity.

Scrambling with the strength left in my tortured limbs, I pulled myself to safety. An aching body was a small price to pay to feel firm ground under my feet again. A blue-black bruise on my right forearm seemed like a badge of honor. I bled from dozens of small wounds, my second best shirt was now in tatters and my head felt like it had been kicked unmercifully in one of West Hamm's worst rugby encounters. I made no effort to move from my rock until daylight.

I awoke in agony. I had been so exhausted that I lay unconscious well past the dawn, roasting in the sun with my untended injuries. Under normal circumstances, I would have viewed the morning as beautiful. But I had been reduced to the basics of survival.

The boulders were so arranged that I saw that I could jump from one to another and reach the shore. They were of volcanic origin, each rife with a variety of sharp-edged, open pocket-like craters that could easily slice a hand open. I only survived my initial contact with the largest one because it was the most worn from the waves, with the smoothest surface.

When I reached the beach, I felt a sense of real accomplishment. It was not made up of sand, but of crushed shell and rock. It had a distinct brown, almost dirty look. I fell to my knees despite the discomfort—what was extra pain to me now?—and kissed the damned stuff.

I was glad that my shoes had survived the ordeal. I wouldn't want to walk barefoot over this brittle expanse. As I crunched my way across this unusual beach, I wondered how long it had been since a man walked here, if ever. The jungle was my objective.

At the time I thought the Fates were apologizing to me for all the trouble I'd experienced in the past twenty-four hours. I found ripe bananas and made a feast of them. I found water.

Next I decided to walk up the coast to see if there was a landing or other signs of a civilization. Here the beach was smooth sand and I gratefully removed my sopping shoes and felt the warm sand under my feet—perhaps the only undamaged portion of my anatomy.

By now the sun was directly overhead. I was glad I had not slept any longer, because I was already sunburned through the rags of my shirt. I cursed the loss of my jacket.

Up to this point, I had not seen anything suggestive of a human presence. There was a variety of tropical birds. Instead of appreciating their bright plumage, all I could think of was how difficult it would be to kill and eat one. Although I did not see any animal life, I felt a presence. I could see nothing, but I couldn't shake the feeling of being watched . . . and stalked.

I had traded the night terrors of sharks for a terror in broad daylight. Just as I could not see a predator in the dark water beneath me, so I could not see what might be padding softly just beyond the line of foliage separating the jungle from the beach. Could there be a sleek and silent leopard that had picked up my scent? The heat of the day did not prevent my shivering.

Presently I arrived at a small inlet that apparently formed a deep water lagoon. I ascertained this from the fact that there was a well maintained dock jutting out into the water. From the length of it, one could surmise that it was built to accommodate a boat of medium size and length. The inlet was shaped naturally like the mouth of a snarling animal with two thin peninsulas curving out into the ocean. The shape provided a convenient breakwater and created a calm lagoon where vessels could moor.

The dock was in good condition, proving that people had been there recently. But there was one sign of human activity that did nothing to set my mind at ease. Someone had painted triangles and circles all over the dock, and letters I did not recognize. There also seemed to be some kind of squid, but the artist wasn't very good— this squid seemed to have some human proportions!

I followed a plainly marked dirt road that left the area and headed into the jungle. It was with eager anticipation that I followed this path, not only because this must lead to a habitation, but also because the moment my foot touched the path I felt as though my unseen companion had stopped following me.

The road that led inland was well maintained and it was clear why it had to be; it was heavily rutted by the wheels of many wagons, or perhaps only one wagon that followed the same route. The surface was as hard as baked clay. The island must be subject to torrential rainfall followed by periods of hot, scorching sun. The flora was thick on both sides, green walls to mark my progress. I had no intention of straying off the path.

After twenty minutes of this, the road suddenly split off to the left. The new path seemed less used. The jungle had made inroads and had all but taken it over again. It did not have the deep ruts dug into it and seemed to lead off in a direction quite opposed to where the main road was headed. The only explanation was that this side road did not lead to the main settlement. I was not in an exploring mood just then. I wanted to find the center of human activity on this island.

Another thirty minutes passed before I saw any further proof of human habitation. I remembered the story of Captain Marsh about the terrific storm that swept these islands years earlier. Perhaps the monster had been swept out to sea from this very island!

The first buildings I laid eyes upon formed a front line that seemed to form a protective battery between the main house and the road leading in. They were small stable-like constructions that rested side by side on either side of the road—three each. The walls of the buildings facing the road were solid and thick with the exception of several small openings that might just be large enough through which to aim a gun.

Beyond the front line of the structures, whose purpose I could not ascertain, were a series of corrals, which were empty with the exception of two sturdy looking horses that were tethered to a post outside the fencing furthest to my right. Beyond these lay a garden of some majesty; beyond that was a mansion.

The mansion was something transplanted from another time and place. It was antebellum by design, but already showed signs of decay with crumbling arches and windows so clouded with age as to be useless. None of this meant a damn to me at that moment. The mansion was a palace of the gods to me. It meant food, a hot bath, a good night's rest, a smoke, a roaring fire, music. Did it mean even more than that? Who might be the master . . . or mistress of this mausoleum in the heart of the jungle?

My heart was in my throat as I grasped the brass knocker and brought it down as hard as I could. Three times I did this before hearing footsteps from within. At first, I anticipated the owner or servant to be accompanied by a large dog, as I thought I heard the pad of several scuffling feet. After listening to a seemingly unending series of well-oiled iron bolts being unlocked and drawn back, the thick door swung open and I saw that I had been completely wrong; well, almost completely.

There, in the doorway, stood the most startling personage I had ever seen. In the course of my travels, I'd come across many unpleasant specimens, but nothing prepared me for the grim visage peering at me from the still white collar of a butler's uniform.

Under a shaggy mop of coal-black hair was the one good feature of the face: his large, soulful brown eyes. But the nose underneath was a horror. At first I thought its twisted configurations might be the result of having been broken several times—I am a follower of the pugilist's art. Closer scrutiny revealed it to be a natural outgrowth.

The lips did not correspond to any recognizable human type. They extended a short distance beyond the nose as if they could scarcely contain the great quantity of teeth in the mouth. The chin seemed to be all crumpled up, as if covered with scars, but this was another misleading impression. The fleshy mass was indeed of a whole with the rest of the poor wretch's appearance.

Instinctively, I reached for my gun, forgetting for the moment that I had lost my weapon in the sea. The odd butler made no countermove, but remained impassive. The next move was mine. As I had my doubts that he could even speak, I broke the silence with, "Excuse me, but I'm stranded on your island."

I don't know what shocked me more: the fact that he answered so promptly or that he was articulate given the handicap of his canine teeth. "Not my island," he said. "Belongs to the master."

"Is your master at home?" Even as I asked the question, I felt the dread of being watched return as if I'd regressed to childhood and there was a devil creeping up behind me. It took all my will power not to turn around and see if a great black leopard had finally emerged from the underbrush . . . but I wasn't about to take my eyes off the malignant fellow right in front of them.

And then the problem resolved itself. The butler gave a start as he stared at something behind me. When I heard the sounds, I joined him as witness. The courtyard in front of the house was suddenly the scene of a frenzied battle between two aberrations of humanity compared to which the butler would have fit right in at Buckingham Palace. The first of these monsters was vaguely anthropoid and might have been mistaken for a gorilla except for the undeniably human head and human proportions of his limbs. The second was less hairy, but in certain ways even more bestial, so distorted was the head from the human norm. It was as if an inverted triangle of flesh had been placed on a human neck and made to snarl and bite.

They started the fight with butting heads and then seemed to remember that they had arms and claws. The noises they made started out animal and shrieked into a parody of the human. The bellowing and screeching would wake the dead—but instead roused the attention of someone very much alive.

From where I stood, I had a perfect view of the bottom half of a staircase down which marched a perfectly shaped pair of female legs. As the rest of her came into view, I was so taken by her that I couldn't tear myself away from the sight of the woman to continue watching two inhuman monsters fighting a few yards away.

She was tall and lithe in a long dress that clung to her curves as if in worship. Her long, black hair seemed to move as if having a life of its own. As she walked past the butler and me, I caught one quick glimpse of her green eyes. She didn't seem to notice either one of us. Her attention was entirely focused on the combatants.

Not until she raised her right hand, did I notice that she carried a long black whip. I had not lived a sheltered life and my travels offered opportunities in some of the finest bordellos in the world. Until that moment I had thought of myself as jaded. But mere proximity to this incredible creature made me wild to have her. Forgotten were all pains; exhaustion vanished in a rush of adrenaline to match the surging ocean waves. There was some kind of musk about her, some natural perfume of desire, that made her the sexiest woman I had ever encountered. And I'd always admired women with high cheekbones.

The goddess wasted no motions. She cracked the whip within a few inches of the heads of the combatants. Such was her control that the monstrosities seemed to freeze in place, staring at each other with blood lust in their eyes. But they knew she was there. They were afraid.

She cried out commands in phrases that meant nothing to me, but then she switched to English. I remained confused.

"What is the law?" she demanded.

The one that looked like an ape answered: "Not to go on all fours; not to suck up drink; not to spill the wrong blood."

"What else?" she asked him, whip still held high.

"Not to eat the wrong flesh. Are we not the children of She whose name we dare not speak? Are we not servants of the Book?"

"And who am I?" she demanded of the other one.

He knew his catechism as well as the ape. "Yours is the hand that makes, that wounds, that heals. Yours is the House of Pain. Yours is the wisdom of the Book."

"Go now," she said, "and sin no more."

The two creatures almost fell over each other in their headlong rush back into the jungle. The astonishing woman finally looked me in the eye and I felt like an awkward adolescent as she announced, "I am Dr. Moreau."

That name stirred something in me, but her appearance banished lesser explorations. Later I would worry about who she was. She looked me up and down the way a bold man admires a woman. My eyes returned the favor, following the lines of the hard leather handle of the incongruous whip. I noticed that she wore a necklace with the same strange squid design I had noticed painted on the dock.

"Who are you?" she asked.

"John Reynolds. I'm afraid that I'm shipwrecked." I was ashamed to admit the manner in which I'd been cast adrift.

"Of course you are," she smiled. "No uninvited guest reaches this island any other way."

"I've never apologized for being shipwrecked before."

She laughed. It was deep-throated and musical. Suddenly she lifted her whip and I thought that she was about to strike me with it. The black tip snaked past my ear and snapped somewhere behind me. I glanced around and saw the biggest damned rat in the world run squealing back into the underbrush. The vermin must have been inches from my bare feet when she spotted it.

"You use that like a born aristocrat," I told her. It was meant as a compliment.

Anger flashed in her eyes even before the words lashed my ego. "What do you know about aristocracy? The most meaningless concept in the pathetic history of man!"

"I apologize if—"

She heard nothing but her own inner voice: "Blood lines are what you make of them!"

Then she finally seemed to hear herself and took a deep breath. She was much calmer as she continued: "A strong hand is the only way to deal with natives. Experience has taught me that. As for my dexterity with the corrector, anyone who grew up with horses would do as well."

"Did you?" I asked lamely.

When she wasn't angry, she had more smiles than a West End actress had hats. But this one was sinister: "I mastered the use of the whip on a handsome, muscular brute who used to be a horse."

It was impossible not to notice the animalistic qualities of the pathetic natives of this island. I assumed they must suffer from some disease or inadequate nutrition. Already I'd begun to construct a theory that the monster discovered by Captain Marsh had been a particularly unsavory specimen washed out to sea and made more fearsome by exposure to the elements. Or a deliberate hybrid, sewn together by some long lost carnival.

So what the hell did Dr. Moreau mean by a brute that used to be a horse?

She seemed to read my mind. "Mr. Reynolds, are you going to stand out there all day trying to solve a mystery? Or will you accept the hospitality of my house?"

She didn't have to invite me more than once. I thanked her and followed her inside. The interior was comfortable despite the sweltering heat of the day, because of large ceiling fans placed throughout the house that helped immeasurably with cross ventilation.

No sooner were we inside than she took me by the arm. I appreciated the strength of her fingers. "Your visit is most auspicious, Mr. Reynolds. May I ask you a personal question?"

"Anything to oblige so gracious a hostess."

"Are you a brave man?"

"Within reason," I answered carefully.

Again she smiled. "My dear sir, anything can be done within the confines of reason!"

An we engaged in this odd conversation, she led me into the dining room. The servant was already there. Somehow he seemed less bestial after the interlopers in the courtyard. He laid out a table of fresh fruit, cold fish and a red wine. Above us the largest ceiling fan I'd seen so far did its silent work.

No sooner were we seated than she let a most interesting cat out of its bag. "I like you. Only a man with strength and intelligence could reach this island without a good boat. I want us to be friends." She sipped her wine, watching me over the rim of her glass. "And friends don't keep secrets from each other. You've already noticed that this island is one gigantic mystery. I will not play with you. I will tell you everything, right now, because I prefer your voluntary assistance with a little project of mine."

She had the grace to let me digest her words along with the excellent cuisine. Then: "You're English, aren't you, Mr. Reynolds?"

"Aren't you, Doctor?" There was no doubt that she had received a proper education. Her exotic qualities suggested that she was

Eurasian, an intermingling of two mighty strains producing a unique beauty. Sitting this close to her was a physical strain, so desperately did I wish to leap across the table and feel her lips on mine. The proximity was in itself invigorating. The woman's perfume made me dizzy and again I was struck by the strong impression that this over-powering essence was her natural scent.

She stared at me with an amused expression. While I twisted and turned on the hot coals of frustration, she was cool and in control.

"Does the name Moreau mean nothing to you?"

I had to admit that something had been whispering in the back of my head since she first introduced herself. Then I remembered! The Moreau case had been a scandal before the Great War.

"Yes!" I nearly shouted. "Dr. Moreau was an Englishman, a vivisectionist who was banished from England because of his cruelty to animals."

"Is that all you remember?" she asked as she leaned over and refilled my glass. She was generous in many ways.

"I remember that he had a theory of evolution that would stagger Darwin."

She clapped her hands. "Top marks! And how did you learn about that?"

"The newspapers were full of the story several years later when a man named Prentiss . . . no, that's wrong, it was Prendick, who claimed to have visited Moreau's island and . . . I'm a fool. *This* is Moreau Island."

"Of course."

"And you?"

"I'm his daughter, naturally. Do you remember what Prendick claimed?"

I finished my wine in one gulp. "No one believed him. He said that Moreau had found a way of turning animals into men. Maybe he could have persuaded more people, but the war came along and everyone was otherwise engaged."

"The theory is more complex, Mr. Reynolds. All the higher life forms tend toward self-awareness, intelligence; something manlike in millions of years. My father thought that he could accelerate the process through advanced surgical techniques he learned from his vivisections. He also studied genetics. He was Mendel with a scalpel."

"And you're Florence Nightingale with a whip," I contributed.

"Excellent!" She sprung out of her seat with feline agility and came up behind me before I could even think of a response. Her hands were at my throat and . . . she started to give me a massage. I was so relieved, and so excited, that I didn't complain about my sunburn or the abrasions that she wasn't even trying to miss.

"Thank you," I thought to say.

"Doesn't this hurt?" she asked with a touch of satisfaction.

"Only a little," I gasped.

"My father also had theories about pain. He liked to say that the study of Nature makes a man at least as remorseless as Nature. He said that a sufficiently evolved human being has so little need for pain that he can easily ignore, through will power, its trivial effects."

Her long fingers dug into my shoulder at this last comment. I winced. "I don't think I'm all that advanced."

She slapped me on the back, which hurt more than the massage, and then returned to her seat. Part of me wanted to get up and slug her. The trouble was that the other part wanted her to come back and do it again.

"Well, you needn't worry about that. I, too, am a doctor, but not of the same kind. My father went as far with the physical as he dared. The House of Pain proves the limitations of that approach. I inherited his wealth and a desire to carry on in, shall we say, more spiritual avenues."

"Spiritual?"

"Yes, and that is where you can help me, Mr. Reynolds. That is if you're willing to make love to me."

Suddenly my deepest longing was brought out into the open! I couldn't believe she was offering herself to me just like that.

"I don't know what to say."

"Perhaps you would care to sleep on it?" she asked slyly.

"No, doctor. I accept."

"Good. You can rest tonight and you will have the opportunity of making love to me in the morning."

That seemed the oddest aspect of her offer so far. "There's no need to wait, really. I feel fine."

She simply shook her head and gestured for the servant to attend me. "Draw our visitor a bath and prepare a bed for him. He can wear some of Mr. Montgomery's old clothes. I believe they will fit."

"Who's that, if I may ask?"

"He was my father's assistant. He's dead now. They're both dead."

"I'm sorry. May I ask what happened?"

She sighed. For the first time, I saw her frown. "My father needed more subtle tools for his unsubtle work. When Edward Prendick came, my father made foolish plans that led to his own destruction. Thankfully, he left thorough records so that I could carry on his work. There was no need for me to reinvent the wheel. But his children made short work of him, Mr. Reynolds. As young as I was, I knew I had to seize control of the situation. Prendick and I found them howling over the blood-smeared remains of his body. His handiwork in flesh and bone had repaid the compliment by separating his constituent parts as a tailor might take apart a suit of clothes."

"I don't know what to say."

She stared at me. "Sleep well, Mr. Reynolds."

I wondered if after she was my lover, I might work up the nerve to ask her to call me John. How long after that would it be before she shared her first name?

She left the room. The next step was obvious. The servant waited for me to follow him upstairs. Now that this utterly mad world had been explained, I recognized the non-human aspect of her butler. He was the faithful dog. It made perfect sense within a context that destroyed my every conception of sense.

I almost fell asleep in the warm bath water. The servant roused me. My premature death simply wouldn't fit into my mistress's plans.

Before my head ever hit the pillow, I was asleep. I was too exhausted to dream. Besides, finding myself in a ready-made nightmare didn't leave much to invent!

In the morning, I awoke more refreshed, but as hot and sticky as if I'd never bathed. The faithful servant was at hand, pointing me in the direction of a shower I had failed to notice the night before. The mansion certainly offered amenities.

The humidity seemed worse today than before and the shower barely made a difference. The fan in my room did little to move air that was so thick I felt I could cut it with a knife. There was no point in toweling off when I stepped out of the shower. The butler laid out a white Panama suit for me and I put it on wet, knowing that my perspiration would leave the material soaked in a minute regardless of what I did.

I was about to slip on the white shoes provided when the taciturn servant said one word, "Stop." He picked up the shoes, turned them over and struck them together. A scorpion fell out of one and tried to scurry away before the butler's booted foot crushed its carapace. Then he returned the shoes, which I carefully examined myself before slipping them on.

Downstairs, Dr. Moreau waited for me. "You must forgive my haste, but we must reach the place by a certain time."

"The place?" I asked. It would take a lot to spoil my buoyant mood considering what this morning promised. "We're not going to stay here?"

Taking me by the arm and smiling radiantly, she was irresistible. "Please forgive my few quirks. I'm sentimental about making love in my favorite spot on the island."

"But what about breakfast?"

"Trust me, Mr. Reynolds. . . ."

"Call me John."

"Trust me, John. It will be better if we dine afterward."

"You haven't told me your first name."

Another enigmatic smile preceded, "That's right. I haven't."

As we ventured down the path in the lazy light of the humid morning, I had a good view of several of the island's denizens. They made no move to follow us, but they stood as if sentries and watched us pass. I was sure that it was not only the power of suggestion that made me recognize the shadow of each animal self lurking behind semi-human countenances. Here pawed a bull with stubborn insistence; there prowled a cat on two legs, caught between a purr and a hiss. One huge fellow with black fur, black as an ocean wave at midnight, was surely the remnant of a bear.

I had not seen her into her workshop, nor did I have any desire to do so. I would follow this woman anywhere so long as it wasn't to the House of Pain, which thankfully receded behind us with each step.

Curiosity in a situation like this was an occupational hazard, and I had to know something: "What are you a doctor of, if not medicine?"

"Here I learned Father's surgical techniques, but when I traveled to the university for a formal education, I chose the path of a scholar, John. Ancient languages are my specialty. When I realized that my father had penetrated into something beyond the mere physical world, I sought to find the key. I found it in the *Necronomicon*."

"What's that?" I asked.

For the first time, her womanly assurance seemed to desert her, replaced with the quality of a little girl: "The truth, John. Simply the truth. 'Nor is it to be thought that man is either the oldest or the last of earth's masters.' Father found the human in the animal. He was too much of a Romantic to see the animal in the human. And yet man and animal are linked in their inferiority."

I stopped walking and made her look at me. "What you are talking about?"

Some of her mastery returned. "We serve greater powers and these powers will bring thought to all life on earth. Not only to animals and men. The insects and the fish, too. Even the plants will be advanced with the knowledge to serve the Great Old Ones and open the gate. My father's work is sacred to the future. Yog-Sothoth is the key to the gate whereby the spheres meet! The earth will once again belong to the Old Ones."

As I saw a wild fire dance in her eyes, I found myself wondering how intimate I wished to become with her, and how much trouble it would be.

Any hesitation was quickly answered by the realization that we were being followed, not by those who had watched us before, but by denizens of the island with far more animal in their eyes. A lifetime of rationalizations finally ran out. I was this woman's prisoner and would have to do whatever she wanted.

We reached the fork in the path I'd noticed the other day. We followed it to a lonely hilltop that rose above the jungle. Upon this hill were stone monoliths and formations that I was certain had some astronomical importance. Perhaps they were like the charting system Captain Marsh had used on his cursed voyage that I never should have undertaken if I'd had any sense whatsoever.

She pointed to a large stone table. Clearly this ancient sacrificial altar was to be our bed. Adding to the charm of the situation was the collection of her beastmen surrounding us, no doubt to make certain that I would not attempt escape.

"I need your seed," she said huskily. She stripped bare and was even more beautiful than I'd dared dream. Ever since I'd been on my own as a kid, I'd tried to make the best of a bad situation. Realistically, things could be worse. I wasn't too sure what the cosmic significance might be, but, on a purely personal level, I thought the situation wasn't all that horrible.

Her fingers were nimble as she undid my belt and then went on from there. She guided me over to the altar, to *her* altar, and then, just as I caressed her breasts and prepared to do my duty, she stepped back.

"I need your seed," she said. "Every version of myself needs your seed."

"What?" was all I could think to say.

The line of beastmen parted and six figures in dark robes joined Dr. Moreau and myself in the circle. As they dropped their garments, I felt seasick again—a disturbing sensation on dry land.

"What are they?" I screamed.

They were six female figures, each a caricature of the beauty that was Dr. Moreau. Each was deeply mired in the animal: one feline, one canine, one a grizzled ape, one a pig, one a goat, one a collection of pieces that never, ever should have gone together this side of hell. In each horrific body was the rough sketch of the perfection that was the laughing woman standing beside me. Each face was hers, no matter how distorted, however far from the perfect profile of my goddess. The family resemblance was unmistakable.

She whispered in my ear, "These are my sisters. I desire that you share your seed with all of us. The results should be interesting."

I'd never felt such revulsion in my life. "But how can they be your sisters? How can you come from the same father?"

"He was the father of us all," she said simply. The other versions of herself began chanting the one word, 'father,' until I wanted to put out my ear drums.

The woman I knew as Dr. Moreau showed kindness to me for the last time. "Poor John Reynolds. I never said that I had a mother." ✳

The Web

by Gary Myers

Zach must have been watching for me from a window when I arrived. I had no sooner left my bike under the porch light than the front door opened and he came out to meet me.

"Hi, Zach. You said you had something to show me."

"Hi, Kevin. It's on my computer. Come on up."

He turned back inside and started upstairs to his room. By the time I caught up with him he was already sitting in front of his computer. As I came up beside him I looked at the monitor to see what all the excitement was about. But there was only a screen saver, a funnel of shooting stars.

He started talking as soon as I came in.

"I was fooling around on the Web, looking for naked chicks, bomb recipes, stuff like that. I was about to log off when a word in an address jumped out at me. I opened it up and found—this!"

He hit the space bar and the starry screen saver disappeared, revealing a page of text. It was very ordinary text, black on white like a printed book and about as exciting. Or so I thought until I began to read it.

"The *Necronomicon?*"

"Funny, that's just what I said. I guess you know now why I called you over tonight."

I guessed I did too. Zach and I had plenty of reasons for being friends, but our closest bond was our common interest in the stories of H.P. Lovecraft. We would spend hours at a time discussing his weird conceptions, from the titanic entities of godlike power, to the monstrous races that served and worshipped them, to the ancient and forbidden books in which their histories were preserved. We knew that these books did not exist, any more than the gods and monsters existed. But that would not interfere with our enjoyment of a well-executed hoax.

I began again, this time reading aloud.

"'The *Necronomicon* of Abdul Alhazred has become well known in recent years, through the writings of Lovecraft and others, as the primary reference for the student of occult knowledge, practical magic and pre-human history. Yet the book itself has been long suppressed by the self-appointed guardians of morality and culture, to keep the rest of us in ignorance of the "dangerous" truths it contains. But "that is not dead which can eternal lie," and a hitherto unknown copy of Alhazred's great work has recently come to light outside the guarded circles of church and university. We hope to publish this complete *Necronomicon,* in a new translation, in the near future. Until then we are making available to the modern disciple of Tsathoggua, of Great Cthulhu, of Yog-Sothoth and the other Old Ones, this collection of essential spells culled from its pages, to arm him for the coming conflict between the forces of light and freedom and those of darkness and oppression.'"

That was all. Except that beneath the text were two buttons, one marked *exit* and the other *continue.*

"What is it?" I asked. "Some kind of game?"

"I don't know. I was waiting for you before going in any deeper. But now that you're here—"

He clicked on the continue button, opening a new page. This was a menu in the form of a table of contents. At least, its items looked more like chapter titles than program names. Most included Lovecraftian names like those we had read in the preface.

"Here's something that looks interesting," I said. "'To pierce the veil of Azathoth.'"

Zach clicked on the item, opening a window with a single start button under a block of text. He began to read the text aloud in his best dramatic voice.

"'Azathoth is the Greatest God, who rules all infinity from his throne at the center of chaos. His body is composed of all the bright stars of the visible universe, but his face is veiled in darkness. In the face of Azathoth, so it is written, the answers to all the great mysteries of the universe are waiting to be read. Yet only three men in the history of the world have possessed the strength of heart and clarity of mind to pierce the darkness unaided. All others must avail themselves of the power of the Mystic Eye.'

"And so on and so on," he ended, falling back into his natural voice. "The rest is just instructions for drawing this Mystic Eye thing on the wall. But I think we can ignore that part, since the computer won't know whether we draw it or not."

"Besides," I said, "your mom'll kill us if she comes home and finds us drawing pictures on her wallpaper."

He clicked on the start button. Almost at once a message box appeared on the screen:

PARAMETERS INVALID. JOB CANCELED.

"Parameters?" said Zach, seriously annoyed. "What parameters? We didn't give it any parameters."

"Maybe the program can't run without the Mystic Eye," I suggested.

"Yeah, right. Or maybe it's a dud. Let's go on to something else."

He backed out to the menu and we started looking for another item.

"What about this one?" he said. "'To quicken the fecundity of Shub-Niggurath.'"

He opened the window and read:

"'Shub-Niggurath is the Mother of All, the great goddess whose teeming womb gave life to the Oldest Ones. The endless round of birth and death, of creation and destruction, is but a reflection in the material plane of the cycle of her eternal menstruation. Her avatars are as innumerable as her children. But the greatest of these is the Black Goat of the Woods, whose thousand young await rebirth in the service of the sorcerer who can quicken their mother's fecundity.'"

"I don't know about quickening fecundity," I said. "It sounds pretty gross, and not in a good way. Besides," I continued, reading over his shoulder, "it says here that the spell can only be run at the dark of the moon."

But Zach clicked on the start button anyway. Almost at once the same message box appeared on the screen:

PARAMETERS INVALID. JOB CANCELED.

Zach pushed himself back from the desk.

"This is bogus! Is every spell just a hokey excuse for why it doesn't work?"

But I was still studying the screen.

"Here's something we can try," I said. "'To summon a Doel.'"

"What's a Doel?"

"'What can be said of the Doels?'" I read. "'They are the parasites that suck at the hearts of suns, and the vermin that gnaw the corpses of worlds. As grave worms riddle the carrion dead to find out their deepest secrets, so the Doels bore through space and time to discover the secrets of the infinite.'

"And that's all," I ended lamely. "But at least we don't have to paint ourselves blue and offer up the blood of a virgin. We just start the program and the Doel comes."

"I'll believe it when I see it," said Zach, pulling himself up to the desk again.

For the third time he clicked on the start button. For the third time the message box appeared. But this time it contained a very different message:

PARAMETERS VALID. JOB STARTED.

Then the screen went blank.

"Great!" said Zach. "The damn thing hung the system!"

"I don't think so. Listen!"

The monitor was dead, but the system speakers were not. There was a low hissing noise like the start of an old-time record, and then the chant began. The chant sounded as thin and distant as an old-time record. It was so garbled and distorted that I could not understand a word of it. But I soon realized that the fault was not with the recording, or even with the chanter. It was with the words themselves. They were not English words, or Spanish words, or words of any language I could recognize. Some of them should not have been pronounceable by any human tongue.

Zach and I looked at each other. We did not speak, but I knew what we both were thinking. The chant was unintelligible. It was indescribable. It was everything a Lovecraftian incantation should be. But it was not very interesting. Surely there must be more to the game than this?

There was. For now the chant was accompanied by a vibration, a sort of low rumble that I felt more than heard. At first it was so faint that I could almost believe I was imagining it. But the chant grew louder as it went on, and the accompanying vibration grew stronger, until I could no longer doubt that it was real. Was the vibration part of the chant? Or was the room around us vibrating in sympathy with it? I could not tell. But the vibration gave no sign of ending anytime soon. It only grew stronger the louder the chant became. And the chant was painfully loud already.

Then things really started to happen. The room lurched under me, throwing me violently to the floor. The lights went out at the same time, plunging us into darkness. And with the darkness came a violent crash, loud enough to drown out even the sound of the chant.

When the shaking and crashing were over and only the chant remained, I raised my head and looked around me. The room was less dark than I had thought, for the computer screen still glowed faintly from the top of the desk. Zach was kneeling in its light beside his toppled chair, holding onto the desk for dear life. He looked over his shoulder at me with an almost comical expression of terror on his pale face. I wondered how I could see his face so clearly when all the light was behind it. Then I realized that all the light was not behind it. Some of it was behind me.

But I found more than the light when I turned my head. The violent shock had partly collapsed the wooden floor. Now it slanted downward toward the center of the room, tilting the remaining furniture crazily. Most of the furniture was gone. It had disappeared down a ragged hole about six feet across which now opened in the middle of the floor. And it was from this hole that the cold gray light was coming.

"Kevin, are you all right? Kevin, what is it?"

"I'm all right, Zach," I answered. But I did not feel all right. There was something about the light in the hole that frightened me more than the darkness, the noise and the devastation put together. These were subject to natural explanations, but the light I could not explain at all. I was afraid to see what might be making it. But I was more afraid to turn away without seeing. I dragged myself to the broken edge and looked down.

Once Zach and I had played with the idea that Lovecraft's gods and monsters really existed, and that Lovecraft himself was only the medium through which they made their existence known. We knew at the time it was only a game. But what if it was not? What if pursuing our fantasy had led us to something like the truth? What if the *Necronomicon* was real, and real cultists had published parts of it on the

Web, to assist their fellow cultists or ensnare poor innocents like Zach and me? Was Zach's computer calling a real Doel to us now?

The hole went straight through the floor to the living room beneath. The floor of the lower room was half buried under the wreckage of the upper one. And out of the wreckage, directly under the hole, the hideous thing was rising. Most of it was still buried, so I could not see its shape. But what I could see was huge and pale and coldly luminous. It was mostly a mouth, but a mouth as big and round as the rim of a hot tub, and as bottomless as a well. It glowed inside as well as out. The mouth was empty of teeth and tongue, but the throat was full of downward-pointing spines to keep anything that went in that way from coming out again. And this was what the thundering chant was calling!

"Zach! Shut it off!" I yelled. "For God's sake, shut it off!" And I threw myself back from the edge of the hole and scrambled toward him on my hands and knees. He had not seen what I had seen, but the tone of my voice alone was enough to rouse him into action.

"I'll shut it off," he yelled back, then reached for the computer's power switch and snapped it to the off position. The chant faltered in response, but almost immediately it started back up again. "Shut off, damn you! Shut off!" Zach screamed, snapping the switch again and again. But it had even less effect than before.

I looked back over my shoulder at the ragged hole. The light above it was brighter now, showing that the glowing thing was getting closer. There must be some way to stop it. Maybe the switch was shorted out so that the power could not be turned off. But even a shorted computer could not run with no power at all. Pushing Zach out of the way, I reached under the desk and jerked the power cord out of the wall. Again the chant faltered, and again it came back stronger than ever.

I stared at the limp cord in my hand. How was this possible? Where was the power coming from? Or if the system was running without power, how could we hope to turn it off? I looked again at the glowing hole. The light was very bright now. In another moment that terrible mouth would be coming through the floor. But there was one thing left to try. I pulled the desk away from the wall and pushed it toward the hole with all my strength.

The desk moved with gathering speed across the slanting floor. It slid down to the broken edge and dropped quickly over it, taking the whole system with it. I heard the components crash together inside that gaping mouth. I heard the chant rise above the noise, only to fall away again as the speakers tumbled deeper and deeper into that bottomless throat. And suddenly there was no more chant. There was only silence and the cold gray light fading into darkness.

Some minutes later I slid on my belly to the broken edge. I looked over it timidly, afraid of what I might see. But the monster was gone. In its place was only a circular hole, a cylindrical well plunging down and down to the center of the earth. For a moment I thought I saw a faint light glowing in its lower depths. But it faded out so quickly that I could not be sure.

Zach had slid down next to me and was looking over the edge with me. Now he turned to me and said in an awed whisper:

"It was real, wasn't it, Kevin?"

"Yeah, Zach, it was real."

"What happened to it? Why did it go away?"

"I don't know. Maybe it had to answer the call no matter where it came from. Even if it came from the center of the earth."

"But if Doels are real, what about the other things in the *Necronomicon?* Are they real too? Kevin, are you thinking what I'm thinking?"

"I'm way ahead of you! We've got to get back on the Web!" ✳

Passing Through

by Robert Weinberg

I began my graduate studies in comparative religions in 1967 at Miskatonic University, in Arkham, Massachusetts. My thesis was an analysis of witchcraft practices and goddess worship among primitive societies. Miskatonic, with its fabled library of occult reference volumes, was the perfect place for my research. An honors fellowship, which enabled me to devote my entire time to my studies without teaching was the other factor in luring me from my home in upper New York state to the quiet streets of Arkham.

All my life I had been a loner and the clannish attitudes of most of the students at M. U. did nothing to break through this reserve. There was little on-campus housing available for graduate students, so I took rooms in a small boarding house a few blocks from the university. Arkham, with its strange, almost decadent atmosphere, was a far cry from the wide open country of my youth, and I found myself spending nearly all of my time working on my thesis.

The so-called "forbidden tomes" were kept in a locked vault in the basement of the Miskatonic Library. Dr. Morgan, a gnarled white-haired old man who spoke with a slight lisp, was the head librarian. He made no secret of his unhappiness with my constant study of the musty volumes. Every time I came to the library, he was waiting for me, hiding behind some musty old stack of books. He enjoyed leaping out of a row after I walked by, his shrill voice piping with veiled warnings of "other fools" who had lusted after the ancient knowledge in those books and had come to terrible ends.

"It was that *Whateley* that was their kind," he would mutter as if whispering some horrifying secret. "He wanted to bring them back. But we stopped him. Put an end to his plans, and to him, too. The Old Ones can't be killed so easy. They're still watching, still waiting. Don't be a fool, Watts. Leave those books alone!"

Again and again, I assured Dr. Morgan that I was no practitioner of black magic and that my only interest in the books involved their description of witchcraft practices. He never seemed to listen or understand. The old man's single-minded obsession made him tiresome company. After a while, I took to ignoring him.

Whenever I wondered if I had made a terrible mistake in attending Miskatonic, I would go to the vault and stare at the books that lined the shelves. It was then that I knew that I was exactly where I belonged. The volumes were priceless. I wasn't surprised to learn from one of the armed guards always on duty in the library that several attempts had been made to steal the books. One such attempt was conducted by a certain Whateley from Dunwich and evidently he was the person Dr. Morgan spoke about. However, those events had taken place decades ago. The librarian was worried about troubles nearly forty years old.

One Sunday afternoon in late fall I decided to go to the library and finish translating a particularly difficult passage I had been working on the day before. At the time, I was deep in the *Necronomicon,* a wild mishmash of spells, threats and cautionary tales as compiled by "the mad Arab," Abdul Alhazred. The library contained a copy of the English version of the book, as compiled by Dr. John Dee, as well as the much rarer edition of the book in Latin, translated by Olaus Wormius in 1228 and published in Spain in the 17th century. In one of his few lucid moments, Morgan, who possessed an astonishing knowledge of the forbidden texts, explained to me that the Dee version was based only on fragmentary notes from the manuscript. Thus, the Latin text contained a good amount of material not available elsewhere. As part of my research, I was going through the laborious task of comparing the two editions and deciphering the passages not contained in the English translation.

The library was empty of all but a few dedicated students as I passed from the center hall to the rear gallery and then down the stairwell to the locked vault. I nodded to the police guard who by this time knew me quite well and made for the sealed chamber where the books were kept in special sealed cases. To my surprise, another person was already in the room. More surprising was that he was busily poring over Dee's English translation of the *Necronomicon.*

"What the hell do you think you're doing?" I asked, feeling somewhat put out. As far as I knew, no one else on campus had permission to consult the fragile texts.

The other man bolted upright in shock. He whirled, his eyes blazing. A short, heavyset man with a thick black beard that covered the entire lower half of his face, his voice was surprisingly mild.

"Do you realize that I was just reading the fate of those who cast spells without taking the proper precautions? Being devoured by a demon who creeps up unaware on the practitioner. Sir, you could have given me a heart attack!"

I had to laugh. "Sorry. I really didn't mean to startle you. That volume isn't one to make surprises welcome. But you still haven't answered my question. I thought I was the only student on campus with permission to use that volume. I had notions of consulting it today."

"Aha, then you must be Alaistar Watts." There was a note of intense pleasure in his voice. "I was hoping to run into you on campus some time, so this meeting is a stroke of luck. Dr. Morgan told me of your extraordinary skills and your devotion to your work."

He held out one pudgy hand. "I'm Arthur Hilton."

I was caught totally off guard by his identity. My surprise must have shown on my face. The bearded man chuckled.

"Yes, the same Hilton who is the world-famous mathematician Miskatonic is so proud to claim as a member of their staff. The Five-Color Problem Hilton. You're one of the select few to discover my secret. Dr. Hilton, graduate of Princeton, Harvard and Yale, is a student of the occult. Better keep that information quiet, though. The administration would be extremely hard on the man who revealed that the university's only Nobel Prize winner has a crackpot strain. Bad for the school's image."

Hilton rambled on and I managed to interject a few remarks of my own. I knew of the man but never dreamed I might actually meet him, least of all encounter him in the vault. The mathematician was regarded as one of the leading theorists on space and time relationships in the world. Only three years ago, his work on transfinite topological sequence spaces had earned him the Nobel Prize in Physics. As Hilton had mentioned, he was without a doubt the most famous member of the Miskatonic faculty.

There had always been speculation in newspaper articles about the professor on why he remained on the staff of the small east coast establishment when colleges all across the country would have welcomed him with open arms; Hilton could have named his price at any university in the world. However, if the mathematician was interested in the books in the sealed room, that would explain why he remained at M. U. Only staff and students of the university had access to the forbidden texts. And no other library in America could match Miskatonic's collection of esoteric works on demonology and witchcraft.

Leaving the vault, we retired to a nearby local coffeehouse for refreshments and conversation. Hilton was fascinated by my research and forced me to explain all my theories in great detail. To my surprise, the professor exhibited an astonishing knowledge of the occult and was able to quote long passages from various mystic texts from memory.

After coffee, we walked to Hilton's on-campus apartment where he displayed to me his small collection of rare books on black magic.

"It was sheer luck that I finally ran into you, Alaistar," he said late that evening. "I'm terrible at foreign languages and I fear that the English translations I've been using in my studies are sadly deficient. What you tell me about the Dee volume confirms my suspicions. Perhaps, with your help, I could finally make some real progress on the project that has occupied most of my time for the past two years."

"Which is?"

"Wait until I have something concrete to show you. At the moment, all I have are my notes and a few theories."

Hilton opened a drawer of his desk and pulled out a thick black notebook. "You've heard, I take it, of Walter Gilman? One of Arkham's most notorious scholars. Everyone knows of Gilman and his mysterious death in the Witch House. Ah, if only that building had not been torn down. Such is life in America."

He waved the notebook in the air. "No matter. Some years ago, in the same vault in which we met today, tucked behind a long untouched bookcase, I found a small binder wedged into a space between the shelves and the wall. It had been there, unnoticed, for years. Inscribed in it were a series of very curious notes. The pad was Gilman's.

"He had placed it between two rare volumes and it had been pushed into the space behind the shelves and lost. Most of the work was sheer nonsense, but the young man did have a glimpse of something . . . strange. Gilman was a mathematical prodigy. His work might actually have led into a branch of my own field of study if he had lived. The problem with Gilman was a lack of understanding of the underlying structure of the field. He was trapped by his own inadequacies. I think I could succeed where he failed."

"I don't follow you. Failed how?"

"In making contact with those beings outside our plane of existence," said Hilton. "Enough for tonight. As we work, I'll explain further. You agree then to assist me in this project?"

"If arrangements can be made," I replied. "Though I have no idea how. I'm no scientist."

"Nor do I want one," said Hilton. "I'll handle all the arrangements."

Arrange he did. Hilton was a power at M. U. and what he said became law. Cutting through red tape like melted butter, the mathematician had me appointed a graduate research assistant for the mathematics department. I became his assistant. My thesis work was put on hold, but I had to admit that the opportunity to work with a world-famous scientist soothed my doubts. Within a few days, I was much caught up in Hilton's work, and all previous studies were forgotten.

The actual purpose of the research was never quite clear. I spent all my time translating passage after passage of the forbidden text, searching for some elusive clue that Hilton needed to tie together his theories about higher-dimensional planes. The bearded professor was obsessed with the so-called "Ancient Ones"—hideous mythological beings who filled the books hidden in the vault. Slowly, listening to his ramblings, I realized that Arthur Hilton, the genius of Miskatonic, actually believed in the existence of those hideous creations.

Inwardly, I scoffed, thinking him a fool. Still, chills ran up and down my back when I transcribed certain passages in the *Necronomicon*. Sections of Von Junzt's *Unaussprechlichen Kulten* gave me vivid nightmares for a week. Still, a few dreams weren't enough to frighten me off. Some of Hilton's determination rubbed off on me. There was a secret hidden in those books, and we had to find it.

Along with our research, the two of us began making short trips into the area surrounding Arkham. Hilton spent most of his time interviewing old locals with bad reputations. I handled most of the secretarial work for Hilton and after a short period, I noticed a pattern emerging in his questions. Arthur was trying to discover an actual method for contacting the Ancient Ones. It was after one such episode, a frightening evening spent in Dunwich with an old crone who whispered of the horror that had taken place there decades in the past, that I confronted Hilton and demanded an answer.

We sat in his office at the mathematics department. Hilton's eyes were alive, sparkling like diamonds. As he spoke, I realized that the man had to be mad. For only a madman could believe what Hilton stated.

"I had the first hints from Gilman's notes, Alaistar. He described passing through a higher plane of existence, traveling to other worlds in our universe by *passing through* a fourth dimension. He was convinced it was done by spells and magic, but I knew that such reasoning was the result of a mind crazed by drugs. There was a much more logical explanation. And I was one of the few men in the world capable of understanding it.

"We are three-dimensional beings. There is no way—I repeat, no way—that our minds, bound by the limitations of our senses, can understand or even conceptualize a fourth dimension. Let me give you an example. In the book *Flatland,* the inhabitants are two-dimensional, having length and width but no height. They are completely flat, thus the title of the story. As their world was a plane, there was no possible manner for them to conceive of the concepts of up or down. They could not rise up from the plane on which they were on. More important, imagine if you will, this two-dimensional world was curved around a sphere. The Flatlanders could only see on their plane, and thus could not understand that it was curved in a third dimension.

"Because they were bound to their plane, there was no method for the Flatlanders to travel in this third dimension. Being creatures of width and length, they could never experience height. Since their world was bound by two dimensions, it was impossible for them to reach a third. At best, all they could do was theorize about it."

"Very interesting," I said. "But what does that have to do with the Ancient Ones?"

"We define a two-dimensional world by two lines that form a right angle with each other," replied Hilton, ignoring my question. "In a three dimensional world, three lines at right angles, like the corner of a room. Length, width and height. Applying that same logic, a fourth dimensional world would be one where four lines can exist at right angles to each other. With our three-dimensional minds, it is impossible to visualize such a construct. More to the point, there is no way for us to reach this higher plane."

"But you said Gilman—"

"Exactly," said Hilton. "Gilman claimed to travel through the fourth dimension. Obviously, not by his own power as he thought. I believe that Gilman was taken into that realm by a being from the higher dimension.

"In his notes, Gilman described frightful creatures he observed during his passage to another world. Incomplete, extremely alien beings. Of course they appeared incomplete to him as he was seeing them through three dimensional eyes. As they were four dimensional, he could only see parts of them. Just as on Flatland, when a sphere comes to visit, it appears to the linear inhabitants of that world as a circle. Gilman merely saw the sections of the four dimensional beings that intersected three dimensions."

"I still have no idea why this is so important," I said. When Hilton got into his lecture mode, he talked non-stop unless interrupted.

"The greatest secret of the universe is hidden in Gilman's notes," whispered Hilton, his face filled with an expression of near-religious awe. "The ability to travel from one spot on our world to any other instantaneously. Or even the secret of travel to the stars. The fourth dimension is curved in ways we cannot conceive. Traveling through it we can bypass most normal space that we would have to cross in our limited three-dimensional world. We could achieve the dream of all science fiction writers. The space warp. We would not traverse space but pass through it."

I stared at Hilton, worried about his sanity. Some of my skepticism must have shown for he started laughing.

"You don't believe me, of course. Why would you? But I'll convince you as I'll convince the world."

"Meaning what?"

"Haven't you wondered what my interest in four dimensional travel has to do with our research in Dunwich? The reason is obvious if you look closely. The Ancient Ones, the horrors described in the forbidden text, are merely four-dimensional beings. Remember the passage in the *Necronomicon* that interested Wilbur Whateley?

"The Old Ones were, the Old Ones are, and the Old Ones shall be. Not in the spaces as we know but between them. They walk serene and primal, undimensioned and to us unseen. Yog-Sothoth knows the gate. Yog-Sothoth is the Gate.

"In a space not as we know, but *between them!*" Hilton shouted. "The Ancient Ones are clearly creatures of the fourth dimension. They're no supernatural monsters. They are merely dwellers on a higher plane that in rare instances intrudes on our three-dimensional world. With their alien shapes and only partial visibility, no wonder that ancient mystics thought them gods."

"Maybe you're correct and they aren't gods," I said. "But their intent is clear enough. They are evil, totally evil. Remember what happened in Dunwich. And Gilman paid the price as well."

Hilton snorted in disgust. "Good and evil are relative terms. These beings can help man if they desire. They helped Gilman, until he went insane. They can help me."

"What are you talking about?"

"You'll see, Alaistar." His tone grew cold, distant. "Soon enough, you'll see."

* * *

After my near quarrel with Hilton, I drifted back to my own researches. I did not see much of the professor, though I did hear stories. He bought an old mansion on the outskirts of Arkham and was having major construction work done inside. No one was sure exactly what, but it involved a large number of blackboards. Finally, one afternoon in mid-spring, Hilton called and invited me to visit his new home.

He appeared hale and cheerful when greeting me at the door. In the kitchen, over a cup of coffee, he continued our conversation of weeks previous as if it had never ended.

"Communication is the key, Alaistar," he said, a fanatic's look in his eyes. "Without communication, there can be no exchange of information. Still, the forbidden texts made it clear that the sight of these four dimension beings, totally alien to our senses, can drive a man mad. After much thought, I have devised a solution to both problems. I call it the black room."

Hilton's sanctum was a large room at the rear of the first floor that had once served as the building's library. The entire room, floor and ceiling and all the walls, had been covered by blackboard slate. The only furniture was a solitary chair in the center of the chamber. Hilton closed the door behind us. It was totally and completely black. There was no light of any sort. Eyes could not adjust to the darkness, as there was no illumination at all. The room was deathly silent, obviously sound-proofed. The only noise was the beating of my heart, pounding like a jack-hammer in the stillness.

"No sight of the creatures is necessary," said Hilton, his voice calm and cool. "Communication will be done using the universal truths of mathematics. Basic axioms will quickly lead to more complex ideas. All writing can be done using chalk on the blackboards. Nothing will disturb my concentration."

I hardly heard what Hilton was saying. All I could think about was the terrifying darkness that surrounded me. The absolute, total blackness that seemed to spill into my soul. It was a black room in thought as well as concept.

"Hilton, I have to get out of here. Or I will go mad!"

Instantly, the door of the room opened and the light from the hallway flooded the chamber. "My fault," said Arthur, sounding apologetic. "It takes a long time to adjust to the black room. My first few times inside, I kept a string tied to the doorknob as an anchor with reality. Sensory deprivation can be deceptively cruel. A man locked inside that room for a few minutes could go mad."

Still shaking, I accepted a fresh cup of coffee and, for a few minutes, we talked of mundane, ordinary matters. Finally, I knew it was time to leave. Hilton wanted to return to his studies. And I wanted to be away from the black room.

"One last question, Arthur. You speak of communicating with the Ancient Ones, using mathematics as your language. How will you summon these four-dimensional beings to your black room? And when?"

"With your translations and the material we gathered in Dunwich," said Hilton, "all of the necessary information is here. The proper words, the supposed magic symbols. Along with Gilman's notes. Together, they make it perfectly clear what to write to summon the dwellers outside."

The mathematician smiled. "As to when, have you forgotten what next week is?"

I left the house feeling somewhat relieved. Despite all of Hilton's talk, I was not convinced that four-dimensional beings existed. Once Hilton tried and failed to communicate with them, it seemed likely to me he'd break free of this obsession and devote his talents to more practical applications.

A student of ancient religions, I knew full well what he meant when he referred to the next week. In seven days, it would be the First of May. It was a day sacred to witches and demons since time immemorial. According to the forbidden texts, it was then that the Old Ones walked the wind.

*   *   *

The day arrived.

I spoke with Hilton that afternoon. He was extremely excited and I couldn't help but feel somewhat sorry for him. In a few hours, I was certain all of his crazy theories would be dashed to bits. I listened in silence as he rambled.

"Tonight, the stars will be right, Alaistar. I have all the proper rituals memorized. That passage you discovered that wasn't in the Dee translation was the key. The section on the Wendigo in *De Vermis Mysteriis* provided me with protection. I'm not a superstitious fool like Gilman. I'm prepared for what is out there. Think of it. In a few hours, I will be in contact with creatures from another plane of existence."

"Call me afterwards," I replied, trying to keep the skepticism from my tones. He noticed it though.

"Still the non-believer? Fine. I have something planned that should cure your doubts for good."

On that cryptic note, Hilton broke the connection.

It was a dark and overcast night. It didn't rain but clouds blocked the moon and stars. Anxiously, I waited for Hilton's phone call. I knew that whatever manifestations he expected, they would occur around midnight. I waited and waited. But no call.

Finally, around four A.M., I knew that something was wrong. There was no answer to his phone. With a feeling of dread anticipation, I got dressed and started my car.

I drove out to the mansion on the edge of town. Lights shone in several windows but the front door was locked. No one answered my poundings. Determined to learn what had happened, I broke in through one of the kitchen windows.

The first thing I noticed was the horrible charnel stench that permeated the entire building. It was that noxious odor that started me shaking. I remembered full well certain passages in the forbidden texts about the "monstrous scent" of the Ancient Ones.

I shouted Hilton's name, but there was no answer. I went immediately to the black room. The door was locked from within. I began banging on it, with no reply. I knew Arthur was still inside. In a near panic, I turned away and looked for something to hammer against the wood panelling. It was then that I found the black notebook. Gilman's notes.

There, in the rear of the book, I found new entries, in Hilton's crabbed handwriting. He had transcribed entire passages from the forbidden texts outlining his theories. Page after page were covered with precise mathematical formulas that only Hilton understood. None of the entries frightened me as much as the last page of the journal.

> Watts still does not believe. Tonight, I will convince him. Once I have established contact, I plan to request Yog-Sothoth take me into the fourth dimension. I will thus pass through our three-dimensional boundaries and travel from here to Watts's apartment without taking one step in normal space.

I ran back to the door and repeatedly threw my body against it. For the first time, I had some small inkling of what might have occurred. My mind refused to accept the possibility of communications, but I had to know. Finally, after what seemed like an eternity, I broke the lock.

The stench was so overwhelming I had to wait several minutes until it had dispelled enough so I could enter. Using a candle I found in the kitchen, I forced myself to walk into the black room. No longer was the chamber dark. The blackboards were covered with strange, glowing writing, mathematical formulas and bizarre characters in a language unknown to man. I recognized dozens of mystic symbols and sigils from the forbidden texts—the signs of the Ancient Ones. Hilton had made contact with the unknown.

I searched the room for some evidence of my friend. In a far corner, I spotted a weird singularity in the walls. As I stepped closer, my mind refused to accept what was there. With a shriek of absolute terror, I collapsed to the floor. It took me several minutes staring at the slate beneath my feet to regain my composure. Gaze fixed on my feet, I shuffled out of the chamber. The one look had been enough. From doubter I had changed to believer. The horror of that single glance has remained with me since. My friends think me odd because I refuse to enter a room without a light burning, that I avoid dark places. They will never know of the horror in the black room.

I staggered from the chamber. The first thing I did was take Gilman's black notebook and burn it. Perhaps it held the secret of travel to the stars. But it also opened a gateway to damnation.

Next, I used the telephone to summon the police. At first, when they heard my story, the officers thought me mad. One look at the horror in the black room changed their minds. Together we destroyed the place and the horror it contained. We blamed the destruction on an out-of-control fire. With the three of us agreeing on all details of our story, there was little investigation.

Since that day, I never again spoke of Arthur Hilton. When asked, I agreed with the oft-proposed theory that he had retired to some out-of-the-way spot to work on some new mathematical theory.

Arthur Hilton is dead. He made contact with the Ancient Ones and that contact destroyed him. Whether such beings are truly dwellers in the fourth dimension or evil gods out of space and time, I will never know. Nor do I have any desire to find out.

Hilton's curiosity was his doom. He wanted to travel in the fourth dimension, and Yog-Sothoth, whatever being lay hidden behind that name, agreed to his request. The Ancient One took Hilton into the higher dimension, the one intersecting our three. But, and I know not whether it was through accident or intent, Yog-Sothoth returned Hilton to our three dimensions *at the wrong spot.*

The horror of the black room was the body of Arthur Hilton imbedded in the black slate of a blackboard covering one of the walls of the chamber. He had been trapped . . . *passing through!* ✳

The Idol

by Scott David Aniolowski

Rivulets of sweat ran down Sam Kinney's fat face, glistened like tiny jewels in the hot August sun. He wiped his brow on an already damp sleeve, panting to catch his breath.

It came in short wheezes. He staggered to a cluster of trees. Even in the shadier spots of the Boston Common it was uncomfortably warm. And muggy. His heart burned in his chest, he could hear it pound. His puffy hands trembled to light a cigar. "Hey kid, slow down," the fat man spit, wide mouth full of cigar smoke.

"Come on, Sam, let's go," came the distant reply.

Sam's eyes stung with sweat, everything was out of focus. He wasn't sure which jogger was his anymore. Teens on bicycles and roller blades swept by, and somewhere a baby wailed, setting his nerves on end. And everywhere pigeons. Dirty, shitting pigeons pecking and cooing. Everywhere. It was like being in that Hitchcock flick, Sam thought. Which one was it? That one with all the birds. But then Sam hated birds. And babies. And if it wasn't for the fact that he made a Goddamn good living off throngs of screaming adolescents, he'd hate them, too. Well, secretly he did.

"Come on, big guy, get a move on," that voice came again, more distant now.

"Yeah, fuck you, too," he mumbled not so much under his breath. He dabbed his greasy face again, tossed the smoking cigar into a trash bin. Then it was off to the beckon and call of his star. Not any star, but The Star. The kid had made a name for himself—and a fortune for Sam—in the span of several busy months. The CD had gone to the top of the charts. He'd made the rounds of all the important late-night talk shows, was soon to embark on a lengthy North American tour.

Sam found Mikey just when that other pants-dropping shirtless white kid from Boston was fading away. He'd discovered him doing some impromptu rap at Quincy Market one day during lunch. The kid was pretty rough, but he drew a crowd. And Sam Kinney knew a talent when he saw it. Well, most of the time. His last client—a professional wrestler—went nowhere fast, ended up sticking Sam with more bills than profit. But a part of being a talent agent was taking risks. You never knew when the next Big Thing might fall into your lap and bring with it Big Money. And with Mikey, Sam had finally found the goose that shit gold.

So he cleaned the kid up, bought him some new clothes, and began an ambitious publicity campaign. Radio play. Television spots. Magazine interviews. Videos. Personal appearances. And the public bought what Sam Kinney was selling. They bought it hook, line, and sinker. Public appearances got to be like frigging Beatles gigs. The clutching hands, the teary eyes. Lusty stargazing adolescent girls screamed and swooned. It wasn't even the kid's singing (who could call that singing?)—it was the kid, himself. Sam was convinced of it. And that's what he sold. He marketed as much of Mikey as he could. He had the kid peel his shirt off whenever and wherever possible. Sex sells. It's the oldest marketing scheme in the book. And the kid's face and half-naked body was splashed across T-shirts, bookbags, buttons, posters, magazine covers. He was The Next Big Thing.

And somewhere along the way to becoming The Next Big Thing, Mikey signed over the lion's share of his growing income to his agent.

There was a high-pitched shriek. The kind of shriek that shatters glass, sets teeth grinding. It was a sound that Sam had come to be used to. The sound of a teenage girl, her love for Mikey. It was the sound of cash registers.

Mikey's adoring fans had spotted him. Sam stopped his ponderous trotting, stared ahead. A sea of grasping arms and writhing bodies was all that he saw. It was always the same. They came out of nowhere. It was creepy. Like hordes of screaming banshees.

By the time Sam stumbled to the flailing screamers a mounted policeman had arrived, was attempting to restore order. Mikey was at the center of the mess signing autographs, kissing fans, smiling ear-to-ear. An anonymous hand snatched the baseball cap from his head; it vanished into the flagellating mass.

"Girls, girls," the big man shouted, began pulling the clutching adolescents away. "You can all have free passes to Mikey's show tonight at the University." He bravely waved a stack of free promotional passes over his head. More screams, a blur of greedy grasping hands. One last candid photo, the crowd melted away back to wherever they always came from. Sam's star was left clawed and tousled but otherwise unscathed (there had been instances where the kid had been picked almost naked by the clawing shrews).

"Just like I figured," the big man purred through a toothy car-salesman grin.

"Huh?" panted Mikey, sun-bronzed skin glistening in the sunlight. He ran a hand through his short bristly black hair, confirmed that his cap was missing. At least they hadn't ripped the gold hoops out of his ears.

"Great publicity, kid. Mikey spotted jogging in the Common. It's important for you to be seen by your adoring fans."

"Whatever," Mikey wiped the beads of dampness from his brow, traced the thin line of black hair that crept from his belly button up to where it spread out to lightly cover his chest. It was wet and shiny like a trickle of black oil.

"Come on, this is it kid. You're a star now." He turned his whole enormous bulk and extended one arm toward a building on Beacon Street, "Can't beat that." There on one full side of a towering structure was Mikey, godlike and larger than life. The black and white image stared down into the park with dark eyes and a seductively boyish grin. He was bare-chested on the building, baggy jeans down low on his hips, baseball cap twisted around backwards. The delicately sculpted contour of every muscle, every hair, was clear and crisp. And above his head in twenty-foot letters was a single word: MIKEY.

The young man just stared up at himself, not sure whether he should smile or turn away embarrassed.

"Not bad for a poor white kid from Boston. Nineteen and a star. What do you think of that?"

Mikey didn't say anything.

*   *   *

"What the hell were you thinking?" Sam screamed, flailed a fat cigar like a knife. He crushed the glossy magazine in his other hand, threw it out an open window. It flapped and tumbled twelve stories to the street like a broken bird.

"I wanted to do it," Mikey screamed back.

"Yeah? Well let me tell you something bigshot, you don't do anything without me saying so. Got it? For Christ's sake, you can't give it away. How the hell do you think I sell you? Huh?" Sam's bloated face was red, slick with sweat. Droplets rained down as his cumbersome bulk shook.

"Yeah, well it ain't no big deal, okay?"

"No? No? It is a big deal. It's a very big fucking deal. You're supposed to be seductive to these screaming twits. A dreamboy. That means leaving something to their horny little imaginations. The spreads in those crappy teen magazines are fine, but *Playgirl?* You're a teen idol for Christ's sake, not a frigging porn star. Do you know what kind of damage something like this can do to your image? And Christmas next month. Just what we need—shit right before the biggest Goddamn shopping season of the year. Do you think parents are going to buy your CD and posters for their little girls if they see you in some magazine with your dick hanging out?"

"I didn't think about it. They called and I said okay. You were away. I thought that was the kind of stuff you wanted me to do." Mikey absently stared into the huge aquarium that nearly filled one wall of his spacious loft. The low steady murmur of billions of tiny bubbles hung like a curtain in the background.

"Well, it ain't," Sam wheezed. He slipped out of his cheap coat, the armpits of his tight shirt were soaked. "Jesus, I can't leave you for a Goddamn minute. I take a couple days off to go fishing and you go and do skin pics."

"Okay," the young man gave in.

"Jesus, what a fucking mess," Sam panted, wiped a fat hand across his dripping forehead.

"Okay, okay. I wasn't thinking."

"You're Goddamn right you weren't thinking."

The teen sat in silence, stared at the bubbling fish tank, at his reflection vague and ghostlike in the glass.

"You'll keep your dick in your pants from now on?" Sam bent to the open window, breathed deeply in.

"Yeah, I said okay," Mikey mumbled.

"Good," he finally smiled after a long moment of tense silence. It was a strong silence. It was a weak smile. "Good," he parroted himself. The red was beginning to wash out of his round face.

"Besides, I don't want to do all that undressing in public anymore." He remained transfixed on the tank, eyes empty, face expressionless. Several brilliant reef fish darted between chunks of coral; clown fish bobbed through waving anemone tentacles.

Sam stared blankly at him for a moment. "What? Why?"

Mikey wouldn't meet his fish-eyed gaze. "I don't know. I just don't," he squirmed.

"Yeah, well that body of yours is our meal ticket."

Silence, just the hypnotic murmur of billions of bubbles.

"Are you okay, kid? You don't look so good." He slapped a puffy hand to the kid's forehead. "Maybe I better call your doctor."

"No." He pushed the flabby hand away.

"You haven't worked out all week." He turned to the expensive gym equipment in one corner. Stark beams from track lights put it on display, made the bulky black machines more art than appliance.

"Yeah?"

"And you haven't shaved in days."

"So?"

"Well, so, you have to take care of yourself. That body of yours ain't going to stay pretty all by itself."

More silence. The kid blindly watched the mesmerizing dance of fish and bubbles. A starfish slid slowly across the glass.

"I'm calling the doctor." He shoved the crumbled cigar in his mouth and grabbed the phone, hand completely engulfing the receiver. Sausage fingers jabbed numbered buttons.

Mikey threw himself from the overstuffed chair, cut off the phone in mid-dial. "No. I don't need to see no doctor."

"Then are you in some sort of trouble? Did you knock up some girl?" he grabbed Mikey's arm.

"No," he pulled away.

"Then what the hell is it?"

"Listen, I just need a break, okay? A vacation."

"Yeah, well we ain't got time for that. You have to be in New York on Friday. Then Rochester on Saturday, and Buffalo on Sunday," he counted on his fingers. "And then we go to Toronto on Monday and Tuesday. Monday and Tuesday, Mikey—two days in one town. Two fucking days. The fans want you and you ain't going to let them down."

"Just a few days. It's only Tuesday—I can still make New York this weekend."

"Where the hell you going to go in only two days?"

"I don't know, I thought I'd go up to Innsmouth."

"Innsmouth? What the hell you want to go to that shithole for?"

"I don't know."

"Why don't we just go to New York a few days early. You can take it easy there. Hang out, go to some of them fancy gyms, do whatever kind of shit you want."

"I can do all that here. I want to go somewhere small and quiet. Somewhere where no one knows my name."

"But Innsmouth?"

"I had relatives there a long time ago. Ma talked about them, and I just thought I'd like to go there. And see for myself."

"See what?"

Silence.

"Well, we ain't going to that shithole. At least not to stay. If you want, we'll go up to Marblehead or Kingsport for a couple days. We can drive out to Innsmouth from there, it's not much more than ten or fifteen miles. But we ain't staying in Innsmouth."

Mikey looked up at Sam, made eye contact for the first time. The corners of his mouth curled up into the sincerest smile Sam had ever seen on the kid. "Thanks," he almost sobbed.

"Christ, don't get all mushy on me. I'm still pissed about those skin pics. And I still think you should see the doc. But if taking a couple days off will put you right, then that's what we'll do."

"Yeah, okay. Thanks, Sam." He folded his arms around the fat man's girth and squeezed.

Sam wriggled out of the hug, turned away. "Yeah, whatever. But," he rotated back, jabbed a stubby finger into the teen's chest, "if you ain't back to your old self after this trip you stop fucking around and see the doctor."

Mikey sighed agreement.

"After all, I got to take care of my star," he half-smiled, tousled the kid's short hair with a nervous hand.

*   *   *

The drive up the North Shore from Boston to Marblehead was a long thirteen miles. Mass. 1A North rambled and turned slowly through an assortment of quaint old New England towns with an assortment of annoying modern traffic lights. The late autumn sun hung low and sleepy in the darkening sky as they turned onto the rte. 129 in Swampscott, headed into Marblehead. Thick drapes of heavy November clouds finally closed, banishing the day into darkness. Mikey quietly gazed out the car window as they made their way along the coastline. The ocean was black and still, a sharp sickle moon vainly struggled to cut through the thick night veil.

Rte. 129 became Atlantic Avenue, and they were in Marblehead. Sam turned his jet black Mercedes off Atlantic and onto Washington Street. The old New England town was dark and quiet. Globes of pale light hung from crook-necked posts above narrow twisting streets. Tall slim buildings sat on the brink of winding alleys, only thin pedestrian walks standing precariously between doors and street. There were few signs of life in the sleepy town beyond warmly-lit windows and the occasional cat that crept through lifeless gardens, along cracked red brick drives.

"This is it," Sam nodded toward a large house, "58 Washington Street." He held a crumpled slip of paper in the dim greenish light of the car dashboard, read the cramped scratching. "Yep, 58."

Welcoming light spilled from the building's many small-paned windows. A single lamp hung over the mahogany-hued door, flanked on either side by tall white columns. Mikey slid out of the car, stretched his legs. He inhaled deeply, clearing the cigar stench from his nose.

"Nice town." Wisps of steam ringed the kid's head as he spoke. He wrapped himself in his oversized jacket. A few early snow flakes danced on the cold night wind, bare-branched trees creaked and moaned in their sleep.

Sam ignored him, not knowing whether he was serious or joking. He opened the Mercedes' trunk, pulled out the bags. "Here, get your stuff," he puffed, then checked that the car doors were locked for the third time.

The fat man rang the house bell when he found the door locked. The door swung open almost immediately, a lovely woman stood there, hands clasped, motherly smile. "Mr. Kinney," she said more than asked, extended a delicate hand.

"Yeah, that's right." He stumbled into the entry hall.

"Come in, come in. It's rather nippy out tonight," she smiled.

Mikey squeezed in behind his agent, quietly slid the door closed. A comforting fire crackled in a hearth in the front parlor. Deep rich oriental rugs covered most of the mellowglow, wide-board, pine floor. Delicate paintings, antiques, and brasswork decorated the burgundy-hued room. Overhead hung a small brass chandelier, flamebulbs glowing brightly.

"And this handsome young man must be your . . . son?" The woman smiled at the teen.

"No," Mikey hurried, absently took a step away from the big man.

Sam shot the kid a look, raised an eyebrow, "Mike . . . Michael's my nephew. I brought the kid up from Boston to do a little fishing."

"Really? How nice," she beamed. "I don't know how much fishing you'll get done, though. This time of year most of the tourist places are closed up. Most of the charters aren't running now."

"We're going up to Innsm—" Mikey started.

"We'll find something," Sam cut him off, gave him a venomous stare.

"Of course," she coughed, waved off a cloud of cigar smoke. "Well, if you'd care to sign in I'll show you gentlemen to your room."

Sam signed the inn's directory, waved a gold credit card in the woman's face. She snapped the plate through the credit card machine, gave the pair a key to the front door.

"Continental breakfast is included," the lovely innkeeper explained as she lead them through the enormous 18th century house and to their room on the third floor.

"Thanks," Sam closed the door. "Muffins and coffee. Swell," he grunted, tried to catch his breath from the climb up so many steep flights of stairs.

The accommodations were quite fine for a bed & breakfast. A large green-hued bedroom with a pair of canopied four-poster beds. A blaze glowed in the room's bedside fireplace. And more oriental carpets, pine flooring, finely tooled furnishings. Their private bath was completely mirrored on one wall, potted ferns ringed the large green-veined marble tub. The perfumy scent of potpourri struggled to mask the old-house-grandmother's-parlor-mustiness of the place.

"It's late. I want to catch a shower and then go to bed." Mikey unzipped one of his bags. Somewhere in the house a clock began to chime.

While the kid showered, Sam unpacked, poked through the room. Pretty nice digs, he thought and smiled. Ain't no five star hotel, but it ain't half bad.

The sound of running water stopped. Outside the wind whistled, the old house creaked.

After another half hour Sam knocked at the bathroom door. "Hey, you drown in there?" he swung the door open. Mikey stood naked in front of the mirrored wall, his face almost to the glass, studying his own reflection.

"Jesus, Sam!" the young man snapped a towel around his waist.

"Well what the hell you doing in here, jerking off?" he blustered back. "You ain't got nothing I ain't already seen."

"I'll be out in a minute," he pushed the door closed on the round face.

The big man was already beneath his blankets when Mikey finally came out of the bathroom. The last glowing embers of the fire crackled in the hearth, bathed the room in a frail ruby light. Shadows stretched into elongated phantoms. The kid padded quietly to the other bed, threw back the heavy quilt. The sheets were icy against his bare skin. He lay there listening to the sounds of the house: the dying embers popping, a clock chiming, the wood floors creaking. And Sam's labored breathing, deep and steady like a hibernating bear. Outside the wind continued to whistle through bare tree branches, rattle the shutters.

"Sam?" Mikey whispered after he'd laid in the dark for what seemed like an hour. The last embers had crackled out, died.

The fat man snorted a reply, rolled onto his side.

"Sam," he repeated, suddenly noticed how his heart raced, his mouth was dry.

Another moan from the next bed.

"I think I'm changing," he gulped in breath, swallowed hard.

Sam groaned. And then the snoring began.

The kid stared up at the shroud-like canopy above his head. Outside a branch knocked, a few dead leaves scratched at the glass. And the sharp lunar crescent peered through the small paned windows like a giant squinting eye.

* * *

The morning was a clear and crisp one. Lacy frost etchings decorated the windows of Sam's big car, slowly melted away in the just-warm rays of the November sun. There was real life in Marblehead this morning. Business people hustling to get to work in the city. Children heading for school. Old timers walking their dogs, taking leisurely strolls through the twisting streets. Everyone smiled and nodded to Sam and Mikey. A few stared. A few pointed.

Mikey was quiet all the way to Innsmouth, just stared out the car window at the passing towns. Salem. Beverly. Arkham. Kingsport Head rose in the distance, ringed with wispy morning fog.

"What's your problem today?" Sam finally coughed, mouth full of half-chewed blueberry muffin. He dusted crumbs from the black leather upholstery between his legs, onto the carpeted floor of the car. Two more home-baked muffins sat on the seat next to him, pirated from the inn along with a hastily-swallowed black coffee. "I don't know what your big Goddamn hurry is. We got two days here."

The teen just sighed in response.

More silence. Sam played with the car radio, tuned in a classic rock station out of Boston. Mick Jagger's voice cut through the thick silence.

"Gimme, gimme shelter," the fat man crooned along with the radio, mouth still full of chewed muffin. "Hey, how about if I do some backup on your next CD?" he flicked the brim of Mikey's baseball cap with a finger.

"Yeah, right," the teen finally cracked a smile, pulled the brim of his hat down over his eyes. "You sound like a pig in heat."

Sam laughed, mumbled some incoherent words in time with the song. "Jesus, what the fuck is Mick saying?"

Mikey shrugged.

"Never could understand that guy. How the hell did he get to be so Goddamn famous? He can't even sing through them big fat lips."

Mikey laughed, sang some incoherent out-of-tune lyrics to the song.

"Is he saying 'just a kiss away' or 'just piss in my face'?" the fat man puffed out his lips, bulged out his eyes, got right in the kid's face.

Mikey held himself as he laughed, stomped his feet, threatened to piss his pants. Then he looked up, the laughter stopped. The expression washed out of his face, his eyes widened just a bit. There in front of them like a shadow was Innsmouth.

The old town spread out ahead of them, larger than the kid had expected it to be. The place was decayed and falling into ruin. Gambrel roofs drooped, completely collapsed in some houses. So many peaked gable windows were cracked, missing. Boards warped, were missing all together from sides of buildings. And Mikey couldn't count the number of windows and doors that were boarded over, fading realtor signs standing blind guard on dead weedy lawns. The tired old structures huddled together under a shroud of mist from the frothing sea. There was some sign of some recent construction. A dead McDonald's sign rose up in the distance, its yellow and red plastic busted and dark. Mikey recognized the signature architecture of another fast-food restaurant, also dark and boarded up. A grey melancholy hung over the place like the sea-mist, the air thick with the smell of fish. A lone boat bobbed on the ocean, just off Innsmouth's sagging docks. Oddly, there were no gulls wheeling, squawking.

Sam auto-locked the car doors, steered down Federal Street and into the belly of Innsmouth. Smoke curled up from a few cracked chimneys, a few faceless pedestrians ambled between dark, twisting streets. They passed an old Masonic temple, its facade cracked and weathered, sign above the door peeling and faded beyond recognition. Cracked, warped trees lined desolate streets, their last few leaves brown and withered. Overgrown lawns of dried weeds and grey grass trembled, snatched up bits of wind-blown litter and leaves. Mikey thought he saw dark furtive shapes peering from cracked windows as they slowly rode past.

"What a dump," Sam snorted.

They made their way to the downtown business district. More dark and deserted buildings, their wounds patched with fungus-sprouting boards. Finally Sam pulled up in front of a diner, only the

word RESTAURANT still legible above the door. The place was
obviously a converted residence, similar in architecture to their
Marblehead inn, but in a state of decay. One of a pair of columns in
the front was missing, only a rough stump left. The tall narrow,
small-paned windows were caked with grime or boarded over; the
glassless lamp over the front door hung precariously by a few frayed
wires. Across the unpaved street sat a large weathered building identified as The Gilman House Hotel. Things seemed slow at the hotel;
Sam wondered if it was even still open for business.

The pair spent the day cautiously picking their way through narrow twisting streets, poking in the few remaining shops. Sam's head
constantly swivelled to keep an eye on everything, everyone. Mikey
took everything in, was mostly oblivious to his companion's unease.
They wandered past great Georgian and Federalist mansions, many
dark and closed up. Along unpaved, lampless alleys. Through overgrown, weed-choked greens. Down warped and rotting docks where
the fish stench was almost sickening. All the time the townsfolk kept
a cautious distance. They were an odd, unfriendly lot who kept
mostly to themselves. Pedestrians crossed to the opposite side of the
street. Merchants were reticent. Rust-eaten cars cruised by, their
vague occupants peering, driving off.

Their last stop was the old Innsmouth burying ground. Shrouded
skeletons capered and danced on thin grey stones. Weather-worn
angels stared down, faces washed away into horrid grimaces.
Generations of families crowded the ossuary; the roll stretched all the
way back to the mid-1700s. Gilmans. Marshes. Eliots. Waites. All
lined in silent stoney neighborhoods. The big man squatted on a particularly firm stone, crossed his arms.

Mikey passed among the markers, intently reading names and
dates. Finally he stopped at one, stooped down. "This is it," his voice
trembled slightly. "My great-great-grandfather," he ran his hand
down the cold damp stone face.

"Is this why you dragged me to this shithole?" He glanced at his
watch, up toward the deepening sky.

The kid didn't reply. Said little all the way back to the car. Sam
reluctantly suggested they get a sandwich and coffee at the diner
before they headed back, his stomach growled its agreement. Mikey
agreed in silence.

The restaurant was a dingy place, dirty and dank. The black and white checked flooring was yellowed and cracked. Paint peeled from walls, the ceiling. Once-fine woodworking was splintered, worm-eaten. A withered old hag perched in a corner booth, bony knees bent to her chest like a gargoyle. And a pair of behemoth women sat in the center of the room, rolls of soft doughy flesh spilling over straining seats; long greasy hair framed puffy yellowed faces; rheumy eyes stared out from behind thick glasses. The weird sisters stared at Mikey and Sam, watched as they sat at a distant table. They smiled, thick tongues sliding side to side in wide gap-toothed mouths. Sam wrinkled his nose at the elephantine pair. They whispered, began to titter. High shrill tittering like enormous rodents.

The hag crawled stiffly off her perch, approached the table. "Yeah, what'll you have?" her mouth was puckered, toothless. Mikey considered how the old woman looked like a Disney witch, with pointed chin and hooked nose.

"Coffee," Sam grunted back, "and a couple menus if it's not too much trouble."

The moon-faced woman sneered, looked down at the kid.

"Pepsi," he looked away.

"Ain't got that," she hissed.

"Just bring him coffee," Sam glared.

The fat jack-o-lantern-faced women stared, giggled.

They ordered their food, sipped their coffee. And tried to ignore the other patrons. While they waited for their food a few others entered the establishment. They were an ugly lot, with stooped posture, wide mouths, bulging eyes. Their flesh had an unhealthy bluish tinge, their hair yellow and in sickly clumps. They were obviously town folk. Some sat at the counter, the rest took a table near the front windows. Like the behemoth sisters, the new patrons all kept an interested watch on Sam and Mikey.

"So you mind telling me finally why the hell we came to this craptown?" Sam stared into Mikey's dark eyes.

The kid turned away. "I wanted to see for myself," he said.

"What? See what? What a fucking dump it is? How ugly the locals are?"

"I think I'm changing," he finally just said, gulping breath.

"Changing?"

The kid just looked at the fat man, eyes soft and sad.

"Are you trying to tell me you're queer?" he asked after a moment of uneasy silence.

"Jesus, Sam! No!"

"I mean, if you are that's okay. No one has to know. It'll be our secret," he wiped his brow, nervously fished for a cigar.

The food arrived. The glowering crone slid the plates in front of them, refilled their coffee mugs, spilled it on the table.

"Shit, that's all you've eaten for weeks. You're going to turn into a fish," he gestured to the plate of steaming seafood in front of Mikey.

"No, Sam, I'm not gay," the teen whispered when the stick-legged woman limped away from the table.

"Then please explain this to me," he gestured with half his sandwich, slopped filling on the table.

"When I was little my ma used to tell me stories."

"Yeah?"

"Stories about my ancestors, and how they . . ." he paused, surveyed the room, lowered his voice, "changed."

Sam just stared, shrugged.

"They were from here. Innsmouth. Something to do with this town. Maybe the old plague. The people change. They change into something else. Monsters or something. It's in their genes." He glanced over his shoulder at the ugly men at the counter. "Whenever I was bad when I was a kid she'd tell me that I was going to change and the people from Innsmouth were going to come for me. They would come and take me out into the ocean."

"Monsters? You think you're turning into a monster? Come on, you're a smart kid—you don't believe that bullshit, do you? For Christ's sake, Mikey, your mother was a Goddamn drunk."

"But it's started. See," he stretched the collar of his T-shirt.

The agent leaned over the table, "what am I looking at?"

"The marks on my neck. The gills. They're starting."

"There ain't nothing there." He felt along the teen's throat. Nothing.

"Those people this morning noticed it."

"Who?"

"Back in Marblehead. You saw the way they stared at me and pointed."

"They stared and pointed because you're a fucking celebrity. Jesus, your face has been on magazine covers and shirts for months. And remember MTV? Videos? Oh, and what about your spread in *Playgirl?* Jesus, there with a fucking hardon for all the world to see." He finally lit the cigar, inhaled deeper than he could remember ever having inhaled. "Those people recognized you. That's why they stared and pointed. Shit, that happens wherever we go. You should be used to it by now."

"Well, what about this?" Mikey pulled a small cloth-wrapped bundle out of his coat pocket, handed it to Sam.

Beneath layers of yellowed cotton strips was a small lump of gold, smooth and maybe greasy-feeling. "Yeah?" Sam turned the thing over in his hand. "What is it?"

"Some kind of old idol," he lowered his voice, huddled to the table. "Innsmouth gold. It was my great-great grandfather's. Ma said it was one of the Innsmouth people's sea gods."

"Sea god? I don't see it. It's just a lump."

"There," he pointed, "can't you see the markings? The tentacles?" he traced his finger over the shapeless nugget.

"It's just a lump," Sam repeated, louder this time. The shrill tittering came again from behind them. And vague mumbling from the counter.

"Here, give it to me. I shouldn't have showed it to you here." Mikey grabbed the smooth chunk away from Sam, stuffed it back into his pocket.

"Okay, so let me get this straight. Because of some drunken ramblings of your crazy mother you think you're going to sprout gills or something and go off to live in the sea? And that little scrap of fool's gold is an ancient idol of some sea god? Please tell me you're shitting with me. This ain't nothing but a fairy tale. Just a line of bullshit she fed you to scare you when you were bad."

"No, I've seen it. I've seen the old photos. And now it's happening to me. It hurts. That's why I haven't been shaving. It hurts my skin. The changes. Just look at me."

"This is why you said you didn't want to take your shirt off in public anymore? Why you aren't taking care of yourself? Because you're turning into the fucking Creature from the Black fucking Lagoon?"

"Sam . . ." he started.

"No. Now that's enough. You're fine for Christ's sake. I saw you in the john last night. I saw all of you, and there ain't a blemish on you. No gills. No scales. Nothing. Now knock off the shit and let's go. You have a show to do in New York and you're going to be ready for it, Goddamn it. Come on."

He stood, tossed money on the table. The weird sisters cracked jack-o-lantern smiles at him. "What the fuck you two looking at?" he growled at them. They just laughed their unnerving little laugh. Sam stared down the wide-faced folk at the counter, the miserable old hag. He pulled on his coat, yanked the kid out of his seat.

Mikey was quiet all the way back to Marblehead. Sam cooled off. He humored his star, offered to check the kid for deformities, blemishes. Said he'd have a doctor examine him. The kid declined. Sam suggested Mikey talk to a shrink. He only got mad, stormed out of the inn. When he finally came back he refused to speak. That night he spent almost two hours in the bathroom.

*　*　*

"This is it. No more Goddamn kids," Sam grumbled to himself, slipped his key into the lock. "Come on, Mikey, we ain't got all day. Get your ass in gear," he bellowed as the heavy door swung in on the cavernous loft apartment. The place was dark, the blinds drawn tight. A tiny red light blinked near the door. The kid's answering machine, loaded with Sam's irate messages. "Mikey, where the hell are you?" he shouted up toward the bedroom loft.

Silence. Just the familiar steady hypnotic murmur from the living area.

"Fucking kid, I'm going to break his Goddamn neck when I get hold of him." He slipped a cigar into his mouth. His face was getting red, he felt hot. He poked his head into the kitchen, the bathroom. No sign of Mikey. Tooth brush; razor; shaving cream: the kid hadn't even packed his toiletries yet. He cursed again, checked his watch. His face got redder. He climbed the spiral staircase to the loft bedroom. The bed hadn't been slept in. Suitcases sat in the bottom of the closet, untouched. "You little bastard, don't you fuck this up," he shouted, voice bouncing hollow in the high ceiling.

It wasn't until he leaned his cumbersome bulk over the loft railing that he found his star.

He squeezed down the spiral metal steps, legs unsteady, moisture beading on his puffed face. Mikey was in the big room, the living area. Sam didn't at first comprehend what he had seen from the bedroom loft. He stumbled into the big room, just stared, cigar falling out of his wide mouth.

A sickly greenish glow filled the living area, bathed everything in ghostly light. The steady murmur was louder here—closer—hung like a shroud over the room. The hardwood floor was spoiled with water, clothes strewn about in the puddle. The front of the wall-length fish tank was crusted with salt streaks. A chair stood there, out of place. And a shape hung in the water, floating, bobbing. A familiar shape.

Mikey stared at Sam from behind the glass, eyes wide and bulging, mouth yawning wide. His swarthy skin was tinged blue, made worse by the fluorescent lights. Colorful marine fish swam and danced around him. Skittering crustaceans nipped at his flesh, burrowed through his hair; starfish sluggishly moved across his naked body, through the stiff bristling hair. Crabs picked at his eyes, darted in and out of his mouth; anemones fastened themselves to his chest. He had no gills, no scales, although he was at one with his living reef microcosm. Mikey was a host. Habitat. Sustenance.

And at the bottom of the aquarium, where his lifeless hand had dropped, it was Mikey's small gold lump, glinting in the pale greenish light. Sam just stared, felt the air drain out of his lungs. He couldn't be sure, but he wondered if he didn't finally see the tentacles, the bulging eyes. ✳

Time in the Hourless House

by A. A. Attanasio

The more one knows, the less one understands.

—*Dao De Jing*

T he Elder Gods lived there. Signs of them were to be found everywhere. But no one had actually seen them. I arrived, as most do, by losing the way. In my case, I'd made a wrong turn on a raindark street under a lamppost stoned blind.

Lean cats watched from between gnarled ashcans, their hot eyes aglow with the faint lightning that trembled like stuttering neon in the narrow sky. Head bowed under the sifting rain, I paid more heed to the black cobbles and their oily haloes than to my surroundings.

When I did look up, I noticed curious rainworn architecture, pale gables of crocketed marble and gargoyled eaves. A chalken frieze of griffins and winged lions surprised me, so incongruous did it seem in my small metropolis of trolleytracks, townhouses, and chimneypots.

That was warning enough for me, and I turned about, determined to go back the way I had come before losing my way worse. But the alley lane seemed wholly unfamiliar. The cobbles had sunk to a cinder path between anonymous warehouses of gray, powdery brick. The rain had cleared off, and a large moon of tarnished silver drifted in a day sky above the dismal buildings. Disturbed by what I saw and did not recognize, I would not go that way.

In the direction I had been walking, beyond the eroded marble edifices of angelic beasts, the alley opened onto warrens of withered weeds and ashy sleech. I wandered across that barren landscape toward a bleak pastoral of rubble overgrown with sedge and sumac.

Gradually, the terrain became more wild and profuse. Sunlight stenciled shadows in a dense wood of narrow trees. A small wind blew, tainted with leafsmoke. Through the skinny trees, I spied a black pond, where a century of rain had collected, the drowned trees leaching the water to the color of night. Garish birds preened pink feathers among the cane brakes, and I surmised I had left my world entirely behind.

My heart thudded dully in my chest, for I had read the arcane books that described this otherworld. I knew of the malevolent and dissociate aspects of this realm. Little doubt remained that I found myself among these sullen precincts as punishment for having read the forbidden texts. I knew that in the land of things unspoken, knowledge itself predicates violation. I had been summoned to these purlieus of the unimaginable by an unguessed kinship between mind and happenstance.

That strange equality had already been described by Ralph Waldo Emerson, who wrote in *The Conduct of Life* that "the secret of the world is the tie between person and event . . . the soul contains the event that shall befall it . . . the event is the print of your form. Events grow on the same stem with persons."

Until the day that I found myself trespassing alien ground, I had considered Emerson's philosophy intriguing but not compelling. When I climbed the shale steps of a dried creekbed among the slender trees, their yellow leaves pouring around me in a sudden turn of cold wind, I knew what I would find atop the ridge. And so, though frightened, I was not terrified when I scrambled over the flat rocks, climbing from stone pool to pool to a chine of heather swept by brisk sunlight and cloud shadows.

Atop that vast high country, I could peer down the curve of the world, and I saw in the blue sky, weird stars, red and green. And among them, loomed planets and moons pinioned in comet vapors bright as a webwork of incandescent cirrus. Notions of immensity, that on earth only the ocean could conjure, awed me. From atop my shelf of rock, I gazed a long time at that celestial vista and no doubt muttered to myself woeful thoughts and all things contained of dread therein.

The icy updrafts of gray mist eventually called my attention to what lay below—a stone path fiery green with lichen that descended through a high forest of pine into a dell of deformed apple trees, a gloomy orchard lit with mist and attached to a vineyard autumn had blackened. At the end of the bereaved valley, a grim house stood. Broad steps, tall fluted columns of rococo plinth and cornice fronted an immense and stark facade.

This was the Hourless House that I had read about, where the Elder Gods dwelled. I was not appalled that it possessed neither the physical stature nor the ancient traits necessary to house such preterit beings colossal of both space and time. This house, and all else since my wrong turning in the alley, was woven in the thin thread of dreams. Yet, I knew well, I knew very well indeed, it was therefore no less real.

Under the star-filled heavens, I climbed down the lichenous stone trace, cold, chilled by more than the wind, a blue animal trembling softly at what I realized awaited me. Ahead loomed the home of dark legends. From its ruined pillars dangled black ivy and gray dodder.

As I approached among the deformed trees of the apple garth, silver footsteps followed. The wind ran past with a figure of mist, then hung among the boughs in the shape of a dead woman. My soul, I understood, depended from those branches, faceless under her long hair, colorless locks aswirl like smoke.

My soul in the leafless tree, creaking the dry wood with her lonely weight, turned slowly. Her silent scream scattered crows from the orchard, and they blew across the sky like faded chords of music, black notes scattering among the slant clouds.

In the decayed vineyard, a dead angel sprawled. His raiment lay tattered and rain-bleached, impaled upon slatted ribs, one extra rib than man in that weathered brisket. Black mandrake sprouted among wingbones and what faded and frayed feathers remained. Thatched hair yet clung to his dried skull, and a perennial grin of perfect teeth greeted me from within a face naked of flesh. This was the source of the woodsmoke I had smelled earlier. The carcass actually smoldered on its bed of loamy compost, seething barely visible fumes of decay that lofted a fragrance of charred leaves. Appalled by this grotesque sight, I did not linger in that arbor of eternal autumn but hurried on to the Hourless House.

I climbed past cracked urns, up dilapidated steps, and entered the foyer. Stricken bats gusted from their coverts in the vaulted ceiling. Dead cold spots in the air identified where other presences stood, entities of other realities, other times, who had arrived at the same house but by different reckonings.

Warped parquetry squeaked underfoot when I advanced into the main reception room. Shards of glass from broken panes glinted among the dust of bat droppings and furry lumps of inchoate dead shapes. No one emerged to receive me, save the invisibles that moved about as I did, felt only as cells of bright chillness and never seen.

Newel and finial stood intact upon the banister, and I mounted the slow curving stairs to the upper landing, where the balustrade had collapsed leaving behind only a few cracked spindles. Foliate scrollwork decorated the mouldings of the waterstained walls and the prolapsed and broken plaster ceiling. I called out the barbarous names I had learned in the arcane books. I called those ponderous names through the long, echoing rooms. As I climbed to the second landing, then the third, I called the thick names. I called them.

And they answered me.

"We are here!" they chimed as one, their cry awobble with echoes like submerged voices. "Here! We are here! Come to us!"

And I obeyed. I had read the arcane books. I knew the profoundly terrible import of those texts. And so I knew as well the frightful nature of those voices. Such dark knowledge did not impede my mesmeric advance. I climbed the broken stairs and the ladder of cobwebbed rungs to the topmost gallery. Under the mansard, the ceiling pressed close, and I stooped to grasp the glass knob of the small door behind which voices whispered frantically, gibberishly sharing anticipation of my arrival.

The door opened upon them—the Elder Gods.

I stood astonished. They are not titanic beings as the texts describe. They are small as dolls, and in the umber shadows their smiles are sad and evil. Dark, anarchic, restless thoughts pollute the curdled brains inside those bulbous heads. And a putrid stench, a rancid reek of cheesy flesh and carnal sulfur, packs the alcove where they squat.

Rickety limbs twitched at the sight of me. Then, all those grotesque dolls fell silent, bald, dented heads bobbing, hollow eyes lidded blackly gold as toads' eyelids, dazed, concussed, dreamhooded, as if attentive to other voices or beholden only to their own minds' shapeless shapeshifting, whole worlds playthings in the gray-green smoke of their staring thoughts. Whole worlds—my world, your world, too, the worlds of every sentient being, provoked from nothing by these squalid, grinning things.

That dark encounter lasted but one unspeakable moment. I slammed the door, shutting away the abhorrent sight, and crashed down the ladder and the stairs. Terror propelled me across the dung-strewn reception hall and out into the bracing wind and the ruined land.

I would have kept running had I not read the esoteric literature. I knew what I feared and feared to know. I knew. There is no way back among the scattered black ponds and the scrawny woods. In a distant city after the rain, the shape of my absence goes on. But I will never find or fill that shape. For I am here now under the red and green stars of a day sky strewn with moons and planetary phases— and my soul hangs from a twisted bough, and the dead angel in the black vineyard grins, grins fiercely at the secret meanings of all that I know and fear to know. *

Special Order

by Henry Lee Forrest

Looking back, I find myself wanting to say it wasn't fair. There should have been premonitions, hints, forebodings. I could anyway, I suppose. . . . No. Not really.

When I first picked up the envelope, all I thought was that a piece of junk mail had gotten into the pile by mistake. It was addressed in an odd script that suggested a laser printer and a bored salesman with a large font library. Then I looked again and realized that it was handwritten, in flawless nineteenth-century copperplate.

The return address said, "Crossroads Emporium, Antiques and Oddities"—Maine? I thought I knew all the book dealers in Maine. No matter. In form, it was just like any other book quote:

In reference to your want list of May 16 we are pleased to be able to offer the following . . .

"What is this?" I spluttered. Everyone in the search room turned. I have been known to get upset, but I'm not usually loud about it.

Seeing the reaction calmed me down quickly. I apologized and turned back to the letter, trying to understand. It didn't take long, unfortunately.

"Faith," I said quietly.

The room went from curious to tense in zero time. Danielle Stewart hopping mad is a curiosity, if disturbing. Danielle Stewart quietly upset makes people very nervous. I've never understood it.

Fortunately, they also seem to know when I'm not upset with *them*. Faith answered without a qualm.

I continued. "Remember the man who came in for a book search last month? Smith, the computer says his name was. Tall, skinny fellow, weird eyes, sounded like he had a throat full of gravel?"

"Mn-hm." Faith saw where this was going already.

"And he wanted a search on a book that didn't exist?"

"Yep."

"According to the computer, we took his money anyway." My voice got even quieter. "Why?" I'd already guessed, of course, but for some reason I found myself wanting to hear it.

Faith obliged me. "Orders. *Der Maus* said if the guy wanted to spend his money looking for a nonexistent book, that was his affair. Three bucks is three bucks, I guess." She looked as if the words tasted bad. "Why do you ask?"

"Because I have a quote on it."

"A quote?" She stared at me, as if trying to decide if this was a joke. And she knew I don't have a sense of humor. "Somebody sent in a quote? On a *used copy of the* Necronomicon?"

"That's right." I turned back to the terminal—might as well eliminate the easy outs first. Calling up the database Abram had sweated into being, I started typing in the keywords, idly wondering if the system would crash again before I finished. Our employer was into state-of-the-art. He was also into cheap. The two were not especially compatible.

Behind me, Lee had wandered over, wanting to know what we were talking about. Faith was willing enough to oblige. "—by H. P. Lovecraft," I heard, not really listening. "In the stories, just reading the thing would drive you crazy. Nobody sane wanted a copy, of course, but in Lovecraft's work that left a lot of people interested."

"Cheerful stuff, huh?" Lee grinned.

"Oh, yes. The Stephen King of the 1930s. A good chuckle on every page—not!"

Necronomicon, the screen said cheerfully, and displayed a list of books published under that name. Big O's coffee-table book of Giger's pre-*Alien* drawings, a mass-market paperback full of ersatz witchcraft . . . the list was not long, and nothing matched either Mr. Smith's demand or Crossroad's description.

I sat back, a little disappointed. "Well, if it's a hoax, it's not an obvious one. Not any of the published titles, anyway."

"I thought you said it didn't exist," Lee said.

"It doesn't," I said, "but that doesn't mean nobody ever used the title. It was just too memorable to pass up, I guess, once the copyrights lapsed."

Faith frowned over my shoulder. "What about that hardback—"

"The gift book? No." Lee still looked lost. "Someone printed a book for the novelty market," I explained. "Leather-bound and written in Arabic script—about forty pages, printed in different combinations. The last page ended in the middle because the writer was supposed to have been carried away by something horrible before he could finish it. Supposed to be pretty, if you like the grotesque.

"No, the customer was specific and what he described doesn't match anything published. He wants the 'real' thing." I shook my head. "I can't believe the Mouse took his money."

"You can't?" Faith smiled sadly. "What about this 'Crossroads' outfit? How convincing are they? And how much do they want?"

"Very, and lots. They and the Mouse ought to get along fine." I got up and handed her the letter. "And speaking of our beloved employer, I'd better go talk to him. I am *not* going to take responsibility for this one." As I left the search room, Faith was reading the quote. Fortunately I had the door closed before she reached the price. The search room doesn't open on the main store, but it's within earshot and the Mouse would not have approved. Hoots of near-hysterical laughter are not Consonant With The Dignity Of This Establishment.

*   *   *

The storefront was wood, painted white and ever so slightly weathered. The old-fashioned multi-paned windows were full of old books and curious things, propped up or scattered about on fixtures that were clean, but not new or polished. I stepped through the entrance and nodded to the earnest young clerk at the front desk. He was ringing up a sale on a terminal the desk tried valiantly to disguise.

Inside, the front of the store was light and airy, with more curios than books. Halfway back, a step up brought me to the book floor, its wallpaper a shade darker, the shelves higher and more crowded, dust jackets and bindings a colorful contrast to pastel walls and dark wooden cases. To my right was the "study," where the first editions were kept; ahead, the owner's office. As I crossed to the office, a very correctly-dressed young man escorted a customer into the study, no doubt to discuss a purchase—or perhaps a search. The chairs in there were quite comfortable.

All very attractive at first glance—the very image of an obscure little English shop on an obscure little English side street. Only the size didn't quite match, and this is America, after all. One must make allowances. The plaque outside, at least, was perfect: small, discreet and unassuming:

MARLOWE AND SONS
BOOKS
Curios, Collectibles,
Rare and Out-of-Print Books

Of course, the big signs out on the mall floor more than made up for the discreet brass plaque. Still and all, it was one of the more impressive facades I'd seen in a mall store. The "little shop" illusion; the careful use of color and stepped floors and lighting to make you feel like a trespasser anywhere but in the front section (but not *too* out-of-place—just enough to make you want to either buy something or leave); the careful arrangement of books and curios to disguise the fact that most of the curios were straight out of a catalog and most of the books were remaindered coffee-table specials; even the name—Our Beloved Employer's name was McKee, and he had no sons—the entire "shop" was a triumph of looks over substance. Much like its owner, I thought, as he graciously granted me an audience.

He was in shirtsleeves, his coat hung carelessly on a chair—within easy reach in case he needed to look plausible for a client. His sleeves were rolled up, but the cufflinks were near to hand. His tie was impeccable, the tack a small cross (which also added to his plausibility, in some quarters). His "Yes, Danielle?" was the perfect balance between *Is something wrong?* and *This had better be important.*

There was a time when I'd been impressed. Then I'd been promoted to head of the search department, and started getting my orders firsthand.

"Mr. McKee, about this search for the *Necronomicon*—a dealer says he has a copy of it."

"Well, call the client and sell him the book," he said, carefully not adding *Why are you bothering me with trivia?*

"Sir, you know this book does not exist—this has to be a fraud of some kind."

He waved it away. "This business is built on trust, Danielle. The dealer says it exists, so we must assume it does. Sell the book."

I tried once more. "But if it doesn't exist, wouldn't we owe the client a refund?"

He looked on me with sorrow and long-suffering patience. "What is standard procedure, Danielle?"

I gritted my teeth. "When the client sends the check, we attach it to the dealer's quote," I recited, staring at the wall. "We send a check to the dealer. When the book comes in we deposit the client's check and mail the client the book." I looked back down. "That won't work this time, sir. The dealer won't take a check—or cash, for that matter."

"What's that?" I finally had his full attention. "What does the dealer want?"

"Silver. Two thousand ounces of silver. To be paid in one-ounce units. '.999 fine, mixed units preferred,' the letter said."

He thought about that for a full three seconds. Then he shrugged. "No problem. Make it clear to the client that we are not responsible for the dealer's fraud. We simply send the money to the dealer."

We know this has to be a fake, I thought, *but we won't tell you that. We'll take your money, and our one hundred percent commission, and charge you for shipping and handling. If you're gullible enough, we'll keep the commission. If not, the money the dealer got out of you is not our problem. Neither is shipping and handling. Either way, We Are Not Responsible For The Dealer's Fraud.*

"Yes, Mr. McKee," I said, and went back to the search room. There'd been no surprises. That didn't make me feel any better.

*   *   *

According to the Library's Ready Reference section, silver was $4.93 an ounce today, and usually ran between $4.00 and $6.00. Call it $5.00, times two thousand, plus our markup, plus handling . . . I blinked at the number that came up. Ridiculous. But I had my instructions. Besides, I thought as I dialed, he'd never go for it at that price, so my conscience would be clear . . .

The phone rang once, and the gravelly voice I remembered said, "Yes?"

"Mr. Smith, this is Danielle from Marlowe and Sons. One of our scouts has found a copy of the book you were looking for, and I would like to describe it to you."

"No paperback," the voice said, and I was suddenly very glad it wasn't one.

"No, sir, this is not the paperback. Let me read to you what the scout says. It is the . . ." I squinted a little—copperplate is hard to read if you're not used to it. Pretty though . . .

". . . the Dee English translation, complete in one volume, full leather binding—the traditional leather, he says—marbled end papers, deckled edges, folio, and is in very good condition. It is a manuscript, of course, not a printed copy. Rubrics, embossed titles, page 619 is torn and there is some staining to several pages. Says here it was copied from the San Francisco copy approximately 1900. On a scale of 1 to 10, with 10 being just like new, this book sounds like it would be between 7 and 8. Does that sound like the book you want?"

"Ya. Could be. . . ." His voice had an odd lilt, if gravel could be said to lilt. "Where is it?"

"Cro——." I nearly bit my tongue. What was wrong with me? Never reveal your sources—that was Rule One here. I took a deep breath and started over. "Cros——," I said, and dragged myself to a halt. Then I tried once more, thinking about each word before I said it, saying each word with infinite care. "One of our six thousand scouts has located it for us, sir," I said. "He is a new scout; he is unfamiliar to us; and I do feel that I should warn you that since we have not dealt with him before, this sale is at your own risk. That is, you send us a check for the amount and we will order the book. We can only guarantee that we will order it, not that he will deliver it. Of course, once it comes into the store, we will inspect it, and if it is in the condition described we will ship it on to you immediately."

"How much?"

I tried to sound casual. "Twenty-two thousand dollars."

"I'll send you the money." No hesitation at all.

"Thank you, sir," I heard someone say, "and if I may check your address to make sure . . ."

After a moment, I decided the voice was mine. I'd gone through this close-of-sale routine so many times I could have done it in my sleep—which was fortunate, because at the moment I wasn't at all sure I wasn't dreaming. Twenty-two thousand dollars! How many weeks worth of sales had I just made here? . . .

"Don't mail the book. Call me. I will come for it."

"Yes, sir. Thank you, sir. Do you have our address to send the—"

"Yessssss," he said and hung up. Just like that.

*   *   *

The next few weeks were busy. Faith, having met her sales quota for the month in less than three weeks, was graciously allowed to take the week of vacation time she'd scheduled. Lee, who'd been a stock clerk the whole time she'd worked here, was put on the sales floor. Since she wasn't new to the company, she was expected to meet the same quotas as the other salespeople immediately.

This was, of course, impossible. Which of course, was what the Mouse had planned. He'd been looking for a way to fire her for cause for some time. She was overweight, you see, and this offended him.

When Faith got back, she gave her notice—in two weeks she would be an honest bookseller, she said. Meanwhile, the two of us covered for Lee while she job-hunted. All in all, not a dull month.

In my copious spare time, I got in touch with an old friend who worked at a pawnshop. Once it had been into electronics; now it was into jewelry, coins, and precious metals. When Mr. Smith's check arrived, I was ready. A week after it came, I gave Chris a check. For that amount (plus the deposit I'd mailed him when Mr. Smith's check came in) I received the following:

1. Some teasing about my taste in obsolete VCRs (I prefer beta format);
2. Two thousand troy ounces of silver, in assorted coins and one-ounce ingots; and
3. A surprisingly enjoyable lecture on the silver trade—tips, tricks, and history.

The first and third items I kept. The 140 or so pounds of silver I shipped to Maine, at considerable expense. The book arrived a few days later.

*   *   *

The mail had arrived five minutes before opening, as usual, but I didn't get to it until the afternoon. That was the day the Mouse fired Lee (waiting until she'd made the trip in, of course). Faith gave me a saint's medallion as a going away present and I put it in my sweater pocket. To add to the general confusion, although it was Faith's last day, he sent her home, too. Perhaps she was too cheerful about it or something. In any case, I spent the entire morning on the sales floor covering for them both.

When I finally got into the back room, I found the book with the UPS shipment. The package, surprisingly heavy, was wrapped in brown paper and twine. Inside the paper was a wooden box bound with straps of metal—I had to borrow a crowbar from Joe in mall security to get it open.

The box was lined with metal on the inside as well. In it was a handwritten receipt and another package of brown paper. Inside that package was a bag made of a strange silvery cloth. I'd never seen anything like it—it wasn't just silver-colored; it looked as if the threads themselves were made of metal.

Mr. McKee had been hovering over me for some time—even here we didn't see too many $22,000.00 books. Now he pushed Abram out of the way and snatched the bag out of my hand. He opened it, much more quickly than I would have, and drew out a large book, about the size of a family Bible. It was bound in a pale, smooth leather that I didn't recognize, with archaic-looking lettering and some sort of design I couldn't quite make out embossed—no, and not painted . . . it almost looked as if it had been *tattooed*—into the leather.

The edges of the boards were rimmed in a dark metal that looked a bit tarnished, and there was a clasp closing the book. It was hard to see much more than that, though, because of the wrapping of cobweb-fine silver threads that made up the last layer of packing. They came together in a knot over the front cover, a knot covered with wax and stamped with a seal. Just like in a Regency romance or something. The seal looked like an elaborate rendering of a Star of David, but I'm not sure. Mr. McKee broke it before I could get a good look at it.

The Mouse usually treated his books like merchandise. Not this time, though. He slipped this one out of its silver-mesh wrapping and caressed it, almost gloatingly. Abram sneezed, but the Mouse didn't say a word about decorum and handkerchiefs. He just stood there, running his fingers over the cover, tracing that obscure design again and again. Since he wasn't paying attention, I went back to the search room to get my sweater. When I got back, Abram said Mr. McKee had gone back to his office with the book. I checked the thermostat—nobody had changed it—and followed him.

When I entered his office, I found him poring over the book, lost to the world. Odd. He didn't read much, most of the time.

"Sir?" I said.

"Yes, Danielle?" he said after my fourth try. He did not look pleased to see me.

"Mr. Smith asked to be notified upon arrival of his book," I said, holding out my hand for it.

"I'll take care of it," he said.

"But sir, I'll need to check the book against the quote—" He glared at me. I shrugged and left.

The rest of the week was no better. Lee and Faith had contributed most of the good cheer in the store. The new people were decent enough, but they could have been selling tires for all I could tell watching them.

The Mouse spent all week in the office with the door closed. That was no great loss, but the only way to the employee bathroom was through that office, and he had the "Do Not Disturb" sign up.

We had the air conditioner people out twice that week. They couldn't find anything wrong, but they agreed with our customers and our staff: the store was far too cold. Replacing the thermostat didn't help.

*   *   *

As shopping malls go, Lexington Court was old, very old. When they laid the first foundations, science fiction had enclosed whole cities, but never just the stores downtown. And as for real architects. . . .

The court the mall was named for, the roof, the upper and lower galleries, the acres of store space—all were afterthoughts, tacked on wherever a place could be found when the architects came up with the latest improvements. I suppose that was part of its charm: It didn't *look* like everybody else's shopping mall. It just grew.

The service areas were something else. The store access corridors, the loading docks, the physical plants of a shopping mall are never pretty—why waste paint on something your customers will never see?—but Lexington Court was in a class by itself. Our service corridors were as much an afterthought as the stores they accessed, put in wherever there was space. They ran behind and around and under the stores, with no obvious rhyme or reason, like an octopus embracing a pretzel.

Stepping out the back of a store put you into a maze of dark tunnels, the newer ones walled with unpainted plasterboard, the older ones with cement blocks, or brick, or—in a few places—blasted through bedrock and left as they were. The older the corridor, the darker and dirtier the walls and the worse the lighting. In the lower levels, some were floored in cement and had gutters running down the middle, full of oily water. I kept expecting to find torch sockets.

I took the trash out one morning and found a rat on the Dumpster. It was a big thing—I could have sworn it was two feet long. Just sitting there, watching me.

"Hey!" I yelled. It just looked at me. "Go away!" It preened its whiskers and I got the distinct impression it was sneering. Looking around, I thought I saw more eyes in the darkness behind the Dumpster, and chose the better part of valor. Dropping the trash bags where I was, I backed out of the cement corridor into the better-lit plasterboard, and thence into the mall itself, shutting doors as I came to them. Then I headed for the court, looking for a security guard.

When I found one, it was Joe, thank goodness. I'd known him since I'd started working here, and we got along quite well, and—well, he was my father's age; I didn't feel as silly telling him I'd been scared by a rat. If it had been one of the younger men—oh, forget it.

As I'd expected, he just grinned and said in his deceptively soft voice, "No problem, Ms. Stewart," and escorted me back down the service tunnel to the Dumpster. The rat was still there. It ducked and ran when *he* yelled "Hey!"; but it didn't really look scared, and I still felt as if it was watching me.

Joe looked after it, frowning. "I'm going to report this, Ms. Stewart. Ain't like the creatures to be that bold. Might be rabies or something."

I shivered as I dumped the trash in. "Thanks for escorting me," I said.

"My pleasure, ma'am. I should have remembered you don't jump at shadows." He grinned. "Next time, though, you ought to be more assertive. Yell 'Botherance!' or something. That'll teach 'im."

I probably turned pink. Good thing this was one of the badly-lit places. "Joe, I told you. If I use a word to myself, I might use it with a customer, and—" I stopped when I saw the grin widen. He'd done it to me again.

*   *   *

The day did not improve. The store was still freezing. Abram was still sneezing, but only at work. Probably an allergy—he still sang in the choir every Sunday—but no one knew what it was. The Mouse was still spending his days blocking access to the restores. And Mr. Smith called to find out where his book was.

"Mr. Smith?" He hadn't given his name, but there was no mistaking that voice. "Your book did arrive at the store, and you should have received it already."

"Then where is it?" he grated.

"Let me check the shipping records and call you back, sir," I said quickly.

"Why shipping? I said call me."

I bit my lip. He *had* said that. "Just a precaution, sir. It may have been shipped by mistake. I'll find out what happened and call you back as soon as possible."

"Yesssssss," he said. I made sure I had his number and hung up. I was shivering again.

I checked the records. The customer hadn't been called. The book hadn't been shipped. It hadn't been stocked. It hadn't even been checked against the quote. That left one place to look. I knocked on the Mouse's door.

The office had a queer smell, and it was even colder than the rest of the store. There must have been something wrong with the lighting, as well; when the Mouse looked up, his skin seemed yellowish and his posture was—well, *wrong*, somehow. Shadows, I guess, but it gave me quite a start.

The book was on his desk, open. "I'm taking care of this book personally," he said when I asked about it.

"Sorry, sir. Mr. Smith called about it, and I couldn't find any records of—"

"I said I'm taking care of it myself!" he almost snarled. "It just hasn't gotten to Mr. Smith yet. Get out." He turned away, hunching a shoulder. Was he losing weight?

*   *   *

Joe started meeting me in the parking lot and walking me to work. "One of the guys took a derelict to the hospital last night," he said when I asked him why.

"Now, Joe . . ."

"Don't you 'Now, Joe' me, young lady. You didn't see this guy, clothes soaked with drool and blood and—and other things." Joe had definite ideas about what you said to ladies. That's what made the "botherance" jokes so funny. "He was babbling and carrying on like nothing I ever saw," he went on. "Eyes wide open, never blinking, muttering about eyes and dark and arms. Big sores all over him— I've never seen the like.

"Or—well, maybe I have."

He was staring straight ahead, across the lot, through the walls of the mall ahead, seeing nothing I could see. "Korea, wintertime, I saw some people with frostbite didn't get treated for it right, they had sores like that. Like the skin got rubbed off and the meat was just left there. Oozing blood and pus and—a lot of them had to have amputations . . ."

Suddenly he was back with me. "Oh. Sorry, Ms. Stewart. Forgot where I was. Anyway, I don't know what could do that, but I don't want you finding out by yourself."

It was irritating—as if I couldn't take care of myself! On the other hand, this was Joe. He had a Silver Star at home that he'd earned in Korea. He'd never talk about how he earned it. Just like Dad. Dad had been career army, and he'd talk about it all day if you let him. But he'd never talk about the fighting. Joe was like that.

The rats were getting bolder. Joe had to throw a rock to get one off the Dumpster that morning. "Darn nuisance," he said. "And the management won't let me bring an air gun. Think I'll start carrying a sling. I used to be pretty good with one."

"With a sling? That must have been hard to learn."

"I had incentive. I ate what I killed."

"I thought you grew up in New York."

"I did."

"But—"

"I learned that in Korea." And he wouldn't say another word.

On second thought, anything that scared Joe was something I didn't want to find myself. I stopped complaining.

* * *

Rumor said a rat had bitten a baby in the food court. Joe said no, it didn't have to. Just showing up it had caused a stampede, and two people had been trampled in the rush. Both ended up with broken arms.

Shoplifting was up fifty-nine percent. There'd been three snatch-and-grabs in the past month. Someone had started attacking people in the parking lot on our side of the store. Alternating male and female victims, every three days. The victims were found wandering the parking lot or the service corridors, badly cut up and speaking gibberish, like that derelict. One had died in the hospital. The mall management was hiring off-duty policemen.

One of the new people figured out his chances of actually making Mr. McKee's sales goals, and quit. Abram's allergy was getting worse. We'd had the air conditioner turned off for a week, but the store was still freezing. And Mr. Smith called about his book again.

Mr. McKee wouldn't talk to him. I couldn't explain anything. Mr. Smith hissed at me over the phone. Mr. McKee shouted in my face. By the time I put down the phone I was ready to cry, I was so scared, and I didn't know why.

* * *

I was never so glad to see a weekend. Cleaning my apartment was a pleasure. The concert at Abram's church that night was a delight (and I don't *like* Renaissance sacred music!). Tripping over Faith and

her roommate, Carolyn, on my way to congratulate the choir was
sheer joy—but that would have been true anytime, so I guess it
doesn't count.

They talked me into going out for a pizza with them (it wasn't
hard). The pizza was marvelous, of course. (Was it better than the
chain usually puts out, or was I just easy to please? I don't know.)
Faith told me all about the trials and tribulations of running your
own bookstore. Carolyn told me all about the trials and tribulations
of living with Faith as she tried to run her own bookstore. I told them
all about the trials and tribulations Faith was missing by running her
own bookstore. That got their attention.

I told them all about it—the rats, the attacks in the parking lot,
the air conditioner, the Mouse in his office. Faith was fascinated. "He
never comes out at all?" she said.

"Only to chew someone out when they make a mistake. How he
knows when they do I have no idea."

She grinned a little. "Must make it hard to get to the bathroom."

"No great loss. Nobody uses that bathroom anymore. Too cold
and it smells funny."

Her lips twitched. "They often do."

"Not that kind of funny. That wouldn't be unexpected—" I got
that far before I noticed them both trying to keep a straight face.
"Never mind." Someday I'll learn to tell the difference between a joke
and a straight line. With the friends I've got, it's a survival trait.

"Speaking of funny smells," Faith said, "Did you ever get in that
copy of the *Necronomicon?*"

"Sure did," I said. "It never got out, though."

Faith raised her eyebrows.

"I was in early yesterday, and the light was on in the Mouse's
office, so I went in to see what the problem was. He was sort of
hunched over his desk reading; and when I said hello, he jumped
about ten feet and screamed at me to get out.

"Believe me, I got. But the book he was reading looked a lot like
the one that Crossroads place sent us. I mean, I can't be sure, but
there can't be a whole lot of books that look like it. So on top of
everything else I have an unsatisfied customer on my hands."

"Mr. Smith, you mean? Danielle, your talent for understatement astounds me." Faith stared thoughtfully across the restaurant. "Such a fuss over an imaginary book. I wonder . . ."

"What?"

"Maybe it's not a fake."

I must have been staring. "Faith—" I started.

"Well, just listen to what you've been describing. Mysterious attacks in the dark. Strange things in the empty corridors. Rats in the walls. Strange men doing incomprehensible things around you. There are things Man was not meant to know . . ."

"You mean like how the Mouse comes up with his sales quotas?" I said, and we all broke up. *Sometimes* I can spot a joke.

We spent the rest of the evening talking about an Indigo Girls concert, and had a wonderful time. On the way home, I stopped by a used bookstore and picked up a couple of Lovecraft paperbacks on a whim. Not as detailed as Stephen King, not as good at setting a mood as Bradbury, but compelling, just the same. And some of it did make me think of Lexington Court these days. Unthinkable evil in an Olde Gifte Shoppe. I laughed, finished off my hot chocolate, and went to bed.

It was a wonderful weekend, but Monday made up for it. We hadn't found a new clerk yet, so I was working the sales floor again. The mall was deserted. The only people in the store were a couple of teenagers. When they figured out I was going to keep being help-ful, they left, and I reshelved the figurine the girl had slipped under her jacket.

I was re-alphabetizing the juvenile section for the third time when I heard a board creak and looked up, right into the cadaverous visage of Mr. Smith.

"My book," he rumbled.

I sat down hard. "Your book?" I squeaked. He was even taller than I remembered—close to seven feet, I swear.

"My book."

I swallowed. "Uh, let me go get the owner, sir."

"Bring me my book." Only his lips moved, or so it seemed.

I rolled to my feet—away from him—and fled to the Mouse's office. It took two tries to get a response. "Go away!" was all he said.

"Sir," I said, "there is a customer here to see you."

"Go away!" was the response.

"Sir, he really wants to see you—"

"WHERE IS MY BOOK?"

If an avalanche had a voice, it might have sounded like Mr. Smith. Heads turned all over our end of the mall. He reached over my shoulder and laid a hand on the door. It popped open with a cracking sound, the lock half torn out of the frame.

"What the hell is going on—" the Mouse said, looking up.

"My book—" Mr. Smith thundered.

"Get out of here!" snapped the Mouse.

"Not without my book." Mr. Smith seemed to gain another six inches.

Mr. McKee seemed to shrink within himself, his skin stretching thin over his face, his lips peeling back to reveal sharp, pointed teeth (yes, I know how this sounds—I knew it then). "It's mine, now," he said. "Mine."

"No, you little fool. Mine." Mr. Smith stretched out a long, bony finger. "Mine by blood and silver. Mine by searching and finding. Mine."

Mr. McKee contemplated the finger, licking his lips as if preparing to eat it. He didn't say a word.

I had long since slipped out of the crossfire. Now I finally picked up a phone. "Mall Security?" I said. "This is Marlowe and Sons. We have a customer creating a disturb—"

Mr. Smith turned and looked at me, and suddenly I understood why people ran that old stock phrase into the ground: My blood ran cold. The phone was squawking at me, but I couldn't understand, or answer.

"Mine," Mr. McKee said, and scuttled forward. "It has called to me. Mine." His eyes glowed red as he advanced. Mr. Smith actually backed up from him, right into me as I stood there like an idiot, holding the telephone. I fell, dropping the phone. He didn't seem to notice.

"What's going on here?" a voice barked. Slowly Mr. Smith turned and looked the two security guards up and down. Then, as if dismissing them, he turned back to the Mouse, gathered his duster around him with his dignity, said, "I will be back for what is mine," and walked out. The guards didn't move. No one moved.

There was a noise out in the court—I think someone dropped a package—and we all jumped. The security guards dashed out after Mr. Smith. I picked up the phone and hung it up. Mr. McKee said, "Mine!", walked into his office, shut the door, and (from the sound of it) pushed a chair up against it in lieu of a working lock.

"I quit," announced our last sales clerk. "That's it. This place is not healthy and I quit." I got up, thinking what an intelligent young man Andrew was, and headed for the search room. When I got to the store entrance, I found Abram in a heap beside the register.

His breathing was quick and shallow, his face swollen and red, like Faith the time she was attacked by a whole nest of wasps. I stood there for a moment, my mind frozen solid, and then memories of CPR classes rushed through my head. I yelled for Andrew to call security or an ambulance or something, and dropped to my knees beside Abram to take his pulse. Of course, I couldn't find it. About that time he stopped breathing.

Somehow I got through the routine the Red Cross people had taught me, pumping his heart for him, breathing air into his lungs, the St. Michael's medal Faith had given me before she left bumping his chest as I moved from one position to the other, praying as I worked like I'd never prayed in church and finding a little room in my mind to be ashamed of that. I don't know what worked, but something did—he started breathing again.

The paramedics arrived within ten minutes, which must have been a record, and took over before I could completely dissolve into hysterics. They took Abram to the hospital, and I filled out what seemed like a dozen OSHA forms while the mall physical plant staff tried to figure out what had caused such a violent allergic reaction. Once I had all the forms done, I kept typing, Andrew's words running around in my head.

This place is not healthy, and I quit. This place is not healthy, and—

*   *   *

It has become fashionable these days to build hotels right next to shopping malls and to put in nice dry connecting walkways so the guests can do their shopping right there in the hotel, sort of. Lexington Court was no exception. After the parking lot attacks started, I'd let Joe talk me into using that route every morning. He would meet me at the hotel end of the walkway and escort me in. As I rode the escalator up from the Lexington Plaza lobby the next morning, I found myself dreading the talk on the walkway as much as the one I'd have at the store.

My letter of resignation was on the table outside the Mouse's office. He must have found it last night. I was only going back to pick up my things and straighten up my desk. What he would say to me I didn't want to think about. What he would say to my potential future employers. . . .

But telling Joe good-bye would not be fun. I hadn't done something like that since—I couldn't remember. Both my parents had come from small families. I'd never had a favorite uncle.

No one was waiting at the walkway. Odd. He'd only missed a day once, and then he'd sent somebody. I went on down, into the mall itself. Still nothing. I adjusted my book bag, looked around, and started toward the store.

There was a scuffling sound behind me. I kept going. It followed me. I told myself to keep breathing, and turned away from the service corridors. I'd always been ahead of most store people, much less the customers; but there'd be people in the court, even this early.

The scuffling got closer, and I could hear breathing. I detoured past a shop window that slanted right, and got a look behind me. Reflected in the glass were a blurred blue uniform and a dark face.

I sighed. Granted I don't get more than half the jokes people try on me, this one was a little much. I'd really expected better from Joe. Right now, though, I was far too relieved to be mad. So I stopped and took a breath, and turned and said, "Joe, you scared the living day—"

It took me a second to realize I was screaming. It wasn't like running away from something, it was more like pulling a hand out of a fire. I didn't think, "I am going to scream." I just screamed, and kept on screaming.

It was Joe. And it wasn't. His uniform was torn to shreds, and there was an ugly red cut on his head that had soaked his hair and bled all down the side of his face, dark red against dark brown. His mouth was slack and he was drooling, and then he started laughing, and his teeth were white against the dark skin and the dark blood and what was left of the dark shirt—

I backed away, covering my mouth with both hands, trying to hold the screams in, and he followed me, God help me, limping, one boot torn off and his foot red and missing a few toes. I could see more wounds through the rents in his uniform. Ugly round things, like bites. What bites in a circle?

"Rats," he said, and for a moment I thought he was answering the question I hadn't asked. "Rats with arms and teeth and eyes and—" He started laughing again.

I backed around a planter and kept going. He kept following me and tripped over it. He couldn't get up, but he kept following me, dragging himself along.

"Cold," he said. "Cold."

"Joe—," I said, and he looked at me. He didn't know me. He didn't know anything that I could tell. But I knew him. I took a step forward.

They tell me I was found sitting on the floor with Joe's head in my lap, singing him a lullaby. I don't remember that. They say I cried when they took him from me, and that it took them ten hours to get any kind of a coherent statement out of me. I don't remember that either, but I believe it. They say they found Faith's phone number on a card in my wallet, and called her. I'll take their word on that. The next thing I remember, I was sitting on a sofa in a small room that smelled of disinfectant, and Faith was trying to get some hot tea past my lips. I started crying, and didn't stop for half an hour.

I was released the next morning. The doctors prescribed a mild sedative and told me to for Heaven's sake use it if I couldn't sleep. Faith was in and out the whole day. If she hadn't had a store to run, I'd have never had the apartment to myself.

As it was, I tried to straighten up, but I'd done too good a job Saturday. I wasn't hungry, so I couldn't cook. It wasn't bedtime, so I couldn't take a pill. And I couldn't just sit there, because I kept seeing Joe, laughing and drooling and bleeding and—

Finally I turned on the computer and called up the outline program. I always thought best on paper or on screen.

I: Odd things at Lexington Court
  a. Rats
  b. Cold
  c. Smells
  d. Shoplifters
  e. Abram's allergy
  f. The Mouse and Mr. Smith
  g. Parking lot attacks
  h. Joe

(Oh, God, Joe. . . .)

It was quite a list. I hadn't really looked at all of it before.

II: Related? Or coincidence?
  a. "Once is an accident; twice is coincidence; three times . . ."

—and this had gone far past three. I couldn't call it chance. Not possible.

III: Cause?

As if I were capable of doubting, or wondering.

  a. The book. The book came first. The book did it.

I suppose I was not really sane just then. Or maybe I was. I had just seen insane, and its face had belonged to the best man I knew. Right now, I could believe anything, and maybe that was good.

Something would have to be done, of course. That was obvious. And I would have to do it alone.

Faith thought I was sick, and she didn't really believe the book was for real. Nothing against her—twenty-four hours ago, neither had I.

Abram—no. He couldn't even get back inside—his allergies wouldn't let him. Allergies. Well, why wouldn't a good Baptist be allergic to the thing? I giggled for a minute, caught myself. Besides, he would never believe it.

On those occasions when I'd resented Abram's bad taste in marrying before I'd found him, I'd always taken comfort in his other great fault: he was convinced Henry McKee could do no wrong. I never had figured out how the Mouse did it, but there it was. Abram would never be persuaded.

And who else? No one. I was alone.

IV: Solutions.
  a. Water.

Water purifies. Water destroys. But slowly. Too slowly. And I would need too much—an ocean, maybe.

b. Fire.

Fire purifies. Fire destroys. And it was fast, yes, and it was portable. Yes. Fire would do, oh yes. But there were sprinklers in the store.

But not out back. I laughed. Not in the old tunnels. Not by the Dumpster, where the rats lived.

The store would be locked, but I had a key. The mall was guarded, but I knew when they made their rounds. The book would be in the Mouse's filing cabinet, and he had the only key. I rummaged through Dad's old toolbox, laughing, and found another key that would serve. Then I gathered the other tools I would need, and waited for night.

*   *   *

I had to wait quite a while, in midsummer, but darkness finally began to arrive. I didn't use the hotel walkway this time—there were fewer people to see me in the parking lot. Besides, the "incidents" only happened at three-day intervals and one had just happened yesterday. . . . I wouldn't think about that. I was quite firm with myself.

The mall was almost empty, as it often was these days. I followed some of the janitorial staff in through a side door—I'd picked my clothing not to clash with theirs, among other things—and split off as they headed for the court. No one looked at me as I turned off the main corridor, and no one was in the side hallway to see me enter the service tunnels. I hid in the shadows underneath a staircase, and waited for closing time.

Oddly enough, I fell asleep. I woke up feeling embarrassed and a little bit silly, but I found I still wanted to go through with it. So I checked the bottle of lamp oil, the matches and the small pry bar in my old, dark-brown book bag, and carefully crept out of my hiding place. No one seemed to be about—I didn't see anyone, and all I heard was the rats scurrying through the walls.

The back door to the store squeaked sometimes, so I took my time opening it. After only a year or so, I slipped through, and froze. There was a light in the Mouse's office.

I wanted to cry. All this, and he was still in there! But the light was odd—it flickered, as if someone was burning a candle. And I heard a voice, rhythmic and droning, rising and falling, never loud enough to quite make out.

I put down the book bag, put on my gloves, and slipped up to the office door. For once it was open. The Mouse was in there, hunched over something on the floor. When he moved I saw it was a book. That book. The book. He'd drawn lines on the floor around it, in red chalk or something. The lines made a pattern like the one I remembered seeing on the cover. There were candles, and a brass bowl with charcoal in it.

The Mouse put down the chalk and put something on the charcoal, and the room filled with thin smoke that smelled acrid and fruity, and he started chanting again. I wondered why the sprinkler system hadn't gone off.

There was something ridiculous about a man in a blue pinstripe three-piece suit doing this, I thought crazily. He should have been wearing robes or something. And he seemed shorter—by a good foot, I would have sworn—and that made no sense either. And he kept on chanting in no language I'd ever heard. How did he pronounce that stuff without hurting his throat? It was cold, and it kept getting colder.

The design on the floor changed, rose up, became three-dimensional, a latticework of lines meeting at impossible angles, like an Escher drawing in laser beams, glowing softly in the smoke. It got colder and colder, until the air froze and ripped open above the book and something oozed through the tear and plopped onto the floor.

It was pink, I believe, or maybe green. About the size of a basketball, but it wasn't round. Its shape kept changing, like an amoeba or pile of snakes, and there were tendrils or tentacles or something that kept forming and disappearing and forming again. It had eyes all over it, even on the tips of the tentacles. One of the suckers on a tentacle opened, and I realized it wasn't a sucker—it was a mouth. The thing oozed and glistened iridescently and smelled like rotting fruit, and the Mouse reached down through the lines and petted it and I threw up.

The Mouse laughed and I looked up again. The thing was growing. It expanded until it was taller than he was, taller than the ceiling that it somehow never touched. It grew until it had filled the cage of lines that surrounded it, lines it shrank from even as it grew.

"Fool!" an avalanche shouted from behind me. I cried out and covered my ears, moving out of the way again.

"Thief and fool!" Yes, again. It was Mr. Smith, of course, his grey duster flapping at his ankles. He walked past me as if I didn't exist. He gave the Mouse no more regard than he had me, simply reaching through the cage of lines for the book. As his fingers touched it, the Mouse leaped, grabbing Smith's arm and burying teeth in his shoulder. Mr. Smith roared, and tore the Mouse from him and flung him against the wall. The Mouse twisted in midair and struck the wall feet first, pushing off against it like a swimmer in a race and throwing himself at Mr. Smith again, gibbering. The impact sent them both reeling, and they fell together against the lattice of lines enclosing the thing in the office.

The lines disappeared as they touched them, and the thing inside grew even larger, filling the office, bursting ceiling and walls, sending plaster and wood raining down all over the sales floor. It was gloating—it made no sound, and nothing about it made any sense as expression or body language or anything, but I knew it was gloating, as it watched the two men struggle, fully half its eyes enjoying the spectacle.

Something brushed my foot, and a rat scurried into the office, followed by another. They launched themselves against Mr. Smith, ripping at his duster. More of them followed, and the coat ripped free. His shirt split and there were tentacles growing out of his shoulders, and he grabbed the rats with them, flinging them aside without looking. The thing that had been in the lines snatched a rat from midair, like a frog grabbing a fly, and hissed with pleasure and swallowed it whole. I could see the rat's outline as it wiggled inside.

My hand hurt, and I looked down for an instant. I had grabbed Faith's St. Michael's medal at some point, and I was gripping it so hard it had cut my hand. I remember thinking about how could an archangel be a saint, and then thinking this was no time for theology.

Or maybe a real good time, I didn't know. Then the thing hissed again, louder, and I looked up.

It had picked up Mr. Smith and the Mouse, and was moving them toward—no, not a mouth. It didn't have a mouth big enough for both of them, so it took them to a bare patch of "skin," and shoved them past, or through, or around, or something—straight into itself. They never stopped fighting.

"God have mercy," I whispered, gripping the medal even tighter. And the thing turned an eye or two and *looked* at me and I screamed, *"Help me!"* and it reached—

There was a swelling noise behind me, and I thought of trumpets, though it didn't sound like one at all, and the thing turned all its eyes toward the sound, and there was a rustle, and I looked and said, "Oh, God, another one—" Then I knew better.

This new thing didn't look like the other one. Its shape was a little more definite, though no more describable. It was covered with eyes like the other one, but they looked different, somehow. It was covered with appendages, and I don't know why I thought of wings instead of tentacles—they didn't resemble either. I could see right into it, like I could into the other, but what I saw, I saw as swirls of color, like slowly turning wheels. It was at least as colorful, and as aromatic, as the one the Mouse had called, but I didn't want to wince or gag.

Don't ask me to explain. I read a book once where the author pointed out that love and fear and seasickness all feel just alike, if you only pay attention to the physical sensations. The odd feeling in the gut; the abstracted, floating feeling; the way all the things you see and hear and smell are so sharp and clear—you know. This was kind of like that. There really wasn't much to choose between one shapeless, ever-changing thing and the other. So why did one make me think of amoebas and slime and snakepits, and why did the other make me think of clouds and rain and flocks of birds against the sun? I don't know. I just know that the one who had just arrived was more terrible, and yet more beautiful, than anything I had ever seen. If it had wanted to swallow me, the way the other one had swallowed the Mouse and Mr. Smith, I would have gone to it gladly.

Somewhere I found the courage to touch it, to take my glove off and touch one of those things that made me think of feathers, and an eye turned and it looked at me, and I felt like I had when I was little and my father had looked at me when he was home on leave, and I'd wondered whether I'd been good enough when he was gone or if he would shake his head and walk away and never speak to me again. He never had, and I'd always thought it was a wonderful thing to have a daddy who loved you even when you were bad sometimes. And now a shapeless monster looked at me and it was just the same, all the way up to the smile and the hug, even though it never touched me.

Then it turned that eye away with the air of a grownup on grownup business, and I remembered where I was. The tear in the air where the first thing had come through was bigger, and more things were oozing out of it: black writhing oily things, and things that walked like bramble bushes, and things that rolled like ball lightning. Over them all towered the amoeba-thing, so tall the roof was gone from the building, so tall I couldn't see the top of it.

The new one suddenly changed, became so solid my eyes hurt looking at it, like blades of fire and dark blue shields. I knew then it was a soldier-thing, and I saluted it the way I'd saluted the coffin when they'd carried it out (all wrapped in stars and stripes and full of something they said was my father, though I knew it wasn't anymore—), and there was a warm wind and an unbearable noise.

The next thing I remember I was standing at attention in the living room of my apartment, my arm aching from holding the salute. The window was far too bright, so I went over and looked out at the night sky. It was brilliant, lit up from the north by what seemed to be a searchlight a half-mile wide.

The authorities are still puzzling over the destruction of Lexington Court. It didn't blow up, and it didn't burn down, but all that's left is a hole that follows the original foundations precisely, neat and square and lined with glass (the experts call it "trinitite"). No debris, no smoke, no radioactivity—the military has a special project to figure it out, and they're praying it was a freak accident.

No two eye witnesses agree on what they heard, and none of them saw anything but a bright light. Oddly enough, no one was reported killed, though one Henry McKee, owner of a store in the complex, has been reported missing. Several people claim to have been in the mall at the time, but they were all found in their homes, and none of them could explain how they got there. Some people are theorizing terrorists who drugged all concerned first and evacuated them. It's not the silliest theory going around, and the military would dearly love to disprove it.

No one ever questioned me about it, of course—I had no reason to be in the mall at that time. No one reported Mr. Smith as missing, but this is a big city; it may not have made the papers with all the rest of it going on.

I refuse to speculate about all this. Maybe it was all coincidence. Or maybe whatever the Mouse did made noise or something, and someone came to investigate. Or maybe I just happened to be thinking the right way—fear, despair, crying for help, and thinking of a soldier—and something heard me and drew the right conclusions. Or maybe my prayer was answered. I have no way to test it, so I'm not going to argue. Draw your own conclusion.

I visit Joe every week. He just sits there when I talk to him. He smiles when I come in, but the staff says he does that for everyone. The doctors have learned a lot, these last few wars, about helping people who've seen unspeakable things. They swear he's improving. I hope so.

I found another job, and I've started going to a different church. Praying to saints is something I feel more comfortable with, these days.

I still see Abram sometimes—he's never had another allergic attack. I get together with Faith and Carolyn fairly often, though certain old times are generally not discussed. And every once in a while I'll read something by Lovecraft, and wonder where he got his ideas, and why he thought *everything* Man Was Not Meant To Know had to be evil. ✳

Lujan's Trunk

by Donald R. Burleson

Nothing would ever be the same again.

True, when Brad Donner moved from Pittsburgh to the little desert town of Corona, New Mexico, he had expected things to be different. He looked out his window now, over a ragged mound of packing boxes, and saw not concrete and glass but sand and cactus and sagebrush, under a turquoise sky too large to be believed. He had expected New Mexico to be another world, certainly, but he could in no way have anticipated what he was really going to find there. Or what was going to find him.

It was late October, but the sun still cast a bright patina of warmth across the land, imparting pointed little shadows to the spikes of yucca and cholla cactus that stood like sentries over the countryside as far as he could see. He had been lucky to rent this little adobe house "out in the county," as people said around here; most of the adjoining land was pasturage belonging to one sheep rancher or another, and his nearest neighbors were almost a mile away, yet for all this wide open space it was only four miles east into town, when he needed supplies. This was genuine seclusion; the only sounds out here were a distant murmur of farm machinery and the occasional nocturnal howl of a coyote. The local joke was that not only could you set off an A-bomb out in this desert—it had been done, as the Trinity Site was only seventy miles or so to the southwest. Brad had wanted privacy, and he had it. This unperturbed little house was going to be the perfect place to finish writing the new novel. And he had to buckle down and do just that, because the royalties from his last two books were wearing a little thin by now.

On his third day in the house he took a break from unpacking and drove into Corona for some groceries he had forgotten. On the way, he noticed an unobtrusive little woodframe house huddled a hundred yards or so off the road, at the end of an unpaved drive; his eyesight wasn't what it used to be, but he thought he saw someone sitting on the porch, an old man perhaps. There was nothing unusual about this, but something about the sight of the person, whoever it was, seemed to give him an odd little chill, as if some deep and obscure response had awakened within him. It was the accumulation of fatigue from moving across the country, no doubt, and he did his best to disregard it, driving on into town and parking in front of the little market where he would be buying most of his groceries. But first he walked to a familiar establishment a few doors down, went in, drew a stool up to the bar, and ordered a beer. Behind him, two young men, one Anglo and one Hispanic, were playing pool and chatting quietly. Brad had stopped in here once before, the day he moved in, and the bartender remembered him; in a town this small, the bartender probably remembered everybody.

"So how do you like the house?"

Brad took his beer, poured it into the glass, and took a sip. "I think it's going to be just what I needed," he said. "When you're used to living in a big city, there's something almost scary about how quiet it is out there."

"Yeah," the bartender said with a grin. "Don't expect to see no traffic jams around here. You probably can't even see another house from where you are."

"No, I can't, actually," Brad said. "Reminds me, I noticed a little place on the way into town—"

The bartender gave him a knowing look. "Old man sitting on the porch."

Brad blinked. "Yeah. You know him? But I keep forgetting, this isn't the big city, you probably know everybody in town."

"Just about," the bartender said, "but don't nobody really know that old guy. Hispanic, calls hisself Lujan, came into town a couple of years ago and moved into that house. There wasn't much moving in to do, because the house was furnished, and anyhow he only had one big trunk, painted all funny, looked like an old circus trunk or something. He just showed up here one day with it. And nobody knows where he's from."

"You know, I don't know why," Brad said, "but when I saw him sitting there—"

"It gave you the creeps," another man at the bar supplied.

"Well," Brad hesitated, "kind of. I mean—"

"Nothing to feel ashamed of," the bartender said. "I guess pretty much everybody feels the same way."

Brad took a long swallow of beer. "What is it about him—"

"For one thing," the other man at the bar said, "he don't never stir out of that chair. Sits on that porch all day long. Maybe all night too, for all I know. I can't think of anybody that particularly wants to go over there at night."

"But that's no reason—I mean, he's probably just some old fellow who came here to spend his retirement years," Brad said.

"Well, that's not all, though," the bartender said. "He don't ever come into town to buy groceries or anything. As far as anybody knows, he don't even eat."

"Come on," Brad said, "he's got to eat."

"Whatever he eats, he don't buy it here, I can tell you that," the bartender said.

Brad considered this. "Maybe he has somebody come in and buy groceries for him?"

"Naw," the other man at the bar said, "old Mrs. Marney down at the market knows everybody in town. People know other people's business around here, too much if you ask me, but that's the way it is. Mrs. Marney would know. Nobody's buying stuff for Lujan."

"Something else funny too," the bartender said.

"What's that?" Brad asked.

"That old trunk of his. People say when he moved in he just parked it right there next to the chair on that porch, never took it inside, maybe never even unpacked it. It's still sitting right there beside him. And you know what else? People that seen the old man close up when he moved in? They say his skin looks odd."

"Ah well," Brad said, "so he's a little strange. Maybe he's sick or something. Still no reason to feel creepy about him."

"Mostly we just don't think about him too much," the bartender said.

Leaving the bar, Brad wondered if he might get another novel out of all this at some point; you never could tell. In any case, he thought he might just pay old man Lujan a visit sometime.

* * *

It took another couple of days to finish unpacking and arrange the house in halfway livable condition, and most of another day to set up the computer and printer and get all his reference books and materials sorted out so that he could get at them. Late that evening, he finally sat down at the computer to work in earnest, starting on the fourth chapter of the novel.

But he found himself staring at a blank screen. *The sun was setting in a sleepy haze on the horizon,* he wrote, and immediately backspaced it out. Where else would the sun set but on the horizon? He stared at the screen for another ten or fifteen minutes before switching the computer off and going to the kitchen for a soda and a handful of pretzels.

What was bothering him?

Somewhere out in the night a coyote howled, long and low and mournful, and Brad drew the shade up and looked out the kitchen window but saw only blackness looking back in at him, so lowered the shade. He sat at the kitchen table and finished his snack before stepping outside and having a look around. A wan yellow gibbous moon was rising like a face of bone over the desert, making strange tendrils of shadow creep out from under clusters of cactus and yucca, and even with the moonlight Brad marvelled at the inky depth of the night sky, frosted so thickly with stars that the familiar constellations were difficult to find. It was true what he had heard, then—you really never saw the sky until you saw it in the desert.

But this bucolic reflection was perturbed, at some level in his mind, by something else, something that kept nagging at him. He pushed the less comfortable thought away and went inside and went to bed.

And dreamed of strange faces, strange shapes, and an oddly painted trunk that he felt unaccountably eager not to see opened.

*   *   *

Waking with a headache and a sense of not having rested at all, he resolved to put a stop to what he knew now was bothering him. He would go visit old man Lujan, introduce himself as a neighbor (though the old man's house was over two miles away), and then he'd be able to see for himself what nonsense it all was.

After all, he reflected, driving toward the old man's house, the region was known for its extravagant legendry; he had discovered this much just by reading, before he decided to move here. There were the La Llorona stories, of a ghostly woman who wandered the arroyos at night crying for her lost children. There were the shapeshifter stories, about Indians turning into crows and coyotes and the like. This tendency toward colorful folktales was one of the reasons why he had chosen to come here, because he felt that such an atmosphere would be fruitful for a writer. The local lore about old man Lujan, on the other hand, was no doubt just the usual tendency of any community to be suspicious of anyone who was different, but Brad might well be able to make literary use of these suspicions sooner or later. It was certainly a good work habit to absorb such rumors and to ponder them at leisure.

Turning up the long dusty drive toward the old man's house, he could see him sitting there on the porch as before, and sure enough, an old-fashioned trunk squatted beside him like some dark, sleeping toad. Brad pulled the car up and parked a respectable distance out from the house, and walked up to the porch. As he did so, the old man watched him but didn't move out of the chair; didn't move at all, in fact. Even on so warm a day, he was swathed in a woolen blanket.

"Hello," Brad said, coming halfway up the rickety wooden steps to the porch and leaning on the rail. "I'm Brad Donner. I just moved into the house a couple of miles up that way, and I wanted to introduce myself."

The old man looked at him without any particular feeling that Brad could identify in the face. People were right, his skin did look odd, sort of rubbery, so that the lizardlike countenance, in its coarse folds, seemed not to reflect emotion clearly. The eyes, dark but alert, peered out from a labyrinthine nest of folds and wrinkles; the fellow was evidently older than Brad had imagined. But at length the convolutions of the face swam apart to form a speaking mouth.

"They call me Lujan," the old man said. The voice was rather thick, almost liquid-sounding.

"I'm pleased to meet you," Brad replied, coming the rest of the way up the steps and extending his hand. Lujan was slow to extend his own hand from under the layers of blanket, but did so, and the hand felt the way the face looked, coarse and rubbery and cold. The hand withdrew, then, back under the blanket. All this time, Brad was observing the trunk also, which was indeed painted lurid colors, showing swirls and patterns that seemed almost to stir some latent memory without quite resolving into any identifiable impression.

Brad could well understand how the old man's arrival in town with such an object would have aroused a certain amount of curiosity, and would have lingered in the memory of townsfolk.

"They tell me you're new here too," Brad said. "Where are you from?"

Lujan waited so long in replying that Brad at first thought that the old man hadn't understood him, or considered the question impertinent. But at length the answer came. "From very far."

Seeing that he would have to be content with this vague answer, but sensing at the same time that the old man was not altogether disinclined to talk with a stranger, Brad said, "I'm a writer, I'm working on a new book—which is why I came out here, it's so quiet, good place to work. Do you get into town much?"

Lujan was again slow in responding, but finally the liquid voice spoke up again. "I never go."

"Well," Brad said, hoping again not to seem presumptuous, "I'll be going in, once or twice a week probably, so if there's anything I can get for you, just let me know."

"*Gracias,*" Lujan replied, "*pero ya tengo todo lo que necesito.* I have everything I need."

Brad scarcely understood how this could be the case, but decided to let the matter drop for now. "Well, again, let me know if there's anything I can do. Say, that's an interesting trunk you have there. Looks like a real antique."

Lujan's head turned, turtle-like, to regard the trunk, then turned back. "It has been with me always."

Brad again glanced over the peculiar painted swirls and suggestions of pattern that covered the surface of the old trunk, and again he had the disquieting feeling that there was something uncannily familiar, or nearly familiar, about those swirls, almost as if some profound repository of inherited memory should respond to them, should know them for what they were, what they represented on some level perhaps too deep for words. He had to look away, finally, because the sight of the trunk palpably disturbed him.

"Well," he said, "I won't take up any more of your time."

"You're very welcome to visit," Lujan said, surprisingly. "We must talk again."

"I'd like that," Brad replied, and realized that he meant it. As oddly uncomfortable as he felt here on the old man's porch, he also felt drawn here, compelled to plan another visit. "I could call you first."

Lujan seemed to be considering this, almost as if he didn't understand it. "I have no telephone," he said after a moment. "Just come, when you want."

* * *

Chapter four was coming along, after a fashion. Brad found that it seemed to require more effort of him than usual to concentrate, and he drew upon such wells of self-discipline as he possessed to make himself sit at the computer and write. Late in the afternoon of the third day after his visit with the old man, he pushed his chair back and regarded the glowing screen with dissatisfaction. The words, the paragraphs, the pages were coming, but somehow he felt now that his dialogue was unnatural, his characters forced and wooden and unconvincing. Maybe he was just being a little paranoid, a little too self-critical. But maybe not. He closed the file, turned the computer off, and went to the kitchen for something to eat.

Munching a sandwich and washing it down with cold beer, he gazed out the kitchen window and watched the sun begin to descend behind a flotilla of clouds. The sunset turned the whole sky first a crimson blaze of farewell, then a kind of salmon-colored wash of light that lingered on the horizon like a memory. It was beautiful, and it made him glad that he lived in the desert, but it failed to banish, altogether, that other thought that kept tugging at his mind. He knew, of course, what the other thought was, but it still took overcoming a certain amount of inertia, or a certain amount of some less clear reluctance—mingled with an odd attraction—to make him face the fact that what he needed to do was drive over and visit Lujan again.

By the time he got there it was getting dark, and when he pulled his car up as before and shut the headlights off, the little cloud of dust that he had raised in driving up was barely discernible in the pallid wash of illumination from the porch light, beneath which the old man sat mummified in blankets, beside his ancient trunk. Brad walked up the creaking wooden steps. "Hello again. I thought we might have a chat. Hope I'm not coming at a bad time."

The old man's wrinkled face seemed even more reptilian than before, in the pale yellow light of the single bulb behind him, and again the maze of folds and wrinkles ebbed away to leave a toothless mouth. "There is no bad time, no good time," he said in that half-gurgling voice. "There is just time. Forever and ever."

"Well," Brad said, taken a little aback, "I guess that's so." He cast a glance at the oddly painted trunk. Somehow it looked all the more sinister under the feeble lightbulb, which seemed to impart a truly appalling quality to the spectral swirls and patterns that covered its rough surface. But the old man was speaking again.

"No beginning, no end."

Brad strained to see the old man's face in the gloom. "I beg your pardon?"

"The Old Ones were, the Old Ones are, the Old Ones forever shall be," Lujan intoned.

Oh brother, Brad thought, what is this all about? "I, uh, I don't understand. Who are the Old Ones?"

"*Los Antiguos,* the Old Ones," Lujan repeated, raising his head slightly to regard Brad more squarely. There was something a little unsettling in the way the head moved, as if the rubbery quality that one saw in the texture of his skin was imparted even to the quality of movement itself. "In the time before all time, in the days *cuando no había tierra ninguna,* when there was no earth, the Old Ones walked in the Great Silence. *No los vemos,* we do not see Them—They walk unseen among us."

"Is this a story they tell here in New Mexico?" Brad asked, feeling more than a little foolish; he simply didn't know what else to say.

"This is a story always told, everywhere," Lujan replied, "by the few who know. Some know. Some few know of Great Cthulhu, some few know of Azathoth at the center of all chaos, some few know of Yog-Sothoth, the One God."

"Whew," Brad said, shaking his head. "I don't know about all this. Now me, I don't mind, but I get the impression that a lot of people people around here are pretty conservative in their religious thinking, Mr. Lujan. I don't think these Sunday-school-going folks—"

"Most people are blind," Lujan stated flatly.

Brad scarcely knew what to say to that. It might have a residuum of truth, but he didn't know what to make of Lujan's reasons for saying it. "What do you call your religion?" he finally asked.

"It is no religion," the old man said, and the eyes, nested within their saurian folds of skin, seemed to grow almost shiny-dark in their intensity. "It is the only truth that there is. The Old Ones are eternal, and one day the gate will open once more to let them in. Yog-Sothoth is the gate."

"I've seen most of the sacred scriptures of the world's major faiths," Brad ventured, "and I can't really say that I recall anything about—"

"Listen to your dreams," Lujan said.

"Sir?"

"Listen to your dreams," the old man repeated, and he appeared disinclined to speak further. After several awkward minutes of waiting in silence, Brad nodded to him and took his leave—but not without receiving one really perplexing impression.

He thought that a sort of shudder had gone through the trunk, making it rattle faintly against the wooden porch on which it rested.

This was just an odd fancy, of course, probably brought on by the weird nature of the old man's talk. But the impression was strong enough to be unsettling, and it was attended by another, vaguer impression, one that wouldn't come clear, one that followed him home and hung like a sable question mark in his mind.

That night he tried again to write, but his thoughts were in turmoil, and he gave it up and tried for a while to read, finding again that his mind kept wandering, wandering back to that peculiar conversation on the old man's porch. The Old Ones? What had that name been—Yog-Sothoth?—he who was "the gate"? What in the world did all this mean? Fatigued both from thinking about it and from trying not to think about it, Brad at length went to bed.

And dreamed a dream of the sky filling with great writhing tentacles as some opening in the very air seemed to gape with horror, showing vistas of restless blackness. He awoke, sweating and trembling, at a little past three o'clock in the morning, and was almost glad that he didn't succeed in going back to sleep right away, because there had been a quality to that dream that profoundly disturbed him. But he did drift back into clouds of slumber, and when he did, his dream was of floating, disembodied and horribly bereft of identity, in a darkness alive with swirling shapes of dread that finally brought him awake again, awake and screaming. It was nearly six in the morning by now, and he got up and took a shower and got dressed and made coffee, and stood in his doorway and watched the sun come up to herald what felt not so much like a new day as a temporary escape from night, and from the horrors of dream.

*   *   *

The novel was not going at all well. The days passed unproductively, the computer screen seemed to glower at him with a terrible sort of irony, as if saying: here you are, privy to some of the most bizarre folk-legendry anyone has ever heard, and you can't seem to write a coherent sentence.

The dreams had grown worse, not in content so much as in intensity. Every night now he seemed to find himself giddily afloat in some restless void where the very darkness writhed with a hideous suggestion of sentience, as if the shadows themselves gathered with purposes of their own, alive and cunning and eloquent of timeless secrets. Some vile name seemed to reverberate in the void, some impression more primal than mere sound, a suggestion of a name older than time. He could almost hear it—

"—oth." The half-sound would linger in his head when he awoke, and would gradually ebb away.

*   *   *

Time passed. He stared at the bright screen, wholly at a loss. Outside, darkness grew upon the land as yet another sunset faded like embers. It was no use trying to write any more tonight. He was exhausted, and some corner of his mind kept threatening to dwell on that—other—impression, from that night on the old man's front porch.

He was halfway out to the car before he realized that unconsciously he must have been planning another visit with Lujan for quite some time. But as he started to climb behind the wheel, he chose to follow a different impulse—he suspected that a long walk might do a good deal to clear his mind. The old man's house was only two miles away, and he was used to longer walks than that. He closed the car door and pocketed the keys and went down the driveway to the road.

Heading east toward Lujan's house, he found himself quite alone on the black ribbon of tarmac that stretched across the land before him, a ribbon of road beneath a bewilderment of icy stars. Parallel lines of barbed-wire fencing marched into the gloom before him like strangely insistent heralds. Except for his footfalls, all was utterly quiet here. There was barely any traffic here even during the day, and none at night. It felt strange to walk along this road in the dark, in the silence of the night, alone. He had never had any reason to walk on a highway at night before, and wondered if he indeed had an adequate reason now. What was this fascination with Lujan?

Was the old man just a peculiar variety of religious fanatic, worshipping some primordial god that no one else had ever heard of? Was Lujan senile, demented, given to puerile fancies?

Or was he a link to some secret so vast, so chillingly bizarre, that the mind could scarcely come to terms with it?

Brad kept on along the highway, finding that his vision gradually adjusted to the dark, though only a faint play of starlight illumined the landscape, as the moon had not yet risen. As his vision cleared, he noticed that despite the clear night sky above him, a black froth of clouds had gathered on the eastern horizon ahead, and he thought he heard a faraway grumble of thunder. As if to corroborate this suspicion, a bolt of lightning appeared in the distance, where the bank of clouds was growing more massive. Brad began to wonder if he could make it to Lujan's house before the storm came on. The lightning flashed again, showing him vistas of range grass and spindly cholla and furtive clusters of yucca and a field of cotton that looked eerily like snow beyond the never-ending barbed wire.

He continued on, mulling over some of the old man's remarks from that time before. *The Old Ones were, the Old Ones are, the Old Ones forever shall be.* It had a sonorous ring to it, as if it were quoted from some immemorially ancient tome. *In the time before all time the Old Ones walked in the Great Silence.* Somehow this didn't sound like merely the ravings of an offbeat religious fanatic. *Some few,* the old man had declared in that gurgling voice, *know of Yog-Sothoth, the One God.* And the old man had enjoined him: *Listen to your dreams.*

Brad's dreams, vague as they had been, came alive to him now, here, on the lonely road in the dark, and he remembered the cosmic reverberations of that horrendously timeless name, which the very thunder in the distant night seemed to mutter aloud. And with this access of vividness of his remembered dreams, he suddenly felt that the very sky above him, still crusted with a multitude of stars not yet eclipsed by the impending storm—that this very sky was a bottomless well of blackness into which he might topple and fall, screaming. This onset of unaccountable vertigo subsided after a moment, but left him so dizzy that he stumbled and nearly fell headlong in the road. Preposterous, the notion that one could fall into the sky, like a pebble dropped into a well. Yet if it was so absurd, this feeling, why was he so reluctant to look again at the fathomless black sky over his head? Why was he almost thankful that the gathering storm, whose lightning and thunder rent the heavens again and again now, would soon mercifully conceal that vault of starry night above him? He had to get hold of his nerves. Regaining his balance after stumbling, he set his eyes once again on the cheerless road.

And saw, off in the distance, a faint suggestion of movement on the tarmac, perhaps a hundred yards off.

Was someone walking toward him?

He couldn't be sure, but when the lightning lit up the sky again, bringing a new crash of thunder, he thought that there was indeed someone in the road.

The image, visible in only intermittent flashes in the coming storm, was confusing. One time it appeared to be a tall, thin man, yet the next time it would appear to be a form more squat, more substantial than before. A moaning voice seemed to float upon the air too, and Brad strained to hear it, but a chill wind had come up, howling, driving across the chaparral like a demon, and he could hear nothing over it except an occasional hint of keening, a sound that chilled him more than the wind alone could have done.

And as the enigmatic figure drew closer and another frenzy of lightning filled the air, he suddenly knew why he had been confused, why he had thought the figure first thin, then fat.

It was a tall, thin man after all, and the thickness of the image was not the man himself, but the trunk. It was Lujan in the road, and he was carrying the trunk as if it were weightless. The old man had come to meet him, apparently.

But why would he do so, and why would he bring the peculiarly painted trunk? And if the trunk was weightless—empty—then what kind of ludicrous business was all this, anyway?

But there was nothing ludicrous in the expression on the old man's multitudinously wrinkled face as he drew near, crowned by lightning, wreathed about by thunder, anointed by wind-driven rain. The face was a picture of triumph.

"You have listened to your dreams, and you know," Lujan croaked, leaning loathsomely toward Brad in the wind and the rain and the insane lantern-show of lightning.

"What—what do I know?" Brad tried to say, but his voice, feeble and hoarse, was drowned out by thunder. Nevertheless, the old man seemed to have heard him.

"You know—*this*," Lujan replied, setting the trunk down on the wet tarmac and opening the lid.

A monumental outburst of lightning clove the night, and Brad looked down into the trunk.

It was the end of all that had ever seemed to him to represent order and sanity in the world.

For in the yawning trunk he found not a few feet of space terminating in a bottom, but rather a limitless extent of restive blackness, as if the trunk were a window upon the hideous and unconscionable void of his dreams, a void where the very nighted chambers of space, the very darkness itself, was alive with a lightless gray slime that stirred horribly awake, avid, conscious. What lay within the trunk was the tiniest vestige of this primordial presence, and what lay beneath it—visible as it moved from side to side—was the nothingness of eternity.

There was another revelation too, one that confirmed the thing he had thought he glimpsed before, on the old man's porch, but he would not dare think about it till later, after Lujan had gone.

Recoiling from the old man and his trunk, Brad would remember nothing of the remainder of that night but a mindless, frantic scramble in the rain and the shrieking wind—was it the wind that shrieked, or did he? Somehow he would get home, out of the storm, and would fall into an exhausted sleep, waking around noon and going to his car and driving back down the eastward highway to where he had met the old man. But when he got there, he found, of course, nothing at all.

Lujan was never seen around Corona again, nor was his enigmatic trunk. Brad would wonder, time and again on sleepless nights in his desert home, what new place the old man had gone to, what new porch he perhaps sat upon, beside his eternal trunk. What face would the old man wear next time, what language would he so haltingly speak? Brad wondered who would be next to peer into the trunk and be changed forever. For he thought he understood at least this much: that it was important, somehow, for "some few" (as Lujan had said) to come to know of Yog-Sothoth in the infinite void—especially in light of that other awareness that had begun, vaguely, on the old man's porch, and had come to fruition in the madness of the storm that final night.

Brad had thought he saw it in the pale glow of a lightbulb, the night on the porch, and he had seen it all too undeniably the night of the storm, out on the highway.

From within the trunk, pale thin strings of substance had extended, subtly hidden in shadow for the most part, running out like slimy gray tubers to connect with the old man's body.

Lujan had not been some human devotee of the primal and soul-shattering Yog-Sothoth. Blown like glass into a semblance of human form, he had been a vestige and a manifestation, speaking and breathing, of that frightful god Himself. *

The San Francisco Treat

by C. J. Henderson

Awhiff—just the tiniest spark of aroma dragged by the breeze whirling through the courtyard. He had only caught the slightest warm and whispering puff . . . and that was all it had taken. The buttery scent of that rice, from so long ago, when the world still had music, a careless pause—a childhood memory. . . .

After so many years of safety, of careful and terrified hiding, now it was over. Now, he was finally doomed.

The San Francisco Treat. . . .

Why? a separate track moaned within his mind, mental tears dripping within his brain. Why me? By this point his left hand kept moving automatically without any thought on his part—back and forth, back and forth, up and down. Brushing, brushing, brushing. . . .

Why did it have to be me?

Philip Reddington did not own a stereo. He did not own a television or a radio. He did not go to movies. He attended no church. When in public buildings he avoided elevators. When speaking on the telephone he did not allow himself to be put on hold. The horrid chance of melody. . . .

It was simply too dangerous.

There were no friends in his life—no one to invite him to parties or dances, bars or concerts or even to their homes, to any place where he might hear a tune. Any tiny scrap of music that might lodge in his head as a happy memory and thus suck him off to Hell. Hell or whatever it was that waited for him the day he finally failed. A day like today.

The flavor. . . .

Philip was twenty-eight years old. The first twenty of them had been normal, average when measured against those of his school mates and relatives and those others who interacted with his everyday life. Then, in his third year of college, it happened for the first time.

He had been laboring in the gym, preparing for the wrestling tournament three days away. Seemingly tireless, he worked with the heavy weights, driving the barbell upward into the air over and over.

Stopping for a moment, one lasting only long enough to add a further twenty pound plate to each end of the sleeve, he tightened the set screws into the collars and began anew. Jerking the steel bar and its iron load up to his chest, sweating and grunting, carefree as only a college athlete can be. And then it happened.

Keep it up. . . . Back and forth, back and forth, up and down. *Brush, brush, brush. . . .*

A song entered his head from somewhere, absently wedging itself into his conscious mind, playing through and then repeating, stuck in his head. It echoed three times, and then, the gymnasium around him simply melted. Philip almost dropped the weight, but the transformation was not so sudden that it took him by surprise. Indeed, in some ways, a part of him had expected it to happen.

He could still feel the floor beneath his feet, could hear the air-conditioners, smell the salty leather and canvas and cotton on his fellows all around him. He simply could not *see* any of it any longer. Instead, he witnessed in all directions a staggering city, an outlandish fracture of minarets and towers and never-ending ziggurats, all passing below him at blinding speed as he flew over them toward some distant ophidian animation—a dark, lightning-filled billow that somehow remained in the distance no matter how fast Philip traveled toward it.

How he kept his wits, he was never certain. Somehow, however, he managed to remain collected. Something within him recognized the discordant jumble of shapes and forms, some unknown instinct buried in his DNA, gifted to him from an ancestor he could not imagine. It told him he had to continue with what he was doing— that he had to keep the tune within his brain, that he had to keep pumping the great weight above his head, that he had to do these things if he was to avoid being sucked over the threshold that had opened beneath his feet. He had to do this—

He *had* to.

Can't be beat. . . .

Philip did a staggering one hundred and eighty seven repetitions. Then he passed out from exhaustion. Most of his fellows in the gymnasium thought him some new Olympian. A few wondered if he might not be addled. For a while, he wondered the latter himself. But, when the same horrible cycle happened again, and then again—

once when bicycling, the other when digging in his mother's garden—he knew that it was more than common insanity.

After the third occurrence, Philip decided he knew the boundaries of his condition. It could only happen to him whenever a tune became stuck within his mind. It could be any melody—all it had to do was repeat three times within his brain and he would be suddenly transported to the tumbling labyrinth and its mad city. If that was all there was to it, of course, Philip might not have been so upset. But there was more.

Something lay beyond the chaotic landscape he had witnessed. Something that dwelt within the deep cobalt maelstrom he as of yet had not reached. Something that needed Philip to stir from its endless slumber.

He *knew* that if he were to drive whatever tune had welded itself to his brain away, that he would instantly streak across the void to that unknown thing. Philip could not explain how or why he was certain he was linked to that unseen lurker at the heart of the absurd darkness. He only knew that to meet it was his finish, and possibly the world's.

Francisco Treat, Rice. . . .

Brush, brush—one, two, one, two—up and down, up and down. . . .

Keep the tune going in his head until he fell asleep, that's all he had to do . . . just keep it going until he passed out and then the mad landscape would disappear. The doorway would shut, the other dimension would vanish—whatever the case, *whatever it was,* if he could keep the tune going, and work himself to exhaustion doing exactly what he was doing at the moment the tune had started, then he would be safe.

But this morning, Philip Reddington was not pumping iron or trenching the earth. He was not tired. He had only been awake for twenty minutes. While brushing his teeth, he had cracked open the bathroom window. Just an inch, just for the breeze, the feel of the morning air. . . .

An aroma stole in through the disastrous space. He recognized it, that wonderful rice his mother had always made every Friday, a treat for those nights when his father worked the late shift. A heaping plate, delicious steam, chicken and peas mixed with the golden, salt and peppered rice—and he and his mother would clank their glasses against the other and sing the rice song. . . .

The flavor can't be beat. . . .

For three hours and twenty minutes, Philip Reddington had brushed his teeth. He had squeezed additional paste into his mouth, spit mouthful after mouthful of minty foam into the sink, always scrubbing, constantly scrubbing—the plastic bristles wearing away, microscopically, pricking and cutting his gums, minty blood drooling over his chin, down the front of his chest. . . .

Within the mirror before him, the raging, iridescent city beckoned, welcoming him, knowing him, sending out waves of terrible invitation. Philip stared helplessly, eyes wide, unblinking. His left arm blistered with burning soreness. His wrist ached with a pain staggering on toward insanity.

How? wondered Philip. How do you exhaust yourself scrubbing your teeth?

By the seventh hour, he knew it was impossible. He was still wide awake, and yet, he could barely go on. His left arm, braced on the counter, his right dragging his hand back and forth, screaming with agony.

Flavor . . . flavor can't can't can't be beat. . . .

No use—can't do it. Not this time, no use. . . .

And then, the inevitable defeat. Minutes shy of the ninth hour, the jingle finally began to fade from within his mind. His shattered brain simply could not whistle its way through the meager collection of notes again. Tears slopped out of Philip's eyes. In a dazzling rush, his memory filled with all the things he had been denied, the possible love and joy, the companionship and exuberant foolishness, the nonsense and tenderness, the melodic flow of life that filled the hearts all around him, but had been forced outside his doorstep by the groping hunger that had shattered dimensions to come hunting him.

As the last notes cracked and fell from his brain, as his numb and shaking fingers dropped his toothbrush, the shapes in his mirror changed drastically. For the first time Philip saw beyond the mad city. Insane geometric patterns began to etch themselves into the glass before him. Discordant piping filled the room and the distant clouds were shattered by onyx lightning, revealing a groping hand attached to a ponderous bulk, a formless eternity that revolved about itself in idiot complacency. Rolling what part of it might have served it as a face over, its attention attracted, the mindless abyss began to focus its sleeping wits. . . .

Philip screamed. He could not remember the tune, could not find another note, could not move his hand, could not think, could not remember—

A crown of dark light erupted from the center of the ultimate personality as it blindly reclined on its dreaming black throne. Fingers reached out across all understanding. Unable to pull away from the terrible sight, Philip did the next best thing.

*   *   *

"And so you heard the scream, saw what happened in your bathroom, and you called us and that was it—right?"

The detective stopped scribbling in his note book as the old woman agreed with his assessment of things. There was no use writing any more. The neighbor knew nothing of value. Besides, the woman did not need to know anything. It was an open and shut case.

Another dead fanatic. No television. No CD player or radio. Foam stuffed under most of his windows and doors, two dozen gross ear plugs in his cupboard, and those bizarre designs carved into his mirror—what was that all about?

The detective thanked the neighbor and sent her on her way. It was time to pack things in. For some reason Phil Reddington had seen fit to drive his head through the mirror of his bathroom, so hard that he broke through the wall into his neighbor's apartment.

Another loner does himself in for some reason known only to him. The plainclothes man had seen a thousand of them.

Quiet. Kept to himself.

"Guess it's best he did himself before he decided to do anyone else," muttered the detective. Then, he noticed something. For some reason, the bathroom window was not foamed like the others. It was even open an inch.

Wanting to do a thorough job, the man pushed the window open all the way and stuck his head outside. He scanned the early evening shadows setting over the courtyard, looking up and down all the walls, listening intently, wondering if there might be some clue as to what could have motivated Reddington's suicide on the evening breeze.

The aroma of spaghetti sauce wafted up to the detective, reminding him of the dinner he was missing, and nothing more. ✳

Acute Spiritual Fear

by Robert M. Price

T he great Gothic edifice of the chapel of Miskatonic University's School of Divinity rose like some primal granite cliff through the frozen fireworks of the brilliant autumn leaves. Philip Brown reflected, on his way to the Great Hall, that sights like these were almost reason enough to have chosen the venerable old New England Seminary. Miskatonic's divinity program attracted few students these days, since most who aspired to the ministry in the Congregational Church, its sponsoring body, were impatient with the conservative traditionalism of the place. Here the debates between Calvinism and Arminianism were still in fashion, and the echoes of the old Puritan divines had not yet completely died away. This was the theological cosmos in which Philip delighted to live.

It was New Student Orientation Week, and as he inspected the various displays of campus clubs, he naturally gravitated to some and equally avoided others without a second thought. The Solidarity with Central America Caucus was not for him, nor the Liberation Army, an updating of the old Salvation Army in light of Latin American Liberation Theology. The Feminist Sisterhood left him cold, too. He was cut from traditional clerical cloth and viewed the role of the minister much as it had existed in the previous century: something of a hybrid between personal counselor and pulpit theologian. Social activism was all right for some, but Philip did not see his call to the ministry in these terms. Nor was this the only respect in which he felt himself an outsider in his generation. Perhaps the old ways lingered longest in New England, but he had to admit that they were passing even here.

Philip had all but decided, by the time he reached the end of the indoor bazaar, that none of the student organizations was for him.

But then he noticed one intriguing hand-lettered sign. It said THE MISKATONIC SOCRATIC CLUB. This name he recognized, for one of his favorite authors, C. S. Lewis, a champion of traditional orthodoxy if ever there was one, had founded the Socratic Club at Oxford. His goal had been to provide a forum for discussing the great philosophical issues of the day. If that's what the name denoted here, he would definitely be interested. He picked up a leaflet which looked hopeful, as he waited for someone to return to the booth. In a moment, a middler or senior appeared with a steaming cup of coffee and offered a friendly hand.

"Name's Glenn Brindley. I discovered the club when I was a freshman, too. It certainly livened up my years here in sleepy old Miskatonic. They started the club ten years ago because some students felt they needed to hear more perspectives than they got in class. Just the old-time religion there, if you know what I mean."

"I happen to like the old-time religion," Philip replied, a tad defensively. "But I see your point. There's a big world out there, religiously like every other way. We need to know about it, I guess."

The other's smile returned. "That's the true Socratic spirit, Phil! We're having a debate next week. Why don't you stop by? The schedule's in that leaflet you're holding."

Philip gave the pamphlet a glance, then looked up. "Eschatology, huh? The doctrine of the end of the world. I just might come! I cut my teeth on that stuff. Hal Lindsey, all that kind of thing."

Glenn smiled knowingly. "Don't tell me; you're one of us 'Afghanistan War babies'?"

A blank stare. "What do you mean?"

"A lot of us were 'born again' back in 1980 when the Soviets invaded Afghanistan. Lindsey and a lot of the other paperback prophets had everybody on the edge of their seats thinking Armageddon was right around the comer. Had *me* convinced. I 'got religion' and started praying hard to escape the Great Tribulation. The whole thing blew over, but, hey, at least it's coming into the faith with a bang, huh?"

Philip laughed, too. "I know just what you mean! I've never heard the phrase, but I guess I'm one of them, too! War babies, that's a good one. You know, Glenn, when I look back at those days, sometimes I feel like a real jerk for getting so excited over a silly scare like that. But I can't deny that when I thought Jesus was coming back any moment, I had a zeal for the Lord I've never been able to recapture since."

"Yeah, right, Phil . . ." the other mused. "I know what you mean. You 'put away childish things,' but you're sort of sorry to see some of them go. And the Lord said that's it's the ones with the faith of a child that make it into the kingdom of heaven. Where do you strike the balance?"

Philip thought a moment. "Sometimes I think that it's striking a balance that *is* the problem. Jesus wasn't balanced. People called him crazy. Mother Theresa's not balanced. Neither was Gandhi. Maybe 'balance' is another word for compromise."

Glenn's eyes were fixed on the newcomer with a certain gleam. "I think you'd make a great Socratic Clubber! And not a bad friend, either!" They shook hands again. Phil went on to the library with a new sense of at-homeness. The Miskatonic campus no longer felt such an alien place. He thought he'd heard there was a student position open at the Hoag Library, and he wanted to verify this. Maybe he'd apply for it.

The next two weeks were a whirl of activity. There were last minute registration mix-ups to iron out, permissions to get for admission to closed classes. Philip felt he just had to get into that seminar on the lesser-known Puritan theologians. He had long been intrigued by the life and writings of the Reverend Abijah Hoadley, a Congregationalist parson who had served one of the oldest standing Congregational Churches in this region. Hoadley had written a lesser-known counterpart to Cotton Mather's notorious *Magnalia Christi*. It was called *Of Evill Sorceries Donne in New-England of Daemons in No Humane Shape* and it promoted much the same sort of fabulous rumor and superstition as Mather's volume. In the places where the two compendia of marvels overlapped, there were curious differences of a striking nature. Philip thought he might try a research paper running down local sources of some of the legends. Had there been any remotely factual basis to any of them?

His classes started out unspectacularly, with the calm dogmatism he had expected and indeed appreciated. Over lunch at the Arkham House of Pizza, a local franchise of a small statewide chain that served up the best Greek-style pizza he had ever tasted, Philip got into a friendly debate with Sue Millman, a fellow first-year student. He had taken exception to Sue's characterization of the faculty as "a bunch of old mossbacks."

"I don't see how you can speak that way, Sue. After all, aren't they just 'defending the faith once for all delivered unto the saints,' as Jude says?"

"That's how they dignify the fact that none of them has read a new book in the past thirty years. Get real, Phil! History passed this place by long ago. They say Dr. Nicole actually falls asleep in his own lectures! Once he was halfway through his notes before he realized he was in the wrong classroom! And old Dr. Kline! You know why he's so sure Adam and Eve were literal people? 'Cause he knew them personally!"

He couldn't help chuckling at this, and that broke the building tension.

Claude LaValle entered the fray. He was one of the few students in the ministerial program who signed up for courses in the seminary's vestigial biblical studies program. He would pursue a career in teaching, not a parish, when he was done. "Sue's right. I'm thinking of transferring over to Harvard Div. The Bible profs here hardly know what historical criticism is. I asked about D. F. Strauss once last semester and Dr. Stuart thought I meant the composer! I even hear there are important biblical manuscripts here that the faculty never even consult, probably don't even know about." Philip had to admit this might be true. He knew they still used the old King James Bible in classes. Even he had switched to the New American Standard Version some years ago.

"I'm beginning to see the need for something like the Socratic Club," Philip suggested. "Are either of you planning to go to their debate this evening?"

"What's the topic?" asked Sue.

"Eschatology. You know, the end of the world."

"Yeah, right. Like I'm going to worry about that. Count me out, Phil."

"Sorry, old man," added Claude, "but I've got prior plans, too."

The trio split up, Philip and Sue heading off to their respective field work assignments. Sue was working with a battered women's center. Philip's task was more traditional. He was filling in for the semester as a youth minister for a small congregation over in Saugus. And if he didn't get moving he would be embarrassingly late for his first session. So he checked for his road map and headed for the parking lot.

As he drove the narrow, winding New England lanes, punctuated as they were with green and white road signs for towns with quaint names like "Pride's Crossing" and "Folly Hill," he almost felt he had left the quiet expanse of Essex County for the living pages of Bunyan's *Pilgrim's Progress*.

He turned on the scraping wipers of his feeble Volkswagen Beetle to scatter the tears falling from the lowering Puritan skies. As he did so, he began to reflect on whether he, too, was something of a "mossback." (Actually that had been only one of the least colorful epithets Sue, an excitingly modern woman in every sense, had used for religious traditionalists.) Maybe the way to recapture some of the excitement that had marked the early years of his spiritual pilgrimage was to experiment with new ideas. But could anything new thrive here in these old precincts of Cotton Mather and Abijah Hoadley?

As was so often true in dying parishes like this one, the youth of the church were few and scarcely interested in their parents' religion. For most, MTV was their church, various decadent rock and roll stars their idols. Philip could see he had his work cut out for him. It was hard to relate to them; when he was their age, he had been busy studying scripture and trying to decipher whether Henry Kissinger or Yuri Andropov was more likely to be the Antichrist. He had precious little in common with the few teenagers who showed up for the meeting. This first session had made that abundantly clear.

So it was not with much enthusiasm that, some hours later, Philip parked outside his dorm and rushed, skipping dinner, over to another dorm lounge where the Socratic Club must already be underway.

He found the door and tried to edge his way in as inconspicuously as he might. He was surprised at the number of seminarians, plus a few of the other university students, crowding the lounge. Who would have thought the end of the world would be so popular a topic? But perhaps the recent turmoil in every corner of the globe, wars and rumors of wars on every newscast, had made it a live question again. Two speakers stood at borrowed classroom lecterns. The first, white-haired Professor Jenkins, was just finishing up. Philip heard enough to know it was the predictable party line: Christ would return at the close of the Millennium when the gospel would have permeated the whole earth, defeating the powers of evil once and for all. He had to admit it did sound a little stale.

As the venerable old academic seated himself uneasily on a flimsy piece of lounge furniture, the other rose to speak. He was a youthful-looking man named Winthrop who pastored a Congregational parish in the nearby town of Foxfield. Philip didn't recognize him, but he thought he remembered the leaflet saying the man was a Miskatonic alumnus. And it was beginning to get interesting.

"Let me suggest a rather different perspective than the one so ably set forth by our previous speaker. I wonder how many of you are familiar with the Gospel of Thomas." Here he raised a thin brown hardcover book and opened it to the middle. "This is a collection of sayings attributed to our Lord, fully as old as our New Testament Gospels, but excluded from the biblical canon in the fourth century. It was rediscovered in 1945 in the sands of Chenoboskion, Egypt. Here's a passage germane to our subject, in saying number . . . um, 51. 'His disciples said unto him: When will the repose of the dead come about, and when will the new world come? He said to them: What you expect has come, but you know it not.'

"Suppose that's true. Suppose in the providence of God this scripture has come to light in our day to warn us we ought not to be looking forward for the kingdom of God, but *backward*. Can it be that the Second Coming of Christ has indeed already occurred? And that, just like two thousand years ago, we, the religious know-it-alls, failed to recognize him?"

The earlier speaker could not contain himself. Rising as if by reflex, he sputtered, "Now, listen here, young man! Our Lord has made it quite clear in Matthew Chapter 24 that his glorious Second Advent would be unmistakable, that his coming would be as when the lightning flashes forth from one end of the firmament to the other, that every eye shall see him!" His face had purpled, and he seemed altogether too outraged to speak further.

The Reverend Mr. Winthrop was not flustered. "Dr. Jenkins, with all due respect, I'd say you have *your* quote from Jesus and I have *mine*. Him who has ears to hear, let him hear." With that, the tempestuous exchange came to an abrupt end.

The student crowd began to disperse, some apparently deep in thought, others no doubt eager to get back to their reading assignments. Those immersed in biblical Hebrew and Greek courses, poor devils, could think of little else. But Philip, who certainly had work of his own to attend to, nonetheless made it a point to seek out the heretical Reverend Winthrop. "Excuse me, sir."

The man turned with an expression of affable interest. "Yes, young man?"

"To tell you the truth, I almost feel guilty talking to you. You see, I suppose I agree with Dr. Jenkins. At least that's the way I've always been taught. But what you say is intriguing, fascinating, really, and I'd like to hear more. Do you have a few minutes?"

The Reverend Winthrop looked at his watch. "Well . . . I do have to be back for a deacons meeting at six, and I've got to check in with a parishioner in Mercy Hospital . . . but, yes, I think I can spare twenty minutes or so. How about a cup of coffee over at the snack bar?"

Once the two of them were seated, ritually consuming a pair of coffee and danishes, Philip spoke all in a rush, as if to a confessor. "It's just that I miss that zeal I once knew when I believed Christ would come again at any moment. I eventually admitted that was naïve, that Christians have been predicting the Second Coming for 2,000 years, and they were always wrong. But what you said, well, it does sound heretical, like Dr. Jenkins said, but maybe Sue is right, and he is a mossback like some of the faculty."

Winthrop burst into laughter. "You said it, I didn't! He was the same when I was a student here. He's a good man, but you're not liable to hear anything new from him, that's for sure."

Philip smiled and continued. "If what you say is true, it would be just electrifying! Amazing! It would be like being back with the original disciples following the Lord Jesus himself!" The wistfulness, the growing will to believe, was evident with every word, and none of it was lost on the older man.

"Congratulations, young Mr. Brown. Unlike some, you can see quite clearly what's at stake here. It becomes far more than a matter of theology, of whose doctrine is truer. We would be talking about the rebirth of the Christian faith. And what does St. Paul say about faith turning into sight?

"Look at the time! I really must be going. But, here, let me give you my number. Let's talk again. Meantime, why don't you look up this verse of scripture and think about it?" He scribbled a brief citation on a napkin, folded it and passed it to Philip.

Back in his dorm room, Philip hastened to his desk and grabbed up his Bible. During the walk back he had tried to place the chapter and verse number, but with no luck. Here it was. Matthew 17:10–12. "And his disciples asked him, saying, 'Why then do the scribes say that Elijah must come first?' And he answered and said, 'Elijah is coming and will restore all things; but I say to you, that Elijah already came, and they did not recognize him, but did to him whatever they wished. So also the son of man is going to suffer at their hands.'"

Philip looked up from the text, perhaps staring into space, perhaps praying. But in a moment his reverie was interrupted by a knock at his open door. "Phil! I saw you at the meeting. How'd you like it?"

"Glenn, I have to admit, it's really set me to thinking. I'm entertaining new ideas I would have rejected out of hand only days ago. And I don't mind telling you it's not very comfortable!"

Glenn sat down on the bed next to him. "I know what you mean, old buddy. I've been there myself. I remember my first semester. I came in here thinking I had it all sewed up. God had called me, and I just needed some practical know-how, or so I thought. It wasn't long before I was doubting everything I ever believed and then some! Theological education does that to you, and it's good that it does, I think. No other way to maturity."

"I suppose you're right, Glenn. But this idea that the Second Coming of Christ has already happened! . . . That he came again and went unnoticed, and, if I'm reading this passage right, that he might even have suffered again. . . . I don't know. That's tough to absorb!"

"Again, Phil, I've been there. I know what you're going through."

At this Philip turned and stared at his new friend with wide eyes. "What? You mean you believe this? That Christ has already returned?"

Glenn laughed and said, "Don't look so startled, for Pete's sake! I was the one who arranged for Reverend Winthrop to come speak, though I did think he'd have a bit more of a chance to air his views!"

"Does the whole Socratic Club believe this way?"

Glenn paused to consider what seemed to Philip a simple question. "I'd rather not speak for anyone but myself. But I'm sure not alone."

"Okay, Glenn, then I've got to ask you this question. I wanted to ask Winthrop, but he had to rush out. You must have some specific idea of who it *was,* don't you? I mean, if Christ returned already, was it somebody you have a name for? Or are you trying to identify him? Waiting for him to reveal himself?"

"Yes to all of the above," Glenn replied. "It's complicated. But let me give you a couple of clues. Maybe you'll guess. We think that the pattern of his coming would be the same both times. So you have to look for a candidate, so to speak, who was born of a virgin, a humble country girl. There would be signs in the heavens to signal the birth, maybe not a star necessarily, but, let's say, thunder and lightning. And that's where Dr. Jenkins's Matthew quote fits in: that's the lightning flashing from one end of the skies to the other.

"And he'd be marked by physical ugliness, because Isaiah predicted, 'He had no form or comeliness that we should look at him, and no beauty that we should desire him. He was despised and rejected of men; a man of sorrows and acquainted with grief; and as one from whom men hide their faces he was despised, and we esteemed him not.' You'd even expect him finally to be set upon by the authorities and killed, then to rise from the dead and ascend into heaven to rejoin his Father."

"And you're saying this has happened to somebody else in recent history?" Philip's initial incredulity had returned with a vengeance.

"I'm saying more than that, Phil." Every trace of casual conversation had drained out of Glenn's voice now. "I'm saying it happened to somebody in this very state. Some of it even happened on our own campus."

What Glenn said began to strike echoes in the recesses of Philip's brain. He *had* heard something, something that sounded like this, but he never saw the significance in it that Glenn seemed to see.

"You're not talking about that Whateley guy, are you? That must have been, what . . . fifty years ago?"

"Sixty-nine, to be exact. What do you already know, Phil?"

"What I saw was some kind of *In Search Of . . .* show on TV. It was one of those Loch Ness Monster kind of things, where they 'investigated' some local sightings of a creature. As I remember, it boiled down to some horribly deformed lunatic, somebody that looked like the Elephant Man or something, right? And he was killed on campus by a Doberman. And this all happened to occur just before a hurricane up in Dunwich, right? The survivors they interviewed were full of wild tales of the guy being born without a human father, having an invisible brother who rose into the sky . . . I'm surprised I remember that much of it, to tell you the truth. All rumor and exaggeration, like the Bermuda Triangle."

"You know what you sound like, Phil? Just like one of those modernists, the Bible critics who have an explanation for everything, 'cause they just can't believe in the supernatural. Do you think Jesus walked on the stepping stones in the Sea of Galilee, too? And the resurrection appearances, they were probably just hallucinations, weren't they?"

Philip was not used to having such accusations leveled at him. It was precisely to avoid that kind of teaching that he had sought out this, the most traditional of theological seminaries. "You know that's not how I believe!"

"Phil, be careful that you don't wind up like the old scribes who dismissed Jesus as a devil and a madman. Don't close your mind like they did. If it happened once, it could happen again. And what if it *has* happened again? Wouldn't you want to be a part of it? I know for a fact you would!"

For this, Philip had no answer. As outlandish as the thing sounded, he still found himself excited by the prospect—just like the old days! He suddenly realized he wasn't really arguing with Glenn; he was really trying to fight down his own rising desire to believe in what Glenn said, what Reverend Winthrop had said. It did make a seductive kind of sense.

"Look, Phil, as I said, I remember feeling just the way you do now. Take some time to think about it, pray on it some. And in the meantime let me lend you this."

He held out a dog-eared copy of a crudely printed paperback book with a stenciled title: *THE DIARY OF WILBUR WHATELEY.* "There's a group of us that meets to study it. Really, it's become a kind of Third Testament for us. You'll see why."

It was time to hit the sack. Both men had early classes the next day.

Morning in the dorm kitchen witnessed a frazzled Philip Brown mumbling a hello to Sue Millman, who seemed enviably bright-eyed. She must be, Philip quipped to himself, living the righteous life, not flirting with heresy like himself. "How's your clinic work going these days, Sue?" he asked with a bit more animation.

Her large brown eyes narrowed, and she brushed her bangs aside. "I'd be lying if I said I enjoyed it. Every day I see women come in bruised and bleeding because they said something that set their husbands off. Most times they don't even know what it was that tripped the land mine. And their husbands, most of them, aren't boozers or criminals. They're doctors, lawyers, professionals. It really makes you sick, and there's no way to distance yourself from it without losing your humanity. But I feel I'm doing important work. I'm even thinking of going into it full time. I mean, instead of the parish ministry. Maybe I'll quit the div school and switch over to Aylesbury State for a masters in social work."

"I'd hate to see you do that, Sue!" said Phil, his interest now patently genuine.

"What, you don't think there's a need for the kind of work I'm doing?" She began to bristle.

"No, that's not it at all, Sue. It's just that . . . I'd . . . miss you, that's all. But you're the one to find God's will for your life, not me, that's for sure." He was turning red, and she saw it. It seemed to amuse her, but for a moment, Sue looked at him with a funny expression, as if seeing him in a new way, assessing him in a new light.

"Well, I guess you're right about that, Phil. Hadn't you better get to class?"

"That's right!" he said, looking at his pocket watch, one of his many odd affectations. "I've got that Puritan seminar, and it's starting right now!"

"Sounds like fun. Don't let me keep you from it," she said with a chuckle. He grabbed his satchel and trotted up the steps and across the wide, leaf-littered lawn.

It was not Philip's best day of the semester. He found himself uncontrollably nodding off in class. One student paper on old Preserved Cromwell of Newport only augmented his drowsiness, but when the name of Abijah Hoadley came up, it woke him like an alarm clock. Cromwell had apparently exchanged a few letters with his colleague. The import of this Philip missed, but it suddenly struck him that Reverend Hoadley had served in Dunwich, the very place from which the mysterious Wilbur Whateley had hailed. It had been called New Dunnich at the time, but he was sure it had to be the same place.

The seminar presentation had more to do with some polemical theological tracts circulated by the combative old preachers, something to do with the Halfway Covenant debate that racked New England Puritanism for a generation. The paper steered clear, perhaps from embarrassment, of the controversy over Reverend Hoadley's pulpit battles against Beelzebub and Dagon. Philip's own research for the seminar had acquainted him with this darker side of Puritan theology.

He left the seminar room after an apology to the professor for his inattention. Philip reflected that he had some time on his hands today. He had planned to drive out to the Wilbraham area to do a bit of research for his project on Abijah Hoadley, but the skies had clouded up already. As he made for his dorm room, the target of the first practice shots of the rain volley that was to follow minutes later, he decided he'd spend the day, after a quick nap, with a different sort of research. He was itching to get into that odd-looking paperback Glenn had loaned him.

Unusual for his cat naps, Philip dreamed. It wasn't the first time he had dreamed himself in the role of one of the twelve disciples, but there was something different about this dream. He couldn't quite focus on the Lord, as if it were one of those too-reverential movies where they didn't show the face of the actor playing Jesus. But now he was going somewhere with Jesus, up a hillside, while most of the other disciples slept. There were a couple of others with him. Upon awaking a few moments later, he would realize he had been dreaming about the story of the Transfiguration on the mountaintop.

In silence the three disciples and their Lord continued till they reached the top. Then, wordlessly, Jesus stood apart by himself and looked up to heaven. Now his face could be seen. He looked as Philip had always imagined him: slender, of medium height, inappropriately European of feature, and with chestnut brown hair and forked beard. But suddenly he was surrounded by a nimbus of light and hard to look upon. Two other figures appeared as if hovering in the air on either side of him, but their shimmering shapes frustrated the eye. Perhaps there was a suggestion of a star-shape up top.

But then it seemed that the Lord Jesus himself changed. He grew to a height of some eight or nine feet. And it was hard to penetrate the light-cloud that enveloped him, but he seemed to have too many limbs, like the statues of Hindu deities, but the arms rolled and flowed with boneless grace. The face, what could be seen of it, seemed vaguely elongated. And the eyes flamed as with a flame of fire.

A peal of thunder spat explosively: **This is my Son; hear ye him!**

And Philip awoke. He jumped from the bed and stood sweating, head aching, heart hammering. It was the most vivid dream of his life. He thought at once to get down on his knees and pray, as he usually did whenever he came to a crisis point. Somehow this seemed to qualify. But it wouldn't calm him. He couldn't seem to get past empty words. So he did the next best thing, went down the hall to the dorm lounge, vacant at the moment, and clicked on the TV. Alpha waves were what he needed, and right about now Philip was willing to take them where he could get them.

After a couple of sitcoms of which he remembered nothing at all, he felt better. He felt he could thrust the disturbing dream from his mind if he could distract himself. So he decided he might as well go back and pick up that Whateley book. See what all the fuss was about.

As he had it in his hand, he realized he might be opening Pandora's Box. But he had come too far to turn back now. He did not try to start from the beginning, but instead felt he stood to get a better idea from a random sample. So he opened the book, which, he now saw, had the loosened spine of a volume much read. Ironically, it reminded him of those early years when, as a young believer, eager to divine the guidance of God, he would "cut scripture," just let it fall open anywhere, assuming the Holy Spirit would pick the page.

"Back from the Zone of the Colossi, just as Grandfather said, in the twinkling of an eye. Folks hereabouts don't know of those worlds. Don't know even of that world they live on. Had no form in that Zone save as vortices—of violet gas. Saw much of the past there, also much of the future. Grandfather says time does not flow there but is frozen like the Miskatonic in February. Now understand that chapter in Dee."

"Mother took me out to the woods, said I'd been spending too much time with my nose in old books. She and Grandfather argued and shouted for a spell, but in the end Grandfather told me to go with her, said we wouldn't put up with sech womanly interference forever. She packed a basket and said she meant to have us a picnic in a clearing she used to visit when she was a young'un like me. Only she got confused and said maybe it weren't there no more. We kept going till she said this one would do. So we sat us down and spread out the cloth and the food. But then she saw what the trees looked like, how the branches wasn't like other trees, how they had little mouths, and didn't stay still. She left it all where it was and got up running. This was funny and I got to eat the chicken by myself."

"Inside the Voorish Dome today. Took shape when Grandfather said them words in the Aklo and danced the Mao Game. I will learn that dance, too. We was up at the hilltop between all the tall stones, and then all at once the stones reached up and closed like fingers when a body prays. Grandfather says it is I who will be the King of the Kingdom of Voor, whence the earth was first stolen. One day I will ride its winds alone."

"Looks as if That above will play host to me fine. I asked Grandfather why he wouldn't use it hisself, but he said, No Willie, it's for ye 'cause it's like unto ye. He said that in that day I should see it is myself and nothing else. Then my

Name from them in Yian-Ho shall be Bugg-Shoggog, and
his will be Kamog. And then Grandfather bowed down in
front of me, and I laughed at him."

Philip's first impulse was to throw the crazy text aside, but he
stopped himself. It wasn't his own book, after all. But there was
something else. There was a sense of something more than strange-
ness. These words were not the product of anyone's conscious artifice.
They didn't make enough sense for that. It was like half a telephone
conversation. You felt you were eavesdropping on something utterly
alien and frightful. And the fact that the diarist didn't seem to sense
it himself, that he was so, well, accustomed to this terrible cosmos of
nightmare hints and cryptic enigmas—that's what made it chilling.
And that chill was almost, no, it *was* spiritual in nature. He couldn't
rightly use any other word for it. Here in this crudely duplicated
paperback lurked the Dark Mysteries, a sense of defiling, demonic
holiness. So he handled the book with a reverence as great as the
loathing he felt for it, and put it back on his desk.

It had stopped raining. More than ever he needed something to
bring him back to terra firma. In another moment, he had it: he
decided there was still time this afternoon to head over to the library
and apply for that opening. As bookish as he was, it would be the
ideal job for him. His field work didn't pay enough to cover his various fees and leave him any pocket money. His head seemed to clear
like the skies above once he got out under them.

As it happened, he was in luck. No one else wanted the job. It
seemed most of them spent enough time among the musty stacks as
it was and couldn't stand spending an extra minute there. Fine with
Philip. He would have to start work next week. That would make his
schedule even tighter, so he'd best get his research done while he
could. Maybe tomorrow would afford a better chance to make it out
to the west of the state.

* * *

The day was cool yet sunny. Philip grabbed a writing pad and a
guidebook. He headed for the Massachusetts Turnpike and rapidly
passed into the familiar mental state he called "driver's Zen." The
miles sped by, and soon he was looking at a local map for the
Wilbraham-Hampdon-Monson Historical Society. He hoped they

might have a collection of the papers of the Reverend Abijah Hoadley, or at least maybe they'd know where to send him next. He didn't trust the telephone, because experience told him you couldn't trust a curator any more than teenage store help to know what they had on hand. He wanted to look for himself.

The inconspicuous white wood-frame building was disappointingly small, but it was occupied. Philip had to wake the curator, who resented it. He was willing for the young man to putter around. "Just don't steal anything." Mere moments revealed there was nothing here. Philip paused on the steps outside to consider how he might salvage the trip. He walked to the gas station across the narrow street and got a Coke out of the machine. It was still a quarter in this backwater.

Then it occurred to him that the Congregational Church in Dunwich itself might well have some relics of its famous former pastor. It had been his last parish, since Hoadley had mysteriously disappeared, most thought killed by Indians whose ways he openly condemned from the pulpit. So he looked at his map again and made a couple of notes.

It proved no easy matter even to get into Dunwich. The roads to the place had only recently been reopened and cleared of encumbering growth. The town had been completely shut off from the outside world for decades. It was only a commonwealth flood relief effort that had caused access to be opened again about fifteen years ago, and the roads were all but unpaved. The rutted paths veered crazily among the steep shoulders of bulbous tall hills, and one rounded corners with heart in throat for fear of invisible oncoming traffic—until one realized there was no such thing. No cars came out of Dunwich, or into it—except for his own.

As he drove over a recently but crudely reinforced covered bridge, he noticed one steeple stabbing crookedly above the low and sagging skyline, and it turned out to crown an old church made over at some point into a dry goods store: OSBORNE'S, a faded sign proclaimed. It had been long ago abandoned. So he drove down the ghost town streets a bit further. No one was in evidence. Perhaps they were such xenophobes that they hastened out of sight upon the entrance of an outsider, like roaches fleeing when you turn on the kitchen light switch.

But turning another block or two, he did manage to find the structure he sought. It was an old meeting house with nothing so pretentious as a steeple, in the unadorned style of the early Puritans. He pulled the Beetle over, noticed the antique absence of a parking meter and carefully climbed the front steps of the church. Modern church buildings had office entrances, but he knew such a relic as this would not. So he pulled at the bell and wondered why he bothered. There was no way anybody but a ghost could be home. If he were lucky it would be the ghost of Abijah Hoadley. He turned to go and call it wasted day.

He had turned the ignition key when the half-oval of the church doors split and then opened wide. Philip jumped out of the car and strode up the steps, hand extended. He faced a small, stooped man who looked little inclined to return his friendly gesture. He was vested as if a service were in progress, though no sound from within suggested activity. And these were certainly no Congregationalist trappings. The robe was faded and colorless, but the bug-eyed man's oblong pate was adorned with a curious golden tiara. Philip's eyes could not trace the delicate workmanship of the thing without impolitely looking away from the man's flap-lipped, expressionless face.

"Help?" grunted the cleric tonelessly.

"Uh, yes, Reverend. My name's Philip Brown. I'm a seminary student with Miskatonic Divinity School, and I'm doing some research on Dr. Abijah Hoadley, who I understand once preached here. I hate to trouble you, but I wonder if the old church might house any papers, you know, sermon notes, pamphlets, letters by him."

"Papers . . . hmmm, might at that. Come on in."

Philip felt a slight sense of foreboding at stepping into the shadowed narthex. It was really pitch dark, though the odd little man didn't seem to mind. In a moment an antique kerosene lamp sputtered into flame, and the peculiar cleric led him past the decrepit sanctuary, barely visible, into the church office.

"Been cleaning it out. About to dump this. This box, old records. Take a look if you want." Philip lost no time stooping to examine what he could see in the flickering dimness. He guessed it was this or nothing. Whatever papers were in the box were so brittle and yellowed that it seemed not unlikely he should find what he was looking for. And yet they could date from any time in over two hundred years since Hoadley's day. What were the chances? Still . . . he remembered how Tischendorf had discovered the precious leaves of the Codex Sinaiticus in the garbage can of St. Catherine's Monastery.

"Since you're only going to throw them out anyway, why not let me take them off your hands?"

The other man signaled his assent (or so Philip interpreted) with a vague wave of the hand. Philip picked up the carton and carried it to his car. Just as the man was about to seal himself back in his empty church, one more silent relic among so many, Philip had an inspiration.

"Uh, one more thing, if you don't mind." The impassive face paused in its retreat into the dark.

Philip was back up on the steps. "Would you know anything about a man named Wilbur Whateley? I understand there was some big ruckus over him back in the twenties. I was curious . . ."

"No, never heard of that gent. Young sir, I dun't know the taown much. Bishop jest sent me here from another town to get th' church goin' agin. Not much interest. Dun't know whut's amiss. A lot o' church-goin' in my town. This Whateley go t' church much?"

"I don't know. Good question. Thanks anyway. Good luck with the church!" Philip drove off with the blank face staring after him.

Hours later, Philip lugged the old box into his room and collapsed onto the narrow bed. He ached from the dullness of driving. Ordinarily he would be sound asleep in seconds. But here came something loud, dragging him reluctantly back into wakefulness.

"Phil! Good! I was afraid I'd miss you! Come on! It's starting!" Glenn Brindley practically dragged his befuddled friend out of bed.

"What? What is it, Glenn? Another Socratic meeting already? For Pete's sake. . . ."

He was soon accompanying Glenn down the hall and out of the dorm. It seemed on balance the easiest thing to do. He was too tired to protest much.

"Hope you don't mind, old buddy; I took the liberty of picking up that copy of the *Diary* I loaned you. Have a chance to look through it yet?"

"Yeah, as a matter of fact, I did. But where is it we're going?" He had begun to get pretty steamed, friend or no friend.

"Think of it as a Bible study meeting, Phil. Remember I told you a group of us gather to study the *Diary*. Well, tonight's something special. We have a guest speaker, and he wants to meet you."

Philip stopped in his tracks. "Meet *me?* You've got to be kidding. I'm going back and get a nap." He turned, but Glenn followed.

"Really! It's a professor, the only prof on campus who sees things like we do. We've told him about your interest, and he says he'd like to meet you, maybe answer some of your questions. Now there's an opportunity for you!"

Philip stopped again. One of the mossbacks? It seemed impossible. "Yeah? Who is it?"

"None of us knows. You see, he can't very well reveal his identity. You and I can accept a new idea and not much will happen. The dean will shake his head if he hears of a student becoming a Modernist or a Pentecostal or something, but the faculty have to sign a doctrinal statement or they get fired. You know that."

"You mean he's teaching here under false pretenses!"

"Come on, Phil! What's the problem? Don't you want to know more about the doctrine?"

A moment of silent musing, then the inevitable: "Sure. You're right, I don't know what's eating me. Just exhausted, I guess. I'll go with you, Glenn. Come on."

They entered one of the classroom buildings that had the hall lights on, but no rooms were illuminated. They entered one of them nonetheless. To Philip's surprise, once his eyes had adjusted to the gloom, the place was full. At the desk, shrouded by strategic darkness, was the heretical professor, the coreligionist, the mentor of the campus sect.

"Ah, I see our new friend has arrived!" The voice was artificially hoarse. Philip could make out little detail belonging to the seated figure. The outlines suggested none of the few professors he knew, but that meant nothing. This was his first semester.

"Glenn tells me he's lent you the book. What did you think, my young friend?"

Philip sensed every eye upon him. He wondered who the students might be. How many of them had been eyeing him for days as a potential recruit?

"To tell you the truth, I couldn't make much sense of it. But I didn't start at the beginning, just flipped the pages and read here and there. But I admit there's a real power to it even without understanding it." It was his answer that made little sense, but in the circumstances he couldn't think of much to say. The shadowed man spoke again.

"And that's what you're looking for, isn't it? Spiritual power. I think that's what we're all looking for. A greater experience of Christ, a Christ at hand, here with us, not two thousand years ago, not just in the pages of the Bible."

"Yes, sir, that is exactly how I feel. Glenn's probably told you. But there's something I don't understand. Why this Whateley man? What reason is there?"

The dark whisperer cut him off. "Son, if you're looking for proof, you're not going to remain any kind of a Christian for long, are you? Do you think you can prove Jesus of Nazareth was the Christ? You know what they used to say, 'Can anything good come from Nazareth?' That's what folks hereabout say of Dunwich today! 'We did esteem him stricken, smitten of God. . . .'" The voice trailed off.

One of the hitherto silent students chimed in here: "It's an act of faith, Phil. You can't escape that. But that's what Christ asks of us, isn't it?" The voice sounded familiar, but without seeing the face, he couldn't hazard a guess.

"Yeah, I guess it is." Phil found creeping over him the familiar feeling of conviction. He had felt it a hundred times over the years of his Christian life, seated in the aisles of a chapel or spiritual retreat: the speaker pressed home the message of repentance, surrender of the will and recommitment to Christ. The laying aside of every proud idol that stood in the way of total dedication to God. Many times he had been obedient to these calls to the deeper life. Now he felt it again, that magnetism of inevitability, that weight on the conscience.

"Tell me one thing, though. I know about the virgin birth, the stories about it, anyway. But was Wilbur Whateley raised from the dead? How could that escape notice?"

"It didn't, young Mr. Brown," the professor replied patiently. "He died, as you probably know, right here at Miskatonic. But certain once-sealed records written by eyewitnesses reveal that the body vanished within seconds. And then, look it up in the local papers if you don't believe it, an entity burst out of confinement up in Dunwich. That was Wilbur, returned in his glorious resurrection body, in his true form. The theological term for it is a 'shoggoth,' the form he had before he condescended to come down among men. He appeared in his greatness to make a final appeal, but again they persecuted him. 'He came unto his own and his own received him not.' Shortly afterward, he left his powerless persecutors behind. Calling on his Heavenly Father, he ascended into heaven, just as he did before, as we read in Luke Chapter 24. Surely you know that text."

The pieces were beginning to fit together at last. It was still terribly hard to believe, to accept, but then Philip had felt exactly the same way when he was first challenged to accept the resurrection of Jesus and the miracles of the Bible back in 1980. He had taken the leap of faith then. Why should it be so hard now?

The professor, as if sensing his hesitation, spoke again: "You work at the library now, don't you Philip? We have someone there who has access to the rare book room. I want you to ask him to give you a look at the Bible manuscript kept there. He'll know the one you mean." He said the name, and Philip recognized it at once. It was the staff member who had hired him only the other day. He didn't doubt there was a connection. Philip was silent for the rest of the meeting, content to listen to the professor's detailed commentary on selected passages from the *Diary*. But he could make little of the arcane exegesis of the equally esoteric texts.

When it came time to go, he was relieved and ached for some sleep. Glenn walked him to his room, keeping up a steady flow of pep-talk chatter. Philip promised him he would seek out the manuscript as early as he could the next day. Finally his pesky friend left him alone and he dove for the pillow.

* * *

Philip appeared at the library yet fully three hours before he was due to work. As a staff member he used his privilege to get into the rare books collection. He found the man who had hired him. The latter now regarded him plainly with a look of silent recognition and led him to a locked cabinet. He opened the doors and from within carefully lifted a huge vellum codex of great antiquity.

"I don't need to tell you how careful you have to be with this. It's old and it's priceless. See, the label says 'Codex Miskatonicus.' Have you heard of it, Philip?"

"No, but I'm not that familiar with textual criticism. I know of Codex Sinaiticus and, let's see, Codex Vaticanus, one or two others."

"Right. They're from the fourth century. The time of Constantine, the first Christian emperor of Rome. This one's from the same general period, at least they think. It's so rare because it's one of the Bibles that escaped burning, maybe the only one."

"Huh?"

"You see, Constantine was the one who convened the Council of Nicea, where they decided which books ought to go into . . . and *out of* the Bible! Once they made the final selection, he had an edition of fifty deluxe codices prepared for his bishops—and then *burned* the others, the older ones that had different books. This is the only one known to have survived."

Philip's eyes were round now. "How . . . how did *we* come to have it?"

"Some decades ago, one of our professors, old Dr. Bowen, found it on an expedition to Egypt. He was looking for an ancient gem of some type, which some say he actually found and kept in a church he pastored up in Providence after his retirement. He had found the Codex almost as an accident and, incredibly, he wasn't really that interested in it! So he donated it to the library as a bequest when he left."

"And it lies here unknown?" Philip marveled aloud.

"That's not such a mystery. This Bible has some striking textual variants, some altogether different books! Local clergy were invited to examine it when it was first brought here. After flipping a few of the pages, they shuddered and urged that it be burned at once. Obviously, the school wasn't going to let that happen to a priceless manuscript, but in the end they did agree to hush the thing up. Remember, the Congregationalist Church endowed this place and still supports it heavily. They couldn't have the local ministers bad-mouthing the seminary. But you're here, as I understand it, to take a look for yourself. Be my guest. But for God's sake be careful, okay?" With that he left Philip alone and returned to his cataloguing.

Philip turned the pages with a sense of dumbfounded awe. He had been vouchsafed a privilege such as few students of the Bible ever had. Luckily he had taken New Testament Greek during his undergraduate years and could work his way through much of the text without great difficulty. The book had been opened to the Gospel of Mark. There were few surprises here, few departures from the canonical text thus far. Here was something: a resurrection story reminiscent of Lazarus, but it ended in a strange way. Jesus, it said, spent the night with the resuscitated man, the two of them clad only in linen sheets, Jesus initiating the man into the Mysteries of the Kingdom of God. That sounded vaguely odd, even offensive. But he could find little else out of the ordinary and was about to turn to one of the other gospels when his eye fell upon what seemed to be the Transfiguration story. Here were some difficult Greek constructions.

One unfamiliar word stumped him, so he got up and fetched a Greek lexicon. He was surprised to see that the word denoted some type of sea creature, a squid or—

Suddenly stunned, he forced himself to read on. It read almost as a transcript of the shocking dream he had dreamed the other afternoon! He tried to proceed further down the page, scanned a chapter in which Jesus encountered Simon Magus and revealed his saving mission to him. . . .

Philip was becoming dizzy now. He shut the book with a thud, the noise not escaping the librarian, who flinched and came running. He began to admonish his new assistant. He really must take better care . . . But when he noticed Philip's ashen face, he calmed himself and quietly urged the young man to take the day off, return to his room and pray about what he had read. Philip left without further comment. He had some thinking to do, once he could do any thinking again, that is.

* * *

Halloween came mid-semester. Philip was not in the habit of celebrating it. His piety had never allowed him to be comfortable making light of devils, witches, and the like. But this year was different. Still not an occasion of revelry, to be sure, but he did have special plans for the evening, at the campus chapel. All Hallow's Eve, All Saints' Eve, was after all a church holiday. It was dedicated to commemorating the holy heroes of the past and their victories over the Powers of Darkness. That's what he and his newfound compatriots would be doing tonight, but that was to understate it. He could hardly contain his excitement.

Sue Millman noticed his anticipation that afternoon and asked whose party he would be attending. None, he had replied sanctimoniously, he was going to church. Sue gave him a puzzled look and left the snack bar.

But now the time had arrived, and Philip picked up his copy of the *Diary* and headed over to the chapel. There would be a preliminary period of prayer and study, kind of a miniature retreat, as they sought to ready themselves for the Epiphany. This should occur at the stroke of Midnight. He did not know exactly what to expect. None of the others were willing to tell him. He wasn't totally sure any of the veterans, even Glenn, had seen one of these events. They had said something about needing Philip to complete the circle of twelve, symbolizing the original disciples. Maybe only the professor, whose identity Philip still did not know, had been here long enough to have seen the last Epiphany of the Returned Christ.

All any of the other students seemed to know for certain was that there would be something analogous to the resurrection appearances of the Gospels. And this was enough for Philip. Tonight he would find out once and for all whether he had been correct in the leap of faith he had at last decided to take. And he felt sure his decision would be vindicated. It would be the high point of his spiritual life. Thus he reflected as the chapel clock struck the quarter before the hour. It was time to make the circle and start the liturgy.

He stood next to Glenn Brindley. Across the nave he could make out the hooded faces of Reverend Winthrop and one other. Squinting, he saw with some surprise that it was Claude LaValle! Claude had never let on that he belonged to the campus sect. Perhaps he was another novice and did not know of Philip's recruitment either, until tonight.

All linked hands and began with the Lord's Prayer. The rest of the litany seemed actually pretty conventional, though he noticed the phrase "Principalities and Powers" kept recurring in it. The circle bent like one of Salvador Dali's melting watches, extending up the chancel steps and into the sanctuary proper. There, still in shadows, the lights turned off up there, was the professor, their mentor and celebrant. After a chanted reference was made to the Nine Angles, or something like that, everyone went silent and waited with held breath.

Philip could hear the distant baying of dogs in the sudden silence. Then the professor began to step forward into the light. Philip was expecting something, something spectacular, but even so, this was a surprise. He couldn't believe a professor who had kept his identity a secret for so long would take a risk like this. Why would he dare being discovered? Suppose some outsiders were secretly watching? He had been afraid of someone recognizing him for the same reason. He was willing to suffer for Christ if need be, but neither was he particularly eager to be expelled from divinity school.

It must have been an effect of the confused lighting pattern in the cavernous place, but Philip thought he saw the form of the professor growing taller as he entered the lit space. But perhaps that was only because he had thus far misjudged the height of a man he usually saw sitting in the shadows. Then the face became visible. There was time only for a brief glimpse. It was definitely no one he had ever seen on campus.

The face *changed*. For a split second Philip had the absurd idea that the man's beard grew longer even as he watched. But no, the face was elongating, like something he had seen in a dream once. . . .

The shape of the figure, who was now raising his voice and saying something in a language Philip didn't know, was vague and seemed to billow out. His liturgical robe, of course . . . unless. . . . There was now plainly visible an extra pair of looping arms, each holding a communion chalice. And now the voice spoke in familiar English, with familiar words: "Peace be unto you. It is I myself. Do not fear."

Philip's spine now froze with the thrill of numinous fear. He dimly heard Glenn announce something about consecrating the body and blood. Philip lowered his eyes. Like Moses in Exodus, he was afraid to look upon God.

Glenn released his hand, which fell nervelessly to his side, and Philip bowed to the ground. Thus he posed in reverent awe, losing count of the minutes. He no more knew what to say or to think than poor Peter did on the Mount of Transfiguration when he had stammered empty words about building booths for Jesus, Elijah and Moses. Best to bask in the divine Presence.

And then from somewhere in the narthex he began to notice the trespassive sounds of yelling and cursing. Philip felt, almost like a physical blow, the sense of sacrilege that some profane person might dare to disturb the holy gravity of this occasion. The noise, instead of abating, was actually growing nearer and more strenuous. Despite himself, Philip could not resist the reflex to look back and see what was going on.

What he saw was Glenn and a couple of the others, with more hastening to assist them, holding a naked and fighting woman. As they came closer, he had the crazy idea that it looked like Sue Millman. They were trying to get her wrists into a pair of handcuffs, but she was going down fighting. It *was* Sue.

Wait a minute! What was going on here? What could she be doing here? Spying on him? Maybe—but *naked?* And what were the other brethren doing with her? He looked back to the One on the chancel steps. That One beckoned hideously with waving arms and empty cups that seemed to be parched for some liquid to fill them. And then he saw the gleam of the knife.

He snapped out of it, almost felt like the deaf man in the gospels who could suddenly hear again. It was as if some spirit of animation had decided to transfer itself from one host to another, for in the same moment Sue went limp, perhaps from some blow he could not see, and Philip was galvanized into motion. Acting on instinct, he jumped up, ran for the knot of robed figures who carried her now-compliant body through the silent nave.

Apparently this move took the rest of them as much by surprise as Sue's appearance had startled him. He barreled into them clumsily, like a ricocheting bowling ball, but the blow was effective enough. They dropped Sue among them—and she landed on her feet. Philip realized she must have been playing possum, hoping for a chance to surprise her captors. Philip had provided it for her, and now the two of them made the most of it. They implicitly agreed not to waste the time trying to fight the larger group, now augmented by the other stunned worshippers. Better just to make a break for it.

Bolting for the twin half-doors, they evaded one or two stumbling attempts to catch at their pistoning legs and cleared the nave, then the narthex, finally bursting through the doorway and into the chill night air. They ran a few more feet before Philip turned about for a glance at the chapel to make sure no one was following. As might be expected, the campus was alive with festive activities, some of them not entirely sober. Those in the chapel, he reasoned, would not pursue them in the open, revealing themselves as a ravening lynch mob.

He paused for a breath and in a moment had stripped off his ritual robe to cover his friend's shivering nakedness. Wordlessly, he took the hand of the traumatized woman and led her back to his room.

In another few moments, Sue, clutching her unaccustomed garment, was her old self again. "What the hell was *that?*"

"I might ask you the same thing," Philip replied, his seminarian prudishness reasserting itself. "I can smell the alcohol on your breath. You were at one of those fraternity mixers, weren't you?" As he said this, he was busy pulling out an old carton from beneath his bunk and hastily sorting through some old papers inside it.

"That's none of your fucking business, Phil! I'm about sick of your pious bullshit! You and the others—you're just a bunch of old . . ."

"'Mossbacks'? Is that the word you're looking for?" mumbled Phil as he scanned a piece of yellowed manuscript.

Both were abruptly brought back to their present dilemma with a sudden pounding on the door. A voice came, Glenn's, speaking in measured tones, as if trying to control itself. "Hey, Phil! Is Sue with you in there? You must have misunderstood! It was just part of the drama of the thing!"

Sue spat back, "What was I supposed to be doing—jumping out of a cake? Get out of here, you bastards!" Then, in a whisper to her friend, "What are we going to *do?* Go through the window?"

There was the muffled sound of a huddle of people deliberating on the other side of the door. Then one voice emerged. This time it was Reverend Winthrop. "Look, you two, let's open the door and talk before the campus police get mixed up in this and we all get into trouble over nothing." No answer.

Another knock came, this one with sufficient force to splinter the door. And judging from the height of the impact point, the blow must have been thrown by a freakishly tall figure. More blows came. Philip was studying another old paper. Sue's eyes widened. "Jesus! What the hell are you *doing?* In a minute they're going to—"

"Sometimes it's the old mossbacks who have what it takes, Sue. Here goes. All I can say is, I hope my Hebrew's good enough!"

What followed was a snaky string of unrecognizable syllables. Among them Sue thought she recognized the divine names Adonai, Jehovah and Tetragrammaton. Then others with a similar ring but no familiar meaning: Buzrael, Lucifuge, Demogorgon. The words made her wince, spun about her the queasy aura of a migraine's onset. She seemed to be missing part of it, as if some other wave than ordinary sound were intersecting the frequency of Philip's voice and canceling it. Then she began to see spots, then the shrinking into tunnel vision. She focused on Philip and saw the tiny lines of blood trickling from his nose and mouth.

Then there was the peculiar sensation of hearing the echo of a mighty scream without the scream itself. And perhaps something had popped disgustingly in the hall outside (though subsequent investigation revealed no residue). There were confused sounds as of stumbling and falling, dragging and footfalls. And the sound of a body falling somewhere behind her.

Sue turned to see the limp form of Philip spread ungracefully on the floor. She tried to get him onto the bed, decided just to prop him sitting against the bunk. She looked quickly about and grabbed up a baseball bat, then tentatively opened the dorm room door. No one. Then she called down the hall for someone to get campus security. No one answered, apparently all out celebrating or praying. Or just too scared to get involved. So she opened the window and called out.

The campus police were not long in arriving, having apprehended a couple of the slower, more dazed cultists as they made their way across campus. It seemed that Sue's disappearance had not gone altogether unnoticed when she had been seen leaving the party with a young man no one in the fraternity recognized. It seemed seminarians just could not help appearing incongruous at such events, so someone noticed a "creep" leading the half-inebriated Sue Millman away and fumbling with her clothes. Though too drunk to intervene himself, the student had possessed the wits to call security from the lounge pay phone. The ruckus at the chapel had sparked another call, so the police had gone there from the dorm.

The scene there was inconclusive though suspicious, so the officers had begun to patrol the campus till they spotted several robed figures in an apparent state of semi-shock. Mere Halloween revelers? Few could speak coherently, yet none appeared to have been drinking. And then they had heard Sue's screamed summons.

It was a matter of just a few minutes till Philip was brought around. He and Sue tried as best they could to explain what had happened, though Sue was almost as much at a loss as the police. Philip spared them those details he knew that, as worldly men, they would never believe. Sufficient to say he'd blundered into what turned out to be a lot more than a Halloween prank. Sue was quick to confirm that her friend hadn't been a part of it and had helped her escape.

In the next week there were more questions to be answered and, this surprised even Philip, there were bodies to be identified. He found himself nauseated at the sight of the strangely . . . *distorted* bodies of Glenn, of Claude, of the librarian he worked for—and of the Reverend Winthrop. No one could say precisely what could have killed them. Oh, it was some sort of severe impact, almost as if the bodies had been selectively crushed at close range, like the old Puritan witch pressings. But in a dormitory hallway? And why were not all of them affected the same way? For some were more mentally affected than physically. Only one or two had after some days begun to return to lucidity, and their memories were spotty, unless they were lying.

No one was expelled from the divinity school, to the initial surprise of the campus community, for the simple reason that none who survived were in any condition to continue there. The parishioners of the Reverend Winthrop took the news with surprising equanimity, almost as if some such denouement might have been expected. The people of Foxfield were always known to be queer in their beliefs and it seemed that nothing surprised them very much.

It took a few days, but at the end of the week Philip was satisfied that all the Miskatonic divinity professors were alive and well, harumphing at all the campus mischief. He was by now persuaded that the rasping mystagogue he had met was not one of them.

The dean had a lot of explaining to do to the grief-stricken families of the slain students, though he had little in the way of explanation to offer them. Philip was just glad that job was not his, though he did try to come up with something to write on a sympathy card to Glenn's mother. Best she not know what devilish business he had been involved in. So he said one late November afternoon, just before

Thanksgiving break, to Sue Millman as the two spent the afternoon in her room talking.

"One thing I haven't asked you, Phil; I know from my work at the women's center that people sometimes need time before they can talk about their traumas. But I'm dying to know. You were affected by that . . . blast, too. I saw you bleeding. You were knocked out. But how come you weren't killed or . . . driven insane like the others? And why wasn't I affected?" She took Philip's hand. "And, well, Phil, what the hell *were* you doing reading those old scraps of paper while they were trying to kill us?"

He laughed. "They weren't just scraps. Those particular scraps happened to be some of the letters of Abijah Hoadley, you remember, my research topic. I found them in that box of documents I scavenged from the Dunwich church. Most of it was old bills and ledger pages, nothing much. But it turned out my hunch had been on target. There were a couple of letters by old Hoadley, even draft pages of his famous book. What I was reading was a letter to him by a colleague, a Dr. Ward Phillips, over at a Baptist church here in Arkham. He knew of Hoadley's one-man crusade against witchcraft in New Dunnich and warned him he was getting in over his head. So he sent him copies of certain old cabalistic spells he said might protect him."

"Must not have worked, though," Sue interrupted. "The one thing I do remember you saying about Hoadley was that he disappeared under dubious circumstances, right?"

"Oh, they would have worked all right. You saw the evidence of that on Halloween night. That's what I was reciting. That's what got rid of our pursuers. Hoadley just didn't use them. The old mossback rebuffed Phillips's advice, said it was all too Popish, too superstitious, and he would rely 'onlie upon the strong Name of the Saviour.' That mistake cost him his life. His soul, too, I'd guess."

"What's the difference?" Sue muttered. "Well, I don't know what to make of it. Maybe you're right, but your 'explanation' sounds just as crazy as what you're explaining."

Philip shrugged. "You've got me there, Sue."

Sue got up to fetch another cup of coffee. She took advantage of the momentary discontinuity to change the subject. "I guess you could see this coming, Phil, but I've decided to leave the seminary. It all seemed less and less relevant the more deeply I got involved with people's problems, out there in the real world. I'm going to look into that Social Work degree I told you about over at Aylesbury State."

Phil rose and looked out the window. "You're right, Sue. That doesn't surprise me. But this may surprise *you*. I'm leaving, too."

"What? Why?" She rose and stood beside him. He turned to face her.

"This is going to sound even crazier than what I just said, but here goes. Right after Halloween, I had to rethink everything. You remember all the business about the second coming, about . . ."

"Yes, I remember," she said, putting a hand on his shoulder. There were deep wheels turning here, and she knew enough to be a sensitive listener.

"At first, given what I saw that night in the chapel, and then what happened in the dorm, I decided I had been lured into a cult. I'd seen the same thing happen to friends of mine who joined the Children of God cult, Guru Maharaj Ji, you know the type. I prayed and asked Christ to forgive me. Especially when I realized what almost happened to you . . .

"But then I remembered the dream, and what I read in that biblical manuscript. Even now it makes too much sense. It all fits together too well!"

"Phil!" she gasped. "You don't still believe it's *true,* do you?" He could sense her body stiffening, reflexively withdrawing from him as if he'd just confided he had a communicable disease.

Philip laughed bitterly. "I *do,* Sue! I do believe it's true! But I don't want anything to do with it! It's like having God appear to you and hearing him tell you his name is Satan. In fact, it's not *like* it— that *is* what happened! The 'real' Christianity: I *wanted* it and I *got* it. But I don't want it anymore. You see the irony of old Hoadley's position. Poor fool! To think the name of Christ would protect him. He needed to be protected from *it!*"

Sue's eyes were round. She had to regather some presence of mind to try and fill the bomb crater of ensuing silence. "So . . . so, what will you do now?"

"I'm open to suggestions. Got an extra copy of that brochure on the social work program?" Smiling a small smile, Sue said that she thought she did. ✳

The Eldridge Collection
by Will Murray

The package was intercepted in Kingston, Rhode Island.

It had been overnighted from Toronto via Worldwide Express. The red and white Worldwide Express jet was tracked en route by an orbiting Zircon spy satellite under the direct control of the Department of Defense's National Reconnaissance Office.

A Worldwide van left Timothy F. Green Airport trailed by a bronze Ford Taurus. It was blocked on Route 138 by a yellow Checker cab. Out of the cab popped a short, dusky man in a severe black suit and tie, showing a leatherette ID case in one hand and a 10mm Delta Elite automatic in the other.

The van driver hit the brakes, thinking, "Hijack!"

The Taurus sheared in on his left, blocking him from exiting his vehicle. A cadaverous man in severe black slapped an ID against his window and shouted: "Exit your vehicle—now!"

The Worldwide courier driver came out quietly, hands raised.

"Department of Defense. You have a pine crate on board," said the tall man in black.

"Crate? I don't remember any—"

They threw him to the ground, cuffing his wrists behind his back. He lay prone while the pair went in the back and carried out a flat wooden box, like a compact pallet.

"Oh, that. That's not a crate. It's a—"

"Shut up!" said the short dusky man.

He shut up.

They took prybars to the sides of the flat wooden box and with a screech and squeal of agonized nails, uncrated a canvas painting encased in cardboard and bubblewrap.

"What do you make of it?" the short one asked the other.

"Looks like the Big A."

"That's my read, too."

"Damn!"

They recreated the painting and carefully laid it in the taxi's trunk. The cab scampered off on smoking tires.

The driver of the Taurus came back, uncuffed the courier and set him on his feet.

"You have been a participant in a sensitive Department of Defense operation. This encounter did not happen. You never saw us. Your supervisors have been briefed. You will say nothing to them or anyone else about what went on here."

"How do I know you're not—"

"Or I can just shoot your Goddamn eyes out here and now."

"I'm cool with this," the driver said.

He was shaking twenty minutes after the Taurus sped away. Nobody ever asked about the missing crate, and he never brought it up either.

* * *

The safe house could only have existed in Rhode Island. It was a dull red Colonial on Church Street in downtown Newport. The paint was peeling on both sides. The owner had had the frontage refreshed with a duller shade of colonial-era red, but had neglected the sides—probably on the theory that the adjoining houses pressed too close to warrant cosmetic paint.

Mel Justice parked the Taurus out front and went in the side door. Osorio's cab was nowhere in sight. Good.

The painting lay on the kitchen table, still encased in rough hard pine. Agent Justo Osorio was on the wall phone, talking to Washington.

"The destination address is the Malbone Museum, Touro Street, Newport, Rhode Island. No, I never heard of it. Look it up."

Osorio nodded when he saw Justice walk in.

"They're running the address on the waybill," Osorio said.

"Right."

Osorio gripped the ivory phone handset until his dusky fingers almost matched the plastic. Then he said, "Okay. We'll handle it from here." He hung up.

"It checks out," he told Justice. "A private art museum. Established 1971. Oriel Malbone, curator. He's in the database as a low-level dabbler."

"Figures."

"I guess we're going to have to go in."

Justice nodded. He picked up the heavy wood crate and set it against the silent refrigerator. Carefully, he lifted the canvas out of its pine sheath.

The painting was an 11 x 14 oil. It might have been new, it might have been old. The colors were bright. The image was garish.

The canvas showed a fragment of interstellar space, framing a vortical disturbance within which squatted a sultanic potentate laughing uproariously as faceless things spun and whirled in orbit about him, piping on flutes composed of snowy quantum stuff.

"Azathoth, or I'm Wilbur Whateley's demented second cousin . . ." Osorio muttered.

Justice nodded. "Yeah. And it's an Eldridge for certain. Look at those frenzied brush strokes."

"No signature."

"He never signed his work," said Justice.

"Check this out."

Osorio's finger indicated a scarlet circle centered in the upper portion of the image area. The circle was not integral to the image, but superimposed over it.

"What do you make of it?" he asked.

"Can't say. A circle. A zero. Maybe an alchemical symbol. I'm rusty on the hermetics."

"Me, too. How's your astrology?"

"Crappy. I was born Mercury retrograde. I can't remember all those trines and occultations and afflicted planets."

"Wasn't there a white numeral 1 on the Nyarlathotep canvas that got away from us in Milan?"

"Not confirmed that it was a 1. Might have been a capital letter I, or a Roman numeral I. The lab said there was no way to differentiate between the two without contextual references."

"Zeroes are Arabic. I'd say this is an O and the Nyarlathotep thing was a capital I."

"If we knew what old Esau was trying to paint when he committed these bastards to canvas, we'd have an inkling."

"But we don't. I guess we just go in and see how much of the Eldridge Collection is in that museum."

They checked their weapons, stowed the painting in the basement and claimed the Taurus.

* * *

The Surveillance and Interdiction van was already on station when they pulled up to the museum, an imposing Greek Revival building with a broken pediment over the pillared portico. It was a UPS van with one visible added feature. A small turret on top that housed the upper lens of a periscope.

Justice got the van on his cellphone.

"What have you got?"

"Damn place is choked with Eldridges," came a hoarse voice.

"Christ! You positive?"

"Of course we're not positive. That old goat never signed his work. But I see a Cthulhu, a Yog and a flock of—"

"Damn it. Don't invoke major entities on an unsecured line."

"—Nightgaunts. I mean, N.G.s."

"How much of the collection do you figure is inside?"

"We count at least 30 canvases."

"Good Christ! Do you think we could be this lucky?"

Justice turned to Osorio. "Intel has it the Eldridge Collection is being reassembled canvas by canvas. Now we know where they're all landing."

"Yeah. But not why."

"So we go in and we find out," Justice said tightly.

They rang the bell. It was a black push-button set in a brass plate, vintage 1933 judging from the tarnish. The door sported a row of leaded-glass fan lights.

An elderly man with a face like a dried turnip opened the tall oak-panel door. He might have been a mummified sea captain of the 1800s with his thinning goatee. He started in surprise.

"Yes?"

"We're patrons," said Justice.

"Viewing is by appointment only."

"We'd like to make an appointment," said Osorio.

"Now," said Justice.

"For now," added Osorio.

"Impossible. Arrangements are made by telephone only." The door began to close.

Justice inserted his foot in the door, and Osorio stuck his service weapon in the old man's face.

"Oriel Malbone, you are under arrest for the illegal importation of banned engineries of magic," warned Justice.

They urged the man in, walking in tandem with his retreating steps. The door was closed.

* * *

In the camouflaged van, the surveillance team waited tensely.

Three minutes and twelve seconds by their synchronized watches, Osorio came out. He looked dazed, and he was wearing the wrong tie.

In the van, the agent at the periscope murmured, "Something's not right . . ."

"What's that?"

"Osorio's wearing Justice's tie."

"So?"

"And his shoes. Take a look yourself."

It was worse than that. Osorio stumbled to the curb. They ran up to his side. Up close, they saw the truth—the unbelievable truth.

"Oh, God. It's Justice."

"Are you blind? It's Osorio."

"It's Justice. Look at his wrists. Pale as muslin. It's Justice—but he's wearing Osorio's head."

A moment later, Osorio stumbled out, looking at the world through the stupefied eyes of his partner. His head did not exactly sit on his neck properly. It was too thin. He looked like a pinhead. And there was a clear neckline demarcation where dark skin turned pale.

An ambulance was called. They loaded the two twitching and flopping agents onto gurneys. Osorio's head came off during the procedure, leaving a nubby stump like a pink matchhead. Justice's head rolled off the other body en route. They were pronounced E.O.A.—Ensorceled on Arrival—and quietly euthanized by lethal injection.

The Malbone Museum was sealed off, its lower windows spray-painted black so that no one could see out—or worse, no agent could look in and risk having his sanity compromised. And the Cryptic

Events Evaluation Section of the National Reconnaissance Office settled down for what looked to be a long grim siege.

*   *   *

Word reached CEES operative James Anthony in Washington, DC.
Section Head Morand walked into his office, shut the door, and broke
the news.

"We've isolated the Eldridge Collection, or most of it. Justice and
Osorio succumbed in the line of duty. Never mind the grisly details.
It's your assignment now. You'll be partnering with Itri."

Anthony blinked. "Itri. Who's he?"

"She. Gina Itri. Boston office. Cartomancy Division."

"A tarot reader! I have to team up with a fucking pasteboard
princess? No damn way."

"This comes from the top. Itri's already on station. You'll liaise
with her in Newport."

The file landed on Anthony's desk. Clipped to the folder was a
plane ticket to Newport. Anthony noticed it was one way. The
Cryptic Events Evaluation Section of the National Reconnaissance
Office stopped wasting money on return tickets after Agent Irby disappeared in Moodus, Connecticut and was later found embedded in a
125-year-old swamp maple as if it had grown around his undecayed
remains since Teddy Roosevelt's day. They never explained that one.

*   *   *

Anthony spent the flight reading the file. Esau Eldridge,
1904–1961. Triple Scorpio. Commercial illustrator. Painted book
plates for privately-printed grimoires during the 1930s, then moved
on to gallery art. His work shocked postwar America, which preferred the safer styles of Rockwell and Lovell. The works that leaked
out of Eldridge's Smuttynose Island lighthouse garret were bad
enough, but rumors were they were merely discarded rejects from his
magnum opus, a series of paintings depicting the Great Old Ones
and their remorseless train. No one knew their purpose. But upon
Eldridge's death, his acolytes and rivals descended upon the isolated
New Hampshire island and spirited away the collection piecemeal.
That was in the pre-NRO days when cosmic countervaillance was a

Secret Service responsibility. After Dallas, NRO was formed and tasked for that mission.

There followed a kind of internecine war between rival Cthulhu worshippers, all vying to reassemble the complete collection. It was nothing less than a Mafia-style power struggle conducted with demons and grimoires instead of hit men and firearms. Bodies turned up in inexplicable places, unaccountably violated. Canvases materialized and dematerialized like wavicles in the quantum matrix.

That disturbing pattern was what had brought in the Cryptic Events Evaluation Section. For better than two decades, they had chased Eldridges, sometimes capturing one, but always losing them to counterforces, sometimes in the form of turncoat dark agents.

Now the paintings were being reassembled in one locale. It was a golden opportunity to seize and quarantine the entire problem.

"But we still don't know what Eldridge was up to," Anthony muttered as the 727 dropped its gear on approach to T. F. Green Airport.

*   *   *

Anthony expected an aging hippie in her 40s. Gina Itri was a feline redhead who looked like a cross between Fran Drescher and a moderately high-priced call girl. She smoked like a Black Mass. And she had a mouth on her . . .

"I'm Itri. Arts and Crafts. Cartomancy Division," she said in a smoky voice.

"Anthony. Intelligence and Enforcement. South Boston?"

She nodded. "You're good, for a non-intuitive."

"I got no use for tarot. I'll say that up front."

"Fine," Itri said, reaching into her handbag. She pulled out the Thoth deck, secured by a black silk ribbon. That told Anthony she was a bitch on wheels. The Thoth was a man's deck.

She started running cards on him. That was another thing Anthony hated about tarot readers. They couldn't take a leak without consulting their cards.

"First," Itri said, "I'm not a mechanical reader. I'm intuitive. In a tight spot, I'll do a one-card pull. But I don't read spreads. I'm not into relying on Chaos Theory."

"Right, right," he said impatiently.

"Aries?"

Anthony sighed. "Yeah."

"I always nail the sun sign. Moon in Capricorn, too. Divorced. No kids. I can see we're going to get along . . ." she said acidly. "I'm Leo, Moon in Scorpio."

"I don't give a rat's ass for astrology, either."

"In that case, you can do all the shooting. And dying."

"That's my job . . ." Anthony said tightly.

She nodded. "I've looked over the seized Azathoth. That's a zero painted at the top. That makes the device on the Nyarlathotep canvas a Roman numeral I for sure."

"The cards tell you that?"

"Yes and no." She held up a card. It showed a yellow-faced green demon or devil. It was labeled The Fool. A tapering scarlet nail touched a zero set in the top border. "Note the zero."

"Noted. . . ."

"This is the first card in the tarot deck, The Fool." She cut the cards blindly, exposing another card. It was titled The Magician. "This is the second card. Note the I."

"I don't have time for this—"

"Stuff it. The Cthulhu painting glimpsed through the Malbone Museum window had a number on it. Guess what number?"

She cut the cards while Anthony frowned darkly.

Up came a card called The Hierophant, the number was V.

"Not—"

"The Fool is Azathoth, the so-called Blind Idiot God. Nyarlathotep is The Magician. Even a stiff like you would get that. And Great Cthulhu is The High Priest, or Hierophant. Want me to spell it out for you in Braille?"

Anthony stiffened. "Eldridge was painting a tarot deck . . ."

"Eldridge was painting the *ultimate* tarot. Maybe the original tarot. No one knows where the tarot comes from. Most of the decks that come down to us, descend from Medieval Italy. They're unrectified, that is, incomplete. And pretty harmless within their limitations as focusing tools for divination. But there's an old theory that the tarot is Egyptian in origin, and it's based on the Book of Thoth." She fixed him with her magnetic brown eyes. "Thoth . . . Azathoth . . . Yog-Sothoth . . . is any of this sinking in?"

Anthony felt the blood drain from his face.

"How bad if the Eldridge Collection has been reassembled?" he croaked.

"No one knows. But we have the Azathoth painting, so we know Malbone hasn't got a complete deck yet."

Itri flipped up another card.

"Take a close look at The Magician," she said.

Anthony did. It showed a brass godlet with rather phallic attributes rampant against a creepy gray backdrop. "Are those *tentacles* in the background?" he asked.

"Coiled tentacles. The Thoth Tarot was envisioned by Aleister Crowley and executed by Lady Frieda Harris in the 1940s. It's thought Crowley was attempting to recreate the original ultimate tarot deck. But he got hung up in the process. Crowley identified with The Magician. Couldn't figure out what magician to use. He ran Lady Frieda ragged painting different interpretations. Just after he produced a limited edition deck in 1944, Crowley died. The Thoth deck remained a rarity until a mass market edition was released in 1969. By then, no one connected it with the Great Old Ones and their spawn. This is believed to be Crowley's preferred Magician card. It has *Necronomicon* written all over it."

Anthony regarded the image floating before his eyes. As he watched the tentacles seemed to . . . writhe.

He slapped the card aside, saying, "Get that thing away from me!"

Itri smiled. "Interesting. You have some latent ability."

"All right. You've done your part. Now I have to find a psychically secure way into that damn museum."

"The cards will lead us."

"Not on your—"

"Unless you want to drive home with someone else's head."

Anthony grabbed his neck. He felt a tightness there. He swallowed his objections.

"You lead. I'll follow."

Agent Itri smiled. "I like a man who understands who's holding all the cards."

* * *

They took up a position behind the Old Stone Mill in Touro Park. It was an eight-legged cylinder of heterogeneous native stone fenced off by wrought iron. Blank windows were set high up at regular intervals like empty-socketed eyes.

"What is this thing?" Anthony asked, looking up warily.

"No one's sure. Some claim it's of Norse origin. In Benedict Arnold's will, it was listed as a windmill."

"So it's just a windmill. . . ."

"That's what Aquidneck Islanders believed until they found its double under 30 feet of water off Brenton's Point."

"I hate elder artifacts. . . ."

Itri was running cards. She started with the Rider-Waite deck, clicking through them until she came to The Devil, a rather hairy bat-winged Satan perched on a block of base metal, to which were chained a nude man and woman, both in attitudes of passive thrall.

"Look familiar?" she asked.

Anthony regarded the card. "Vaguely," he admitted. "Can't place it, though."

"Remember the Cthulhu canvas? It's nearly the same posture."

"Mother of God. You're right!"

"This confirms my college thesis. The tarot descends from knowledge psychically apprehended by Egyptian Cthulhu-worshippers."

"Miskatonic?"

Itri nodded. "Where else would I get a masters in applied cartomancy?"

"I say we burn the damn building down. End this right here."

Itri shook her long red hair. "Can't."

"Give me one sound reason. And don't consult the damn cards."

"Reason one: We don't know how many amateur magicians, adepts, cartomancers or whatever have Eldridge photographs in their collection. We need to record and archive every image in the rectified deck, or look forward to wasting the next 500 years confiscating and burning every Cthulhuvian canvas that comes to light."

Anthony sighed. "Point taken. What's reason two?"

"Reason two is if unrectified decks are out there, the only counterforce is a partial deck under Department of Defense control." She lit up a Marlboro. "Not to mention reason three."

"Which is?"

"I want a crack at working this complete deck myself."

Anthony shuddered. Southie women. They were as tough as advertised.

Itri blew gray tendrilly smoke. "Okay, here's the way it reads to me. Malbone can't see out his windows, and we can't look in. He's got at best a partial deck, while I have Rider-Waite, Crowley's Thoth, and if events get really sticky, a Xultun deck. That just about levels the playing field." She looked at him pointedly. "You man enough to back me up?"

Anthony silently popped his belt buckle and thumbed the reservoir last replenished on Ash Wednesday. He traced a five-pointed star on his forehead, jacked a fresh round into the chamber of his service weapon, and nodded wordlessly.

Itri led him to the cellar entrance. It was a galvanized steel hatch, padlocked. He picked it in thirty seconds, threw the hatch and they descended. The plank door at the bottom of the short wooden steps wouldn't budge.

"Padlocked," he hissed.

Itri ran through her Rider-Waite. "No, just a hasp."

Anthony reversed his pick. The other end was a sharp punch. He dug the tip into the soft wood around the painted-over hasp strapping. When the point scraped hard metal, he put his weight into it. A slow screech of metal declared that he had popped the hasp.

The door came open. Itri cut the cards, saw the Star and seemed satisfied.

"The easy part's over," Anthony muttered as he stepped into the crepuscular gloom. An ancient coal furnace blew hot air, throwing angry orange light. The light showed the dusty orb web blocking the angling stairs to the upper floors.

Anthony advanced, one big hand lifted to swat away the drooping strands.

"Don't touch it!" Itri hissed. "Early warning webbing. I ran into one of these in a 300-year-old grist mill in Foxfield, Mass."

Anthony froze. He saw the spider. It looked dead. On closer inspection, its resemblance to a spider was more general than specific.

Itri took a piece of tissue, masticated it into a soggy ball in her mouth, then spit it into the web. The spider scuttled from its hole, sinking fangs into the moist morsel.

It sizzled, and fell, a sputtering cinder that stank of burnt tar.

"Holy water gets them every time . . ." said Itri, clearing the web away with a dusty ski pole.

"Holy? . . ."

"I gargle the stuff before every operation."

Anthony followed her up the steps, weapon at the ready.

"Holy water never works for me," he said.

"Not against major entities. But the minor ones really bought into that old good vs. evil modality."

*　*　*

Oriel Malbone sat in a throne carved from a single block of imperial jade, his smoldering eyes fixed upon a crystal ball upheld by the inverted talons of an Arabian roc.

The UPS van was still parked across the street, regarding the building with its primitive ground glass lens. No doubt the non-blackened windows were laser-miked for sound. It was getting so that science was catching up to sorcery. . . .

A faint vibration caught his attention. He looked to his left wrist, where a thin strand of spider silk vibrated. It went limp. The cellar web had been breached. Good. Just as the cards had foretold.

Rising, Malbone laid six oversized pasteboards in a circle around his booted feet. Fixing his eye on the Elder Sign card, he stepped off a slow circle until he had addressed all six cards three times three.

Then the hardwood floor began to melt under his feet like so much hot molasses, swallowing his feet. . . .

*　*　*

Itri was picking her way from the kitchen to the cramped angular hallways with their unhappy carvings. There were no doors, making their stealthy progress smooth and silent.

They encountered the first Eldridge at the terminus of the main hallway. It was a massive black canvas, fretted with watery greens and grays that limned a shuddering stone structure.

"R'lyeh," Itri hissed. "The Tower. It always signifies disaster."

"We gotta walk past it to—"

"Waite isn't helping." She switched to the Thoth deck. "Okay, just follow in my footsteps. Don't deviate."

Itri walked toward the painting, holding to the middle of the hardwood floor.

Anthony followed. At one point, his foot slipped and his straying toe encountered empty air. He strangled his curse.

"The floor's an illusion," Itri called over her shoulder. "Only this middle section is real."

"Why didn't you say so?"

"Didn't want you losing your water. I partnered with an I & E stiff in Ubar."

"Ubar?"

"Irem to you. A sand gulper jumped out of a dune and swallowed the lower half of his body."

Anthony nodded. "I knew him. Hurley. Heard he ate his own gun."

"That was the story I & E put out to save face. Truth is, I put him out of his misery with his own weapon. The big baby kept blubbering."

"Bitch."

"What's that?"

"I said witch. You're into Wicca, right?"

"I'm part Gypsy."

"Same difference."

The hallway negotiated, they came to a large room paneled in old teak and ebony dominated by a brick fireplace. In the center sat a jade throne facing a crystal ball about the size of a console television.

Anthony approached the crystal gingerly. "What's with the oracle? Malbone's a cartomancer, right?"

"Divination is divination," Itri said. She stopped dead when she spotted the six cards lying flat on the floor in a circle. Her brown eyes fixed on one card, which looked like a Yin/Yang sign as if it were some kind of symbolic Siamese creature. "Eldridge knew his stuff. The Lovers card is Nug and Yeb."

"Nug and who?" asked Anthony.

"Two of the most obscure yet potent of the Old Ones. If Eldridge painted them from life, he was communing with the highest universal powers in existence."

Itri picked up the cards, extracted an equal number from the Thoth, discarded them, and whispered, "Let's get moving."

"What are you doing?"

"Building a rectified ultimate tarot," she said.

They worked from room to room, Itri consulting her cards before turning each corner, Anthony jumping in ahead, Delta Elite ready to fire. They encountered no one.

The walls were covered in canvases, all hung in heavy ornate gilt frames. And all arranged in orderly numbers. All they had to do was follow the numerical progression to explore the collection and take stock of the museum's holdings.

They came to a card displaying a congeries of bubbles floating in a void.

Itri extracted the Nine of Disks from her Thoth desk. Labeled Gain, it showed a dismal blue, green and gray melange of floating spheres. The resemblance of the two designs was unmistakable.

"Which proves what?" Anthony asked.

Itri moved on until she came to a canvas that could only be Great Cthulhu. He squatted on a block of some base metal, batwings outspread, one hand raised, facing the viewer. Chained to the block were two headless humanoid beings.

Itri pulled her Rider-Waite and without appearing to deliberately select a card, revealed The Devil. Its pose was identical to that of Cthulhu.

"There's no question now. Every tarot descends from a proto-tarot predating the earliest known decks. This is the original deck. This is the key to everything, and Eldridge managed to recreate it through God knows what occult medium."

The progression took them to a winding staircase whose newels were carved in the traditional Kingsport motif. They went up, their feet staying on the fuzzy brown runner to muffle any sound. It felt like they were walking up a long, dead tongue.

"Check it out," Itri said, indicating a canvas depicting a black faceless batwinged creature rising into a moonlit night clutching a naked man and woman by their stomachs. "The Death card is a nightgaunt."

"I hate the Death card," Anthony said.

"It's not what you think," Itri returned. "Only an amateur reads the Death card as Death personified."

"Looks like Death to me. . . ."

"Amateur."

Reaching the top step, they found themselves facing a gilt-framed painting that looked weirdly familiar. A tall grayish cone of a creature squatted on eight elephantine legs, looking out in eight directions with an equal number of blank orbs.

"What the hell is that?" Anthony said.

"Shoggoth."

"Damned if it doesn't look exactly like that stone tower across the street."

"I was thinking the exact same thing."

"Aren't shoggoths amphibious?"

Itri nodded. "That might explain the waterlogged stone tower, too. They're petrified shoggoths. Could also explain that Nazi sub that went down near here during the Big One. A shoggoth got it."

The second floor split in two directions. Every wall was hung with Eldridges. There were only two doors, both shut.

Itri ran cards on the south door, nodded, then performed the same operation on the north door.

"Bedrooms. Empty," she said.

"Secret panels?" wondered Anthony.

She ran along the deck, stopped at The Hermit.

"Plenty of them. All empty."

"Malbone's gotta be somewhere in here."

"I don't see him in the cards."

"Dammit, shouldn't we be looking behind every door, not in your damn deck," Anthony hissed.

"Feel free to waste your time," Itri said acidly.

Anthony hit the north door. It popped inward when his shoulder struck it. A bedroom. The south door opened on a mirror-image bedroom. The last of the canvases sat over each four-poster bed. A row of high vaulted windows looked out upon Touro Park and its strange sentinel of stone.

Itri was tapping one toe impatiently when Anthony rejoined her. "Satisfied?" she asked.

"Yeah."

"Taurus ascendant?"

Anthony frowned darkly. "You tell me."

"Something in your chart made you as stubborn as a bad smell."

They discovered no missing canvases in the minor arcana. And only one in the major arcana.

"Only The Fool is missing," Itri said grimly.

Anthony nodded. "Azathoth. And we have that covered."

Absently, Itri dropped a card. Her hand snagged it before it hit the floor. She looked at it. "The Moon," she said thoughtfully.

"So what? You dropped it by accident."

"Nothing in the universe happens by chance. I wonder what this means. . . ." Itri looked up. There was a box-frame hatch directly over their heads. "Boost me up," she said.

Holstering his weapon, Anthony made a basket with his hands. Itri stepped into it. He lifted her up. She slapped the hatch door up. It fell back, and she pulled herself up and in.

Anthony redrew his weapon and waited tensely. Minutes crawled by. The shoggoth in the painting seemed to be staring at him like a deformed owl at a mouse.

"Itri!"

No answer.

"Itri!"

Her face appeared in the hatch, wearing a wide red grin. She flashed a fan of cards, saying "Jackpot!" then disappeared.

When her legs reappeared a moment later, Anthony reached up to catch her about the waist. Her feet hit the hardwood flooring with a single click.

"What'd you find?" Anthony demanded.

"Malbone's printing press and photographic equipment. And all these." She flashed a fat deck of cards. "Rejects and castoffs, but they're good enough for government work."

"How many?"

"No time to take inventory. Okay, let's go."

"Go where?"

Without answering, Itri ran down the steps. Anthony followed her to the room dominated by the crystal ball. She took up a standing position before it, peering deep within.

Catching up, Anthony asked, "I thought you—"

"I minored in scrying at MU, okay? Now get your ass out of my light."

Anthony retreated to guard the door.

Itri leaned into the crystal. Her supple body stiffened. "Don't look now, but I found our wayward wizard. He's at the safe house. Nice I & E security, by the way."

Anthony rushed forward. "Malbone?"

She turned. "Once he has the Azathoth, he's on his way to a complete deck, minus my six."

"And you have just what—how many?"

Itri said nothing. She was thinking. Quietly, she went picking through her composite deck, an admixture of Thoth and Cthulhu cards. Pulling six, she laid them in a circle before the crystal ball. They were the six she had found originally.

"Let's see if he comes back."

"Back?"

The floor began to run and congeal. A face like a jaundiced carven turnip lifted out of the cold molasses morass. The eyes were wide, but unseeing as if tranced. Tucked under the set beard-feathered chin was the upper portion of a starry canvas bearing a blood-red zero.

Anthony stepped in, leveled his Delta Elite at the rising head and said: "I'll take that."

Itri beat him to it. She wrested the canvas from Malbone's trance-stiff fingers, spun away with it.

Anthony tracked the exact middle of Malbone's rising forehead with a steady gunhand. When the floor solidified under his settling boots, vision returned to the old magician's faded agate eyes. His dry lips formed a malevolent orifice.

Anthony said, "Oriel Malbone, you stand accused of trafficking in forbidden engineries of magic. It is my sworn duty to dispatch you from this earth."

Anthony's finger squeezed the stainless steel trigger. The weapon popped, jumping in his hand. Malbone's head jerked back on its age-wattled neck. Gunsmoke obscured Anthony's view.

He turned to address Itri. She wasn't there.

"Where? . . ."

A cold voice behind him intoned: "Not so quick, my uninitiated pretender to power."

Anthony whirled. Malbone stood there with his deck held before him arrayed in a short fan, a bloodless blue hole in the center of his forehead closing like a meaty iris.

Anthony opened fire. The weapon shook and smoked, creating thunder in the room. Hot rounds chipped jade fragments off the Oriental throne. Struck once, the crystal ball shattered into clear chunks and powdery glass particles.

Yet Oriel Malbone stood unharmed, protected by nothing more substantial than a fan of tarot cards . . .

A cold fear creeping into his bones, Anthony began backing out of the room, calling, "Itri! Agent Itri! Damn it, where are you?"

Floating down the stairs came a smoky taunting laugh.

"Last one into the attic eats the Death card."

"Damn that mouthy bitch!"

Malbone was advancing now, eyes wild, his parched lips peeling back from yellow peg teeth. He was running cards, their faces directed at Anthony as if to ensnare and confuse him.

Every round Anthony sent his way veered in midair to ricochet into teak paneling. The automatic soon ran empty, slide freezing into the locked position.

Malbone cackled a thin laugh as Anthony expertly ejected the empty clip and slammed home a fresh one. He resumed firing.

"You waste your time," Malbone taunted. "I am protected." He revealed the Yog-Sothoth card. It seemed to pulse and shift its bubbling congeries of alien spheres.

Anthony picked his shots. A round seemed to bounce off the old wizard's skull, to gouge a decorative rosette. Another smeared a leaden brushstroke along the fireplace lintel. Anthony began seeing science in the misses, geometry in the ricochets.

At the door, he dropped into a marksman's crouch and blazed away at an imaginary spot to the immediate right of Oriel Malbone's coldly advancing form.

Bullets rained on the fireplace, knocking over brass andirons and fracturing brick. Some ricocheted. One found a soft spot in Malbone's lower spine. Wearing an expression of shocked astonishment, Malbone stumbled forward, cards fluttering all around him like tired origami bats. He clutched at them wildly.

Anthony lunged, stepping on a thin wrist so hard bones snapped. The wizard howled in pain. He let go of a fistful of pasteboards. Without hesitation, Anthony aligned the Elite's muzzle with Oriel Malbone's yawning mouth.

Two rounds fragmented the old wizard's head in a brutal echo of the shattered crystal ball. The thin body collapsed, one yellowing claw crushing a lone card.

Anthony plucked it free, saw it was a nightgaunt—the Death card—and got down on his knees to collect the rest of the deck.

When he had them all, Anthony gave the jittering corpse an angry kick and went in search of Agent Gina Itri.

Reaching the second floor landing, he located her. A fitful green light came down from the attic hatch. It repeated.

"What the hell . . ."

Accompanying sounds told him an ordinary photocopier was in operation.

"Damn! Itri! Get down here!"

Her voice came back, distracted and brittle. "Hold your horses. I'm almost done reducing Azathoth to card size."

"That is a direct order. You are not authorized to—"

"Bite me, okay?"

The photocopier went silent. Attic flooring creaked under a shifting human weight.

Anthony looked at the cards in his hands and felt a chill touch his bone marrow. Between them, they had a full tarot. And for the first time in his life he began to wish he had studied the damn cards.

Itri's voice was thin when it next sounded. "Get ready. I'm coming down."

Anthony took up a position at the top of the staircase, Delta Elite sighted on the square ceiling hatch. When Itri's oval face appeared, he said tightly: "Drop the cards ahead of you, Itri."

"What are you afraid of?"

Anthony's voice was flat and expressionless. "You."

A silence. Then: "All right. Here they come."

A single card dropped down, fluttered momentarily, and made a sharp midair veer. It sliced through the automatic's muzzle like a guillotine. The fore part of the weapon hit the floor with a *clank!*

"Jesus!" Anthony said, recoiling.

The card lay on the floor. It was The Shoggoth. Anthony's eye went from the card image to the original painting framed on the wall just beneath the hatch. The card sported a vertical black line—a printing or photocopying defect. It seemed not to matter, because Itri's voice lifted in some guttural prehuman chant and—

Abruptly the shoggoth in the painting turned to petrified rock. Its weird blank orbs melted into empty stone sockets.

And outside, coming from the direction to Touro Park, came a plodding *thud-thud-thud-thud* of dull, elephantine feet.

"Itri, what the hell do you think you're doing?" Anthony shouted.

"Seizing my rightful power. No one has ever wielded the ultimate tarot. This is the dream of every cartomancer since Bonifacio Bembo painted the original medieval deck. Waite tried, but he got tangled up in useless Jungian archetypes. Crowley came close, but he put too much faith in modern science. Eldridge succeeded only to die just as he finished his masterpiece. His bad karma is my glory."

"Renegade. You've gone renegade!" Anthony said heatedly.

"Your word for it, not mine. I've had it up to here with I & E stuffed suits like you looking down your long noses at my gift. I don't owe the agency anything."

"You know the building is surrounded, Itri."

"And you know I can drop through the floor to Paris or London any time I damn well want," Itri fired back.

"But you won't until you have the rest of Malbone's deck. Come down and get them."

The dull thudding of heavy feet was drawing nearer.

"I don't have to," came the smoky laughing voice from the attic. "Reinforcements are coming your way."

Anthony was not a prayerful man. But he made a sign of the cross. He couldn't see what was bearing down on the house. He didn't need to see it. The stony thing in the painting gave his imagination all it needed to fill in the pieces.

"Last chance to surrender," Itri warned. "Before your brains get scooped out like seeds from a gourd."

Anthony's teeth squeezed tight. "You—"

"I think the word you're groping for is bitch. Or do you mean witch?"

"Take your damn pick," Anthony growled.

"Trade you card for card. No? Try this one."

Another card fluttered down like a falling leaf. A nightgaunt. The Death card. It slid along the floor and kept sliding, homing in on James Anthony like a flat speedy cockroach. It sliced the heel off his left shoe, then came back for the right. Anthony dodged it. The pasteboard continued after him. He stepped on it. Hard.

Under his surviving shoe heel, Anthony felt the card tug and tug stubbornly. The damn thing was not giving up. He relinquished pressure long enough to bring his heel up and down with crushing force. That momentary lapse was his mistake. The card zipped free, pulling Anthony's foot out from under him.

He landed on his backside. Eyes widening, he looked for the fugitive nightgaunt card. Where was it? Where the hell did it go?

He understood he was sitting on the card too late. After he discovered himself skidding along the polished hardwood floor into the north bedroom, where the row of high vaulted windows framed a two-story tall cone of dull gray matter which regarded him with blank orbs like polished ivory balls.

The glass broke inward, impelled by an extrusion like a gray clay limb.

And over his shoulder, Anthony heard a mocking voice say, "I'll take that from you."

Nimble fingers extracted the last of Oriel Malbone's tarot deck from his bone-and-sinew vise of a hand. The nails were scarlet, as if enameled in blood. He caught that much out of the tail of his eye—but the thing in the window continued to hold his frozen attention.

"Only an amateur reads the Death card as Death," Gina Itri was saying. "But only a fool ignores the inevitable. *Ciao.*"

Anthony opened his mouth to scream as the blunt extension reached in to envelop his head. He never got out a single sound.

As the world turned black to his eyes and cold to his brain, Agent James Anthony had time to process a final strange thought: shoggoths tasted exactly like dead wet clams.

Then his pressure-stressed skull cracked, while a cold gray mass slipped down his gullet to fill his lungs and stomach with the dead weight of unliving alien matter.

*   *   *

The Cryptic Events Evaluation Section of the National Reconnaissance Office that day declared the Malbone Museum a Compromised Site and burned it to the ground after the sun had gone down.

By that time, they knew it was too late. For the shoggoth had retraced its leaden steps to Touro Park and resumed its petrified state and stance.

The body of the late James Anthony was discovered at the foot of one of the eight arched feet, his corpse intact, but his head encased in stone as if integral to it. They separated what could be buried from what couldn't. They never explained his fate, either.

When the charred remains of the Malbone Museum were later combed over by a CEES Containment and Contamination crew, they found only blackened gilt frames where the 78 paintings of the Esau Eldridge collection had hung. They were declared officially destroyed. Oriel Malbone's black vitrified bones were ground to powder and scattered off Brenton's Reef.

No trace of CEES Cartomancer First Class Gina Itri was ever uncovered, but in the Washington offices of the agency, her file was quietly transferred from Personnel to the Known Collaborators database.

No matter how many times they moved the file, it kept reappearing in Personnel, one brown eye closed in a knowing wink. ✳

An Arkham Home Companion

by Brad Strickland

W ell, it has been a quiet week in Arkham, Massachusetts, my home town, up there north of Boston where the hills rise wild. It started out as a wet week, with rain all day Sunday and then into Monday, but it cleared up pretty well by noon Tuesday. Of course that meant that all day Monday the New England Bachelor Farmers sat in the Hotbox Cafe and just about drove Dolly crazy complaining about the weather. Dolly ran her legs off pouring that strong black coffee for a bunch of frowning old men who never thanked her, but just went on and on about the rain: "Coulda used some of this back in May. Had a wet spell like this in May, June, ya know we'd have some good crops."

Now, they've *had* a good crop, as a matter of fact, about the best anyone in this town can remember, but when a New England Bachelor Farmer stops badmouthing God about the weather, why his friends begin to think what they're going to wear to his funeral. There is a man who has given up all interest in life.

We had a little excitement that began early in the week, Tuesday evening I think, or maybe it was Monday. No, I'm pretty sure it was Tuesday, because Lyle, the coach of the Miskatonic Mystics football team, was out for a late walk and it was raining Monday Night, so it pretty well had to be Tuesday night, about eleven o'clock, that the Whateley boy, Wilbur, turned into a tentacled horror from beyond the reaches of the Time and Space that we know, right in the Eliza Quiggley Peabody Memorial Reading Room of the Miskatonic University library.

Don't get me wrong, that wasn't the excitement in itself, because we know the Whateleys, of course. Now what happened was that Lyle Mergandanz, the coach at Miskatonic University, had been down in the dumps because our team, the Mystics, have not been doing all that well. We *have* improved since last year, now; last year at this time the team was 0 for 5, but we managed to lose one fewer game this year, and we're 0 for 4. Of course, that's only because back in September that mysterious meteorite crashed into the Mystics' field, blasting out about a thirty-foot diameter crater in the end zone, and the season had to be delayed until they had filled that in, not that the Mystics reached the end zone all that often, don't you know, but for the looks of the thing.

Well, Lyle had been complaining about the team's losing streak at dinner, and his wife, Cathy Lou, whom he met when she was a cheerleader and he was the star quarterback way back in college, Cathy Lou chirped up in that bright way she has and said, "Well, we went to college with Coach Daimler, for heaven's sake. Call him up and ask him to have his boys go easy on our team next Saturday, why don't you?"

And Lyle looked at this lovely, lovely woman, to whom he's been married for twenty-five years now, and he thought, *My God, you're dumb*. But he didn't say it out loud. That's why he's been married for twenty-five years. No, instead of saying anything to Cathy Lou, he went for a very long walk after dinner, and that's why, at a few minutes after eleven P.M., he found himself outside the library of Miskatonic University, and he heard the worst noise coming from inside that building he had ever heard in his life. It was Professor Armitage's big dog, Rameses, snarling and barking as if he had gone crazy.

Now, Lyle knows, of course, that Professor Armitage has made Rameses sleep in the library for years. The Professor has told everyone that it's to protect the University's copy of the *Necronomicon,* but Lyle knows the truth, just like everyone else. The truth is that the Professor sleeps in an old-fashioned nightshirt. He likes to sleep on his stomach, and that shirt kind of rides up sometimes, and Rameses is a very friendly dog. He is also healthy, so he has a very cold nose. So he sleeps in the library now.

Well, Lyle went running in to find out what in the world was going on, and Professor Armitage rushed in about the same time, and there on the floor was Wilbur Whateley, and that dog had just about ripped him to pieces. Lyle knew Wilbur. Everyone did. He was an unusual boy, always had been. He was fifteen years old, and he sort of favored his mother, the albino Lavinny Whateley. Nobody knows who Wilbur's father was, but the boy was unusual. He was fifteen years old, nearly nine feet tall, and he weighed about three hundred and fifty pounds. We knew that, but now that Rameses had torn Wilbur's shirt off, Lyle and the Professor could also see that Wilbur had about thirteen tentacles sprouting out of his midriff.

Lyle and Professor Armitage could see it was too late. Wilbur was obviously a goner, and Lyle stood there and he cried like a baby. He lifted his eyes up and said, "Oh, God, why? Why did you take this boy? Why did you take him, when we *need* a wide receiver who'd stick up above the crowd and have at least a chance of catching the ball?" So it was sad. It was a sad evening.

But the real excitement happened the next morning, Wednesday, when Professor Armitage invited some Harvard professors to come up and help him go up on Sentinel Hill and banish the spawn of Yog-Sothoth to the outer darkness, because of course we don't get visitors from the big city all that often. They had breakfast in the Hotbox Cafe before climbing up the hill, and Dolly thought one of them, the youngest one, was cute. And he was not wearing a wedding band. So while they were busy, Dolly whipped up one of her famous Boston Cream pies, the kind that would make a dead man come to life and ask for a large slice, on the off chance that they might come back.

And sure enough, the young fellow she had noticed did return. He came in after it was all over, and Dolly said, "Honey, you look like you could use a little something. Here, this is on the house." And she put a piece of pie and a cup of coffee in front of him.

But you know, there's something about facing one of the Great Old Ones that put that man off his feed. He drank a little of the coffee, and he looked at the pie, and he pushed it aside and went out.

Dolly started to cry a little as she took the piece of pie off the counter. She dabbed her eyes with a napkin and thought, *What's the matter with me? I'm twenty-seven years old, and no man has ever looked twice at me. What's wrong with me? Am I ugly?*

About then, Lyle came dragging in. He looked awful. He sat down at the counter and said, "How about some coffee, dolly?"

So she poured him a cup and she said, "Wasn't it terrible?"

And Lyle said, "You mean about Wilbur Whateley?" He started to sniffle. "That boy could have made the team," he said.

Well, that wasn't what Dolly had meant. She knew the Whateleys, and she might not have predicted that Wilbur would turn out to be a tentacled freak of nature, but she would have predicted something pretty close to that. Anyway, she said, "I think you need this. Here you go." And she put that piece of pie in front of him, and Lyle took a bite, and he started to smile.

And Dolly felt better, too. She was thinking to herself that Lavinny Whateley had been ugly as sin, an albino, with those little red eyes like a rat's, and skinny, and her nose had been like a pick-axe, but Wilbur had been living proof that Lavinny had found herself a catch. *And if Lavinny Whateley could find herself a catch,* Dolly thought, *there's hope for us all.*

And don't you know, that's the way I feel, too. The rain will pass. The sun will come out. There is hope for us all.

That's the news from Arkham, Massachusetts, where all the women are eldritch, all the men are decadent, and all the children are from beyond the reaches of Time and Space that we know. ✳

The Last Temptation
of Ricky Perez

by Benjamin Adams

Fear was my father, Father Fear
His look drained the stones.
—Theodore Roethke, 1948

Behind the El Paz Taqueria, in the alley reeking of grease and rotting lettuce, Ricky Perez faced the only future he thought open to him.

"It's simple," explained Malo, his thin, handsome features showing no emotion. "You just steal something from the old lady. Something valuable, right? Jewelry or something like that, man, you know. Silver or gold. Then you're in the gang."

Ricky nodded, sweat gathering at his temples. It was an unseasonably warm and humid afternoon for Palomar. He wished he hadn't worn the heavy and uncomfortable woolen blue plaid shirt. This was T-shirt weather. He could hear Snoop Doggy Dogg's funky "Gz and Hustlas" blasting from a car parked out on Layman Street, the low, pumping bass enough to rattle the trash cans in the alley.

He still couldn't believe he was here with Malo and the rest of the Vice Lord Disciples. This was what he'd wanted for so long. A chance for proving he was a man, worthy of respect; not a pitiful cripple, a birth defected mutant. He shifted slightly on his malformed right leg, feeling the extra inch on the sole of his black leather boot grind against the filthy pavement of the alley.

Malo's lieutenant, pockmarked Martín, smiled with a mouthful of bad teeth. A blue-and-black checked bandanna wrapped around his head, proudly announcing his affiliation with the Vice Lord Disciples. Back in the Sixth Grade, Martín had bullied Ricky and stolen his lunch money. It was time to let that be in the past, though. They would be in the same gang. They would be brothers.

But that momentary illusion shattered when Martín opened his mouth. "This cripple's not gonna make it, Malo. You're wastin' our time."

Ricky's heart sank to the bottom of his stomach. Damn Martín! Damn him!

Malo fixed his lieutenant with an icy glare. "His brother was one of us; we owe it to Joaquin's memory."

"Joaquin wasn't no cripple!" blurted Martín.

"Don't call me cripple," Ricky said softly, but steel ran through his words. Everyone turned to look.

There were twelve of them there, counting Ricky; the twelve Vice Lord Disciples. Once his brother Joaquin had been the twelfth: Malo's lieutenant before Martín. Quick Joaquin, agile Joaquin. So fast on the soccer field, so nimble with a combination lock. But not nimble or fast enough to evade a bullet to the back of his skull. A rival gang, Southtown F-Troop, had stolen Joaquin's life.

"Ha!" burst Martín. "You're a cripple and your father was a freak."

"I don't know who my father was, but I know you never saw him. And I'm *not* a cripple," Ricky said.

Martín took a menacing step toward him, but Malo gently held the larger boy back. "Then prove it," the gang leader replied in a voice barely above a whisper. "Tonight. Ten o'clock. Be back here at eleven. Don't fuck up, little man. Don't show me I've misplaced my trust."

*   *   *

Prove it.

The words repeated through Ricky's mind like a damaged compact disc hung up on a deep scratch.

He lay back on the ancient, faded *Star Wars* sheets covering his bed. His mother had bought the sheets at the Salvation Army store on Greist Street not long after Joaquin's death. When Ricky first saw them he'd been horrified, and knew that when he was grown he'd never buy anything used at a secondhand shop for his kids. He said as much to his mother and earned a crack against his face for it. Not another word was spoken about the sheets.

Ricky rolled over on his side and idly picked at a growing hole in the Imperial Death Star. *When I'm in the Vice Lord Disciples,* he thought, *I'll be able to bring home extra money the way Joaquin did—but I won't waste it on a car and fancy clothes, like him. And then we'll have new sheets for the apartment. We'll have new everything.*

I can make Mama proud.

All I have to do is break into that old woman's apartment.

That's all I have to do. . . .

He didn't know why the thought filled him with such trepidation. Old Mrs. Gonsalves had been a thorn in his ass for years. Not just in *his* ass, either—the old woman had been a scourge to all the kids in the neighborhood for as long as he could remember. Always poking her head out of her window and yelling for quiet down at children playing in the street. Getting the kids in trouble, calling their parents when she witnessed harmless horseplay.

There were other old folks in the neighborhood. Some were treated with all the respect due their age; others—the weirdoes, the cranks, the damaged-by-life—were teased mercilessly by the kids. Until their parents heard about it and punishments were meted out, which would tone the bad behavior down for about a day or two.

But Mrs. Gonsalves was different. The kids didn't respect her, but neither did they tease her. She was tolerated because she was feared. There was something odd about her, something that brooked no insouciance.

And Ricky had to break into her apartment and steal something—anything.

He had no choice. Malo and Martín had thrown down a challenge Ricky couldn't ignore for hope it would go away. If he backed out on the gang now, the punishment wouldn't just be ridicule. If any of them caught him alone on the street, he'd be beaten severely. Maybe even killed.

Executed, just like Joaquin. And not even by the F-Troopers—but by the kids he'd known all his life.

No! I won't let that happen! I'll prove myself to them and then they'll have to treat me as an equal—even that pendejo *Martín!*

"Ricky!" His mother's powerful, honking voice carried through the closed door of his room as if it were made of tissue paper. "Time for dinner!"

With a start, Ricky realized he'd daydreamed the entire afternoon and early evening away. Mama always had dinner ready at eight.

In two hours, he'd be busting in on old Mrs. Gonsalves' apartment.

* * *

"Where are you going tonight?" called mama from the beat-up green couch in the living room. Ricky paused by the front door of the apartment, his hand on the knob.

"Um . . . nowhere, really, mama. I'm just going to hang out with some friends."

"You come in here first," ordered Mrs. Perez.

Ricky heaved a sigh and stomped lopsidedly into the living room, his shorter leg vibrating with every blow of his thick-soled boot against the floor.

The ancient console television blared tinnily in the corner, its colors gone all wrong. Above the TV hung a cluster of framed, faded photographs, showing the Perez family through the years.

There were no photographs of Ricky's father. He'd never known the man, had no idea what he looked like. And Mrs. Perez never mentioned him. When pressed by her sons, she never said anything further than, "He was a bad man, a dark man. He was a monster."

A rosary hung from the corner of Joaquin's graduation picture. Mama drew her eyes away from the television and fixed them fuzzily on Ricky.

"What?" he demanded.

"Now—now you tell me to my face where you are going."

"Like I said, I'm gonna hang out with my friends."

She studied his face for a moment. "You be careful, Ricky. You are a special boy. You are not like those others."

"Mama—"

"No, no, you listen to me. You are almost a man now and can make your own choices. But I already lost one son because he made the wrong choice; I cannot bear the thought of losing another one."

"Mama, you're not going to lose me. I'll be right here, taking care of you."

Mrs. Perez looked away from Ricky, toward the row of family pictures. Her eyes lit on Joaquin's graduation photo. She creaked to her feet and walked to the photograph, lifting the dusty rosary from its corner.

He blinked, feeling a sudden speck of dirt in his eye. *Joaquin.*

"Do not make me count the beads once again, Ricky. Make me proud of you."

"I will, Mama. I will."

He turned away so she couldn't see the tear starting down his cheek.

"I'll be back later tonight. Don't worry about me."

Ricky walked back to the front door. In moments he was down on the street, moving as quickly as he could away from his apartment building, the uneven clacking of his soles against the hard, cold pavement like the clicking together of so many rosary beads.

* * *

Old Mrs. Gonsalves lived over on Aster Street in a dissolute apartment building that looked as if it had already been torn down, but no one had remembered to tell it to collapse.

Ricky skittered into the slender alley between the building and the *supermercado* next door. His bad foot hit something heavy and soft that hissed loudly and ran off into the impenetrable darkness at the rear of the alley, back where the Dumpsters were kept.

Three feet above his head was the heavy wrought iron of the building's fire escape. Ricky made a feeble jump and missed grabbing hold of it by several inches. "Oh, *fuck*," he muttered, coming down badly and almost twisting his good ankle.

He leaned against the rough brick wall of the building and wondered what he would do next.

Maybe Martín is right. Maybe I am just a cripple. Anyone else could make that jump. Anyone at all. A three-year-old could do it.

From further back in the alley came a metallic crash and a yowl, followed by an urgent scrabbling of claws on the pavement.

Ricky flinched at the sound. That damn cat he'd accidentally kicked was messing around with the Dumpsters, must have fallen off—

A slow grin crossed his face, and he fought the temptation to smack his forehead. *Duh!*

The Dumpsters!

Ricky walked toward the rear of the alley, his feet knocking aside tin cans and crunching through wads of ancient newspaper. His outstretched hand touched the cool metal of a Dumpster, and he shoved it experimentally. With a creaking groan, it moved a couple of inches on rusty casters.

Good enough, he thought, walking to the rear of the Dumpster. With a slight grunt, he began pushing it forward. *Yeah, this makes things a bit easier. Vice Lord Disciples, here I come.*

It was heavier than he expected. Maybe the alley was built on an upward slant or something.

It stank, too, with the sickly-sweet smell of rot and decay, like Hawaiian Punch gone bad. And another, more sour smell, like—like the smell of Joaquin's body at his funeral—the scent of death itself—

Abruptly, jarringly, the Dumpster quit moving. Ricky pulled up short to avoid colliding with it. "Shit," he muttered, giving the thing an impotent whack with his fist.

He gave himself a new footing and applied pressure against the Dumpster again. It rocked slightly, but refused to budge another inch.

Ricky wandered around the Dumpster, eyeing the casters. Sure enough, one of the front casters had stuck in a small pothole in the alley pavement.

Black thoughts rolled through Ricky's head.

A sudden soft *thud* and *clang* on the Dumpster lid caught his attention, and he looked up. A fat black cat sat there, staring at him with wide black eyes encircled with a thin border of yellow. Half-a-white mustache decorated its quizzical face, but it appeared to have no other markings.

"Ah, Señor Gato Negro," said Ricky gently. "Have you come just to mock me, or do you have any ideas?"

The cat stared back at Ricky solemnly, then looked overhead. He followed its glance, his eyes growing wide as he saw.

The fire escape ladder was just barely reachable from the edge of the Dumpster.

If he jumped.

Ricky glared back at the cat, which was now busily grooming its hindquarters. "Oh, thank you very much, Señor Gato."

The cat gave him a brief, disdainful look, then jumped from the Dumpster lid and disappeared back down the alley.

Sighing, Ricky placed his hands on the sticky surface of the Dumpster and hoisted himself up. He crouched on top of the Dumpster and eyed the fire escape ladder, seemingly a million miles away. Certainly it had appeared closer when he'd still been on the ground.

"If I break my neck, Señor Gato, it's all *your* fault!" he hissed in the direction in which the cat had scurried.

No response. How like a cat.

Ricky drew himself to his full height. Now the end of the ladder was only a foot away. A foot may as well be a million miles, if he missed.

He couldn't miss. Not now.

He sank back down into a partial crouch, then sprang at the ladder.

As his feet pushed against the Dumpster lid, the whole damn thing began sliding away, the stuck caster bouncing out of the pothole at the sudden change in balance.

Ricky's hands closed around the bottom rung.

"God!" he whispered in pain. He had no idea how much it would sting, how the weight of his body would grind his palms against the loose paint and rust on the rung.

But his hands held, despite the burning in his palms and the stinging in his arms. Slowly he began hoisting himself up, rung by rung, until finally his feet rested on the bottom step.

Allowing himself a deep sigh, Ricky looked down.

Instantly he swayed with vertigo. *That's a long way down. A long, long way down. Even if I jump from here, I'd probably miss the top of the Dumpster.*

He closed his eyes and began climbing the ladder, not opening them again until he had reached the safety of the first landing.

Only two more floors to Mrs. Gonsalves' apartment, Ricky realized then.

He was almost there.

* * *

Through the dusty window Ricky saw no lights, no movement within the apartment. Mrs. Gonsalves was probably asleep; old people liked to turn in early, though Ricky had never understood why.

Malo had explained that people on upper floors tended not to have locks on their windows, somehow under the impression that no one would go to that much trouble to break in. Ricky hoped Mrs. Gonsalves was among that deluded group.

He pushed upward on the sash of the window, expecting to meet some resistance.

Instead, the window glided up effortlessly, almost banging against the top of the frame.

Ricky's heart pounded, and he gently let go of the window. It stayed in place. Plenty of room for him to squeeze through. Plenty of room.

He stuck his head through and looked around. The old woman sure had a lot of furniture. It all looked like antiques—Malo was probably right when he thought she had gold and silver stuff. The air smelled . . . dry and dusty . . . but with something else underneath it, like sweet, aged perfume.

Grabbing hold of the edge of the windowsill from the inside, Ricky pulled himself forward. He clambered over the sill and placed his feet on the floor.

He was inside.

So far, so good—

Behind him, the window slammed shut with a loud *crash!* that made his spine stiffen and the hair on the back of his neck stand on end.

At once, all the lights in the room blinked on: ancient hurricane lamps; gaudy blown-glass bowls of many colors; tall, elegant brass poles with fringed shades; and a crystal chandelier swaying softly from the ceiling, tinkling in an unseen breeze.

In the center of the room stood Mrs. Gonsalves, her bright green eyes examining Ricky with piercing severity. Around her ankles rubbed a fat black cat with half-a-white mustache on its face, also staring at Ricky with inscrutable intentions.

"Welcome, my young housebreaker," she said, in the elegant, singsong patois of Castilian Spanish. "We have much to discuss, I think. Yes. We have much to discuss."

* * *

Slender and powder-white, her salt-and-pepper hair piled in a bun on top of her head, Mrs. Gonsalves sat Ricky down in a high-backed chair. Then she sat in its twin, facing the young man across a narrow table of highly-polished dark wood.

Ricky looked down at the table, ashamed to meet Mrs. Gonsalves' eyes. He could see his reflection there; distorted and corrupted by the grain of the wood, he looked like a monster. *Maybe,* he thought, *this is what I look like on the inside. All twisted up, mutated. Just like my leg is on the outside.*

He was aware of Mrs. Gonsalves' gaze burning into him, but couldn't look away from that reflection. It seemingly shimmered, shifting somehow while he watched. One moment he saw in the table a monster; the next, his brother Joaquin's face stared back at him with his own eyes.

"Do not stare long at the table," Mrs. Gonsalves cautioned him finally. "You may not like what it reveals."

"Huh? What?" Ricky jerked back to reality.

"You are Ricardo Perez," Mrs. Gonsalves said.

By the tone of her voice he knew it wasn't a question, so he waited for her to continue. The black cat chose that moment to rub up against the old woman's legs.

"Come up here, Te-Te. Yes; good."

With the black cat in her lap, its wide eyes locked on Ricky, she went on.

"I have seen many of you children grow up, down in the street. Some, I knew, were earmarked for destruction at an early age. I could see it above them, around them, like a dark cloud embracing their every move. Others were good and gracious children; they will live long and happy lives. Some were good and yet are doomed. That, too, I can see. It is the way of the Old Ones. *Ïa! Cthulhu fhtagn!*

"You, Ricardo Perez, have always been an enigma to me. Your future is misty; uncertain. You have choices to make, young man. You determine your own destiny. Tonight, you are at a crossroads, but I fear you may have already turned down the wrong path."

She paused, fingers slowly kneading the fur at the back of the cat's neck.

Ricky felt lost. He couldn't understand what the old woman was saying; her odd Castilian accent put a spin on the words, made them hard to grasp.

"Look, Mrs. Gonsalves, I'm sorry. It was a really stupid thing I did, breaking in here."

"Yes, it was. But this, at least, is one thing in which you had no choice. I foresaw it long ago. I knew that one day you and I would meet this way. Foolish, brash youth. You need not prove anything to anybody except yourself."

"How—how do you know so much about me?" blurted Ricky. Strangely, he wasn't afraid of her any longer. Instead he burned with curiosity, sensing that here was a rare opportunity for learning, for knowing more about himself and his place in the world. Malo, Martín and the rest of the Vice Lord Disciples might as well have been a million miles away, as he stared into her eyes and listened. "Do you—did you—know my father?"

The old woman scowled and shook her head. "No, no. Listen to the words I speak and do not confuse them with your own thoughts. I said there is much unknown about you to me; any truths you hear are only generalities. All I can tell you is that you are your father's son."

But as she said it, he knew it was the first falsehood she'd spoken to him. Disappointed, he looked down at the highly-polished table again.

As before, his reflection glimmered and roiled in the table's high gloss. He saw himself, at first; but then the image shifted and dissolved into that of his brother, Joaquin. This had happened the first time he looked at the table, but something was different now.

Behind Joaquin's face was not reflected an image of the room in which Ricky now sat, but instead the gritty alleyway just behind the El Paz Taqueria.

Further down the alley was a shadowy figure moving toward Joaquin, who chewed nervously on the end of a toothpick and reached up to adjust his hat. If he heard the figure, Joaquin showed no sign, but perhaps he knew who it was.

Martín.

A clammy hand clutched Ricky's heart as he watched, unable to tear his eyes away.

In one casual motion Martín lifted the untucked tail of his oversized flannel shirt, reached into the waistband of his baggy jeans and pulled out an ugly-looking little silver gun, aiming it at the back of Joaquin's head. Martín's pockmarked face showed no emotion whatsoever. Still moving, he pulled the trigger—

Ricky tried screaming, but the sound remained stuck in his throat. He finally pulled his eyes away from the table, but too late—he had seen the awful betrayal of his brother by Martín.

"Life is a series of choices," reminded Mrs. Gonsalves. "The table reflects choices that have been made, that will be made."

"What does it show for—for me?" choked Ricky.

She shrugged. "As I said before, you are an enigma. You are special, Ricardo. The Old Ones have put their mark upon you. Your future I cannot divine. No one may except yourself."

In Mrs. Gonsalves' words he heard an echo of those of his mother: *You are a special boy. You are not like those others.*

He nodded, understanding slowly dawning over him like the warm rays of the summer sun. *The Old ones have put their mark upon you. You are your father's son.*

"My foot," he whispered. "That's the mark you mean."

Mrs. Gonsalves closed her eyes and smiled faintly. "Perhaps you are not so blind after all."

"Who is my father?"

"A dark man," Mrs. Gonsalves breathed through barely parted lips.

Te-Te, the mustachioed cat, suddenly stiffened and hissed in Mrs. Gonsalves' lap, glancing behind Ricky toward the window through which he had crawled. Almost involuntarily, the boy followed the cat's gaze.

Shapes at the window. Two people on the fire escape, trying to jimmy open the window.

"God, no," murmured Ricky. "It's Malo and Martín."

He looked around wildly, for some avenue of escape.

The window finally gave and began sliding open inch-by-inch, creaking in bitter protest.

Ricky's frantic gaze fell on Mrs. Gonsalves, who leaned back in her seat with a slight smile on her face.

"Come on!" he said. "We've got to get out of here!"

"It is of no concern," she replied sanguinely.

Now the voices of the two intruders could be heard. "I told you, I saw him go in here a couple of hours ago," came Martín's thin whine. "He never came back out, either through the alley or the front door of the building."

A couple of hours? wondered Ricky. *But I haven't even been in here thirty minutes.*

"We'll find out in a minute, man; you don't need to keep explaining yourself," hissed Malo.

"I think the little crippled fucker found somethin' and ripped us off, man—"

"That's it!" snapped Malo. "Shut the fuck up, Martín! I'm trying to concentrate. Damn, it's dark in there."

Ricky glanced around at all the brightly shining lights in the room and wondered what Malo could possibly mean.

Mrs. Gonsalves' smile was even wider now. Her green eyes positively sparkled with amusement. She held up one forefinger at Ricky, as if to say, *See?*

The leader and lieutenant of the Vice Lord Disciples finally squeezed through the window and stood in Mrs. Gonsalves' living room, peering around as if mired in complete darkness.

"I can't see a fuckin' thing," complained Martín.

Malo reached out his left arm and *thwacked* his lieutenant across the chest. "Shut up, man," he whispered, his words dripping ice.

Ricky saw a look of pure malice and hatred for Malo cross Martín's face. *He's going to assassinate Malo,* Ricky realized with a cold jolt through his spine.

Just the same as Joaquin.

The gang leader's eyes finally seemed to have acclimated to the darkness he thought filled the room. "What a load of junk," Malo muttered. "Look at this—milk crates, wadded-up newspaper, cereal boxes . . . maybe Ricky couldn't even find anything worth grabbing."

"Then where is he?" demanded Martín.

"Maybe he got delayed somehow," Malo shrugged. "On the way to the meeting."

"I think he chickened out. I think we ought to teach the little cripple a lesson."

"That's not up to you, man," Malo hissed back. "He's Joaquin's brother and we owe him a chance."

Martín smiled viciously. "The way you stand up for him, maybe you're in love with the little fucker." His hand started creeping for the waistband of his baggy jeans.

When Malo finally replied, the sheer venom in his voice shocked Ricky. "You're *out*, Martín. Do you get me? When we get back to the street, you are *so* fucking out on your ass. No one will talk to you. No one will even want to be near you, not even those F-Troop fuckers in Southtown. You're finished in Palomar."

"No, *you're* finished," said Martín, drawing his little silver pistol and leveling it at Malo.

Malo said nothing as he looked from the gun, to his traitorous lieutenant's face, then back again.

The moment dragged on forever. Ricky looked helplessly at Mrs. Gonsalves, who no longer wore a smile. There was something in the look on her face, like she knew what to do, but was choosing not to act. *It's up to me,* Ricky thought. *There's got to be something I can do. Or else Martín's going to get away with murder again.*

Something snapped inside Ricky. He suddenly knew exactly what he had to do. He propelled himself from the chair toward Martín. For once, Ricky's feet worked in perfect unison; no missteps, no stumbles. A human rocket aimed straight for Joaquin's murderer.

Away from Mrs. Gonsalves, the lights faded and died. The room plunged into darkness, and Ricky knew this was what the two gang members had seen, as if he and the old woman hadn't even been in the room. A moment later he barreled into Martín, sending the lieutenant sprawling to the floor. The gun clattered out of his hand and skittered across the hardwood floor.

"Get—get off of me, you fuckin' cripple!" screamed Martín.

"You killed my brother, you bastard!" Ricky knelt with his knees on either side of Martín's chest, raining blows down on the older boy's face.

Ricky's hands became like bludgeons. He barely registered the change as he beat the older boy. Bones shifted and lengthened under the skin. Long stripes of blood appeared on Martín's face as he screamed under Ricky's attack.

In the midst of retrieving his lieutenant's pistol from the floor, Malo's head whipped around at Martín's cries.

"Mother of God—*what the hell are you?*" burst the gang leader.

Ricky glanced up. What did Malo mean? And then Ricky saw his shadow cast by the moon, upon the floor. It was all wrong—his joints bent in strange angles, his head a shaggy mass humped upon his shoulders. *The monster . . . the monster he'd seen when he looked in the reflective depths of the table. . . .*

He looked at his hands. Like claws they were, with fingers nine inches long, coated with some kind of black stuff like the shell of an insect. Glistening with blood and gore from the wrecked, pulped mass of Martín's face.

The Old ones have put their mark upon you.

"Malo," Ricky said. "It's me. It's Ricky Perez." But the sounds that emerged from his throat were scratching, buzzing noises with only the faintest resemblance to human speech.

Malo leveled the pistol and fired. The bullet whizzed past Ricky's head so closely he could feel it, a mosquito made of hot lead.

Ricky didn't waste any more time. He leaped away from Martín's body toward the window over Mrs. Gonsalves' fire escape. He took one last look toward Malo, and saw the shadows of the room advancing toward the gang leader, like black tendrils of darkest night.

Ricky ran down the cast-iron steps of the ladder, taking them two-by-two until he jumped off the bottom. He leapt the final distance to the ground and rolled, scraping his elbows and knees painfully. Then he reached his feet and walked away from the alley and the apartment building as quickly as he could. With every step his bones seemed to shrink and return to normal beneath his torn clothing.

He was half-a-block away when he heard the scream and single gunshot echo down the deserted street.

* * *

Mama had fallen asleep on the tattered green couch, the TV casting its pale blue light over her form like an intangible sheet. As her chest rose and fell she wheezed softly, a slight smell of mint on her breath. In her right hand she still clutched the rosary beads tightly, holding them dear against her chest.

With trembling fingers—his own, normal fingers—Ricky carefully prised the rosary loose from her pudgy fingers. The beads clattered softly. For a moment he contemplated holding them to his lips to kiss the tiny form of Jesus on the cross. *No. That way is closed to me forever now. I am my father's son.* Then he silently stepped across the room and replaced the beads on the picture of Joaquin.

Upstairs, Ricky washed his familiar face and went around the normal routine of getting ready for bed. He winced, seeing the abrasions on his elbows and knees as he undressed. His bad leg ached from the unnatural abuse and strain it had suffered tonight.

He could almost put the whole thing down as a nightmare if it weren't for those cuts and bruises and the unnatural ache in his bones. Every shifting, unnatural pain told him the events of the evening were real, that he had the blood of a monster within him. His father, the dark man.

At least some things never change, he reflected as he took off his special boot, and regarded his deformed foot. The one that curled inward and became a cloven hoof.

He still didn't know who his father was, but at last he knew *what* his father was, and that was enough for a start.

Star Wars or no, the cool comforting sheets on his bed felt wonderful. And the breeze filtering in through his open window felt equally as nice. He felt sleep mere moments away—

Something thudded on his bed, and his eyes popped open. A round, feline face with half-a-white mustache stared into his; unblinking, inscrutable. Then the cat, Te-Te, quietly padded down the side of Ricky's body and laid down next to him, curling up directly on top of Darth Vader's faded form.

"When Mrs. Gonsalves shows up, you're going right back to her," Ricky said with a yawn, scratching the back of the cat's neck fondly.

The cat murmured something vaguely dismissive in return, and soon they were both asleep. Cats know no monsters, after all; they only know who they love. ✳

ABOUT THE CONTRIBUTORS

Benjamin adams believes that in order to get to the essence of Lovecraft, one must appreciate cats. Because there's something cats know that they ain't lettin' us in on. . . .

Scott david aniolowski is an active member of the Horror Writers Association and the editor of *Made in Goatswood, Singers of Strange Songs, Return to Lovecraft Country,* and *Beyond the Lamplight.* His own fiction has appeared in *Cthulhu's Heirs, Made in Goatswood, Tales Out of Innsmouth* from Chaosium, *365 Scary Stories* from Barnes & Noble, and *Deathrealm* magazine. Two of his stories, "I Dream of Wires" from *Made in Goatswood* and "Mr. Bauble's Bag" from *365 Scary Stories* were chosen for the Recommended Reading list in *The Year's Best Fantasy & Horror.* He has also written dozens of articles and scenarios for the *Call of Cthulhu* roleplaying game over the past fifteen years. In the real world, Scott is an executive chef, and a fan of British comedies, Vincent Price films, New England travels, and too many brilliant authors to mention.

A. a. attanasio resides in Hawaii with his family, where he earns his living by his imagination.

Edward p. berglund retired from the U.S. Marine Corps and became an independent paralegal in Jacksonville, North Carolina. He edited the first *The Disciples of Cthulhu* for DAW Books (1976) and the revised version from Chaosium Books (1996). He compiled the second edition of the *Reader's Guide to the Cthulhu Mythos* with Robert Weinberg (1974). A collection of his Cthulhu Mythos stories, entitled *Shards of Darkness,* was published by Mythos Books in 2000. Currently he edits the Cthulhu Mythos-related ezine *Nightscapes* and runs the *Reader's Guide to the Cthulhu Mythos* website, a one-stop guide to the Mythos on the Internet (http://www.toddalan. com/~berglund/). He is an associate member of the Horror Writers Association.

Donald r. burleson is the author of three novels: *Flute Song, Arroyo,* and *A Roswell Christmas Carol.* His short stories have appeared in *Twilight Zone, The Magazine of Fantasy and Science*

Fiction, 2AM, Lore, Terminal Fright, Deathrealm, Wicked Mystic, and many other magazines, as well as in dozens of major anthologies, including *100 Creepy Little Creature Stories, 100 Wicked Little Witch Stories, 100 Vicious Little Vampire Stories, 100 Ghastly Little Ghost Stories, 100 Fiendish Little Frightmares, Horrors! 365 Scary Stories, 100 Twisted Little Tales of Torment, Best New Horror, Post Mortem, MetaHorror, Dark Terrors 4, Return to Lovecraft Country, Made in Goatswood, Singers of Strange Songs, The Azathoth Cycle,* and *The Cthulhu Cycle.* Burleson's short story collections include *Beyond the Lamplight* (Jack O'Lantern Press), *Lemon Drops and Other Horrors* (Hobgoblin Press), and *Four Shadowings* (Necronomicon Press). Burleson and his wife Mollie, who is also a horror writer, live in Roswell, New Mexico, where he writes a monthly UFO column and serves as a Field Investigator and Research Consultant for MUFON, the Mutual UFO Network, and as the director of a computer lab at Eastern New Mexico University.

WALTER C. DEBILL, JR. was born in 1939. He discovered Poe at 10, and at 13, after a foggy night walk to the library, H. P. Lovecraft. After writing short fiction for almost thirty years, he retired from his programming career to write full time. His current interests, besides writing, include foreign languages, music, ikebana, pool and birding. Walt lives in Austin, Texas.

HENRY LEE FORREST is the name under which John *Henry* Campbell, Terry *Lee* Sanders and Oreta *Forrestine* Hinamon Taylor collaborate. All three have been reading science-fiction since they learned to read. They write regularly for the Atlanta Radio Theatre Company, but this is their first published short story.

JOHN CAMPBELL is a recent victim of the telecommunications stock collapse, and is currently seeking new and unexpected ways to keep the wolves from his door. He is of good Southern Scots-Cherokee ancestry (no relation to the late editor of *Analog*), and is the former property of a cat named Astrophe, but is presently between owners.

TERRY SANDERS programs mainframe computers (yes, SOME people still use them) while waiting to become rich and famous.

Anticipated careers include writer, singer, actor, and lottery winner. Other suggestions are welcome.

O RETA HINAMON TAYLOR is married and has two children. She is presently an office manager for an investment firm. She has always hated her middle name, "Forrestine," and is glad to finally find a good use for it.

C. J. HENDERSON, creator of the Teddy London supernatural detective series, has written Mythos based novels, short stories and comics for the past twenty years. A large, looming gray-bearded man, his take on the Mythos is not quite the same as that held by most devotees of the genre. Still, it's driven him insane enough to have written the included story, which he hopes you enjoyed.

B RAD LINAWEAVER is the author of the award-winning novel *Moon of Ice,* which has appeared in both hardback and paperback in America and has been published in England. He's sold about 70 short stories and 300 articles. He is the only author of books based on the *Sliders* television series. He is co-author, with Dafydd ab Hugh, of four *Doom* novels, based on the popular video game from Id Software. As an editor, he has co-edited *Weird Menace* with filmmaker Fred Olen Ray and *Free Space* with Ed Kramer. He shares original story credit on *Jack-O,* the last film of John Carradine. He also had a number of scripts produced on radio (including NPR) and is a frequent collaborator with the Atlanta Radio Theatre Company, which has done a number of Lovecraft programs. Brad also wrote a Lovecraftian story for *Miskatonic University,* "Scavenger Hunt."

W ILL MURRAY is the author of over fifty novels in such series as *Doc Savage, Destroyer, Executioner, Mars Attacks* and others. A frequent contributor to *Crypt of Cthulhu* and *Lovecraft Studies* for many years, his Mythos fiction has appeared in *The Cthulhu Cycle, The Shub-Niggurath Cycle* and *Miskatonic University,* among other anthologies. Much of "The Eldridge Collection" chronicles the efforts of the Cryptic Events Evaluation Section of the Department of Defense to preserve the Earth from Things Out There.

As one of the founding members of the Friends of H. P. Lovecraft, he helped raise the funds which placed a memorial plaque dedicated to HPL on the grounds of the John Hay Library at Brown

University on the occasion of the centennial of Lovecraft's birth. Murray also works as a professional psychic and is a Master Remote Viewer certified by Remote Viewing Technologies International. His most recent novel, *Nick Fury, Agent of S.H.I.E.L.D.: Empyre,* predicted the operational details of the September 11, 2001 terrorist attacks on the US.

GARY (CLAYTON) MYERS (born 1952) fell under the shadow of H. P. Lovecraft at the tender age of sixteen and never completely escaped it. His earliest stories, double pastiches of Lovecraft and Dunsany, began to appear in August Derleth's *The Arkham Collector* in 1970; the complete cycle was later published by Arkham House as *The House of the Worm* in 1975. He recently finished work on a new cycle of Lovecraftian horrors in modern settings; some of these have already appeared in genre magazines and theme anthologies like the Chaosium series. In real life Gary is a computer programmer of over twenty years' standing. He lives in Fullerton, California with his wife Jennifer, their cats Jorkens and Greystoke, and extensive collections of fantasy books and movies.

ROBERT M. PRICE discovered Lovecraft at the ripe old age of 13 when he stumbled upon a copy of the Lancer paperback *The Colour out of Space.* He was hooked for time and eternity. Born in Jackson, Mississippi in 1954, Price moved to New Jersey at age 10. Except for brief sojourns in New England for graduate study and teaching in North Carolina, he has lived in NJ ever since, until just recently he returned to North Carolina. He is married to Carol Selby Price, with whom he co-authored *Mystic Rhythms: The Philosophical Vision of RUSH.* Their daughters are Victoria (age 13) and Veronica (11). Price's articles on Lovecraft and related subjects have appeared in *Lovecraft Studies,* his own *Crypt of Cthulhu,* and in various critical anthologies. His fiction has appeared in *Nyctalops, Etchings & Odysseys, Footsteps, Grue,* and others. He edits Mythos anthology series for Fedogan & Bremer, Chaosium Inc., and Mythos Books.

FRED OLEN RAY has been writing, producing and directing money-making feature films of every kind and nature. Considered an expert in bringing in profitable films on time and on budget he has become, as *Variety* described him, "a Fantasy Specialist." In recent years Fred has made films for Paramount, 20th

Century Fox, and Columbia Tri-Star. These films include *Submerged, Mach 2, Critical Mass, and Venomous.* Fred has featured prominently on such TV programs as *Entertainment Tonight, Hard Copy,* Stephen King's *World of Horror,* CNN's *Show Biz Today,* and was the subject of a half-hour British television series episode hosted by Jonathan Ross called *The Incredibly Strange Film Show.* Fred authored a hardback book entitled *The New Poverty Row: Independent Filmmakers as Distributors,* which outlines the world marketplace from the 1950s till now. He also writes for several national magazines and is himself the subject of numerous magazine articles and interviews, one such in *Entertainment Weekly.* Fred has also written a number of short stories in anthologies, such as *Adventure in The Twilight Zone* and *Strange Attraction.*

B RAD STRICKLAND has written or co-written forty-five novels, many of them books for young readers. He has continued the popular mystery-horror series for teen-agers begun by the late John Bellairs, most recently with *The Tower at the End of the World.* Occasionally, Brad also contributes to Garrison Keillor's radio program *A Prairie Home Companion.* In addition to writing, Brad teaches English at Gainesville College. He and his wife Barbara live in Oakwood, Georgia.

R OBERT WEINBERG is the author of more than a dozen novels and two dozen short stories. He's also written ten non-fiction books and edited over a hundred and thirty anthologies. He's won two World Fantasy Awards and a Bram Stoker Award from the Horror Writers Association. At present, he's scripting *Nightside,* a creator-owned comic for Marvel Comics.

SINGERS OF STRANGE SONGS

Most readers acknowledge Brian Lumley as the superstar of British horror writers. With the great popularity of his *Necroscope* series, he is one of the best known horror authors in the world. Devoted fans know that his roots are deep in the Cthulhu Mythos, with which most of his early work deals. This volume contains eleven new tales in that vein, as well as three reprints of excellent but little-known work by Lumley. This book was published in conjunction with Lumley's 1997 trip to the United States.

5 3/8" x 8 3/8", 244 pages, $12.95. Stock #6014; ISBN 1-56882-104-2.

THE XOTHIC LEGEND CYCLE

The late Lin Carter was a prolific writer and anthologist of horror and fantasy with over eighty titles to his credit. His tales of Mythos horror are loving tributes to H. P. Lovecraft's "revision" tales and to August Derleth's stories of Hastur and the *R'lyeh Text*. This is the first collection of Carter's Mythos tales; it includes his intended novel, *The Terror Out of Time*. Most of the stories in this collection have been unavailable for some time. Selected and introduced by Robert M. Price.

5 3/8" x 8 3/8", 274 pages, $10.95. Stock #6013; ISBN 1-56882-078-X.

NAMELESS CULTS

Robert E. Howard is the world-renowned author of the *Conan* series and the stories that were the basis of the recent *Kull* movie. He frequently corresponded with H. P. Lovecraft, and authored many pivotal Mythos tales. This book collects together all of Howard's Mythos tales, including those which originated Gol-Goroth, the *Black Book (Unaussprechlichen Kulten),* and Friedrich Von Junzt—all the stories that are usually considered his Cthulhu Mythos yarns, plus another batch that make use of Arthur Machen's lore of the Little People and help fill out the picture implicit in a couple of the overt Mythos tales. A third group are tales which Howard did not intend in a Lovecraftian vein but which feature creations later assimilated into the Mythos, whether by Howard, Lovecraft, or later writers. Four Howard fragments are presented here with additional text by Robert M. Price, C. J. Henderson, Joe Pulver, and August Derleth.

5 3/8" x 8 3/8", 376 pages, $15.95. Stock #6028; ISBN 1-56882-130-1.

THE NECRONOMICON
Second Revised Edition

Although skeptics claim that the *Necronomicon* is a fantastic tome created by H. P. Lovecraft, true seekers into the esoteric mysteries of the world know the truth: The *Necronomicon* is a blasphemous tome of forbidden knowledge written by the mad Arab, Abdul Alhazred. Even today, after attempts over the centuries to destroy any and all copies in any language, some few copies still exist, secreted away. Within this book you will find stories about the *Necronomicon*, different versions of the *Necronomicon*, and two essays on the blasphemous tome. Now you too may learn the true lore of Abdul Alhazred. Selected and introduced by Robert M. Price.

5 3/8" x 8 3/8", 334 pages, $12.95. Stock #6012; ISBN 1-56882-070-4.

NIGHTMARE'S DISCIPLE

Even in the modern day, horrors arise in Innsmouth. In this brand-new novel the curse of the Marshes falls upon an entirely new generation when a serial killer terrorizes Schenectady, New York. Detective Christopher James Stewart must follow a trail of mutilated bodies and piece together enigmatic clues before the murderer strikes again. Here is a wealth of terror and exuberant scenes, a detailed Cthulhu Mythos novel of the present day. Warning: contains explicit scenes.

5 3/8" x 8 3/8", 400 pages, $14.95. Stock #6018; ISBN 1-56882-118-2.

THE BOOK OF DZYAN

Mme. Blavatsky's famous transcribed messages from beyond, the mysterious *Book of Dzyan,* the heart of the sacred books of Kie-te, are said to have been known only to Tibetan mystics. Quotations from *Dzyan* form the core of her closely-argued *The Secret Doctrine,* the most influential single book of occult knowledge to emerge from the nineteenth century. The text of this book reproduces nearly all of *Book of Dzyan* that Blavatsky transcribed. It also includes long excerpts from her *Secret Doctrine* as well as from the Society of Psychical Research's 1885 report concerning phenomena witnessed by members of the Theosophical Society. There are notes and additional shorter materials. Editor Tim Maroney's biographical essay starts off the book, a fascinating portrait of an amazing woman.

5 3/8" x 8 3/8", 272 pages, $13.95. Stock #6027; ISBN 1-56882-114-X.

THE ITHAQUA CYCLE

The elusive, supernatural Ithaqua roams the North Woods and the wastes beyond, as invisible as the wind. Hunters and travelers fear the cold and isolation of the North; they fear the advent of the mysterious, malignant Wind-Walker even more. This collection includes the progenitor tale "The Wendigo" by Algernon Blackwood, three stories by August Derleth, and ten more from a spectrum of contemporary authors including Brian Lumley, Stephen Mark Rainey, and Pierre Comtois.

5 3/8" x 8 3/8", 260 pages, $12.95. Stock #6021; ISBN 1-56882-124-7.

TALES OUT OF INNSMOUTH

Innsmouth is a half-deserted, seedy little town on the North Shore of Massachusetts. It is rarely included on any map of the state. Folks in neighboring towns shun those who come from Innsmouth, and murmur about what goes on there. They try not to mention the place in public, for Innsmouth has ways of quelling gossip, and of taking revenge on troublemakers. Here are ten new tales and three reprints concerning the town, the hybrids who live there, the strange city rumored to exist nearby under the sea, and those who nightly lurch and shamble down the fog-bound streets of Innsmouth.

5 3/8" x 8 3/8", 294 pages, $13.95. Stock #6024; ISBN 1-56882-127-1.

THE YELLOW SIGN AND OTHER STORIES

This book contains all the immortal tales of Robert W. Chambers, including "The Repairer of Reputations," "The Yellow Sign," and "The Mask." These titles are often found in survey anthologies. In addition to the six stories reprinted from *The Yellow Sign* (1895), this book also offers more than two dozen other stories and episodes. These narratives rarely appear in print. Some have not been published in nearly a century.

This is a complete collection of Robert W. Chambers' short weird fiction—his published horror, science fiction, and fantasy/supernatural, as well as some self-conscious whimsy. The writing can be facile and out of fashion, of interest to collectors and those desiring to comprehend the writer. But other stories are as delicate and durable as those wrought by Lord Dunsany, and worthy of every reader's time.

5 3/8" x 8 3/8", 652 pages, $19.95. Stock #6023; ISBN 1-56882-126-3.

THE BOOK OF EIBON

Tales of lore tell of the *Book of Eibon,* a tome so ancient that it was originally written in the Hyperborean language of Tsath-Yo, long before Atlantis was born from the sea. It goes by dozens of names and predates even the *Necronomicon* and *Unaussprechlichen Kulten.* Now, Chaosium reveals the true secrets of the *Book of Eibon* for the first time.

The contents of the *Book of Eibon* are primarily the work of Clark Ashton Smith, one of the most famous authors of *Weird Tales* and the inventor of the *Book of Eibon.* Lin Carter, esteemed fantasy and horror editor Robert Price, Richard Tierney, Joseph Pulver, and a number of other authors have helped complete the text, resulting in a tome that reveals all the secrets of the Cthulhu Mythos, from the history of the first alien races to come to Earth, to the histories of the Elder Magi of Hyperborea, and the story of Eibon's life and death.

5 3/8" x 8 3/8", 408 pages, $17.95. Stock #6026; ISBN 1-56882-129-8.

THE THREE IMPOSTORS AND OTHER STORIES

In these eerie and once-shocking stories, supernatural horror is a transmuting force powered by the core of life. To resist it requires great will from the living, for civilization is only a new way to behave, and not one instinctive to life. Decency prevents discussion about such pressures, so each person must face such things alone. The comforts and hopes of civilization are threatened and undermined by these ecstatic nightmares that haunt the living. This is nowhere more deftly suggested than through Machen's extraordinary prose, where the textures and dreams of the Old Ways are never far removed.

5 3/8" x 8 3/8", 262 pages, $13.95. Stock #6030; ISBN 1-56882-132-8.

THE ANTARKTOS CYCLE

Writers are drawn to the unreachable places of the earth—to the greatest mountains and depths of the sea, the most barren deserts, and the white frozen deserts surrounding the north and south poles. In our minds' eyes, the beauty and mystery of the ice descends from Poe to the present and into the future, an infinite realm of wonder—and terror. This collection includes H. P. Lovecraft's "At the Mountains of Madness" and Edgar Allan Poe's *The Narrative of Arthur Gordon Pym.*

5 3/8" x 8 3/8", 578 pages, $19.95. Stock #6031; ISBN 1-56882-146-8.

SONG OF CTHULHU

Lovecraft's most famous portraitist was Richard Upton Pickman, whose ironic canvases of ghouls and humanity's relation to ghouls have become famous, even though they existed only in Lovecraft's keen imagination. Among HPL's characters, Randolph Carter and the tragically destined Edward Pickman Derby stand out. And of course there is Erich Zann, the inhumanly-great violist, whose powers are detailed in "The Music of Erich Zann," included in this volume.

In HPL, the artist is the detached observer of society, a cultural reporter of the sort whose function has since become familiar. But Lovecraft also saw a deeper role, one such as played by Henry Wilcox the sculptor in "The Call of Cthulhu": "Wilcox's imagination had been keenly affected. [He had] an unprecedented dream of great cyclopean cities of titan blocks and sky-flung monoliths, all dripping with green ooze and sinister with latent horror. . . . [and] a voice that was not a voice; a chaotic sensation which only fancy could transmute into sound, but which he attempted to render by the almost unpronounceable jumble of letters, *Cthulhu fhtagn.*"

Here are nineteen Mythos tales, melodies of prophecy and deceit. *Cthulhu fhtagn!*

5 3/8" x 8 3/8", 222 pages, $13.95. Stock #6032; ISBN 1-56882-117-4.

All titles are available from bookstores and game stores. You can also order directly from Wizard's Attic, your source for Cthulhiana and more. To order by credit card via the internet, visit http://www.wizards-attic.com. To order via fax, send your order to 1-510-452-4952, 24 hours a day. To order via phone, call 1-800-213-1493 (1-510-452-4951 outside the United States), 10 A.M. to 4 P.M. P.S.T.